S0-BOD-510

Tyndale House books by Tim LaHaye and Jerry B. Jenkins

The Left Behind series
Left Behind®
Tribulation Force
Nicolae
Soul Harvest
Apollyon
Assassins
The Indwelling
The Mark
Book 9—available summer 2001

Left Behind®: The Kids
#1: The Vanishings
#2: Second Chance
#3: Through the Flames
#4: Facing the Future
#5: Nicolae High
#6: The Underground
#7: Busted!
#8: Death Strike
#9: The Search
#10: On the Run
#11: Into the Storm
#12: Earthquake!

Tyndale House books by Tim LaHaye
Are We Living in the End Times?
How to Be Happy Though Married
Spirit-Controlled Temperament
Transformed Temperaments
Why You Act the Way You Do

Tyndale House books by Jerry B. Jenkins
And Then Came You
As You Leave Home
Still the One

THE MARK

THE BEAST RULES THE WORLD

TIM LAHAYE
JERRY B. JENKINS

Bookspan Large Print Edition

Tyndale House Publishers, Inc.
WHEATON, ILLINOIS

This Large Print Edition, prepared especially for Bookspan, contains the complete unabridged text of the original Publisher's Edition.

Left Behind series designed by Catherine Bergstrom
Cover photo illustration by Julie Chen

Published in association with the literary agency of Alive Communications, Inc., 7680 Goddard Street, Suite 200, Colorado Springs, CO 80920.

ISBN 0-7394-1263-9

Printed in the United States of America

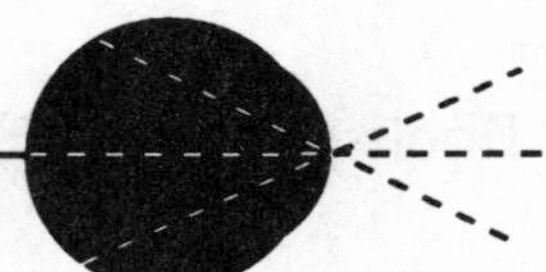

This Large Print Book carries the Seal of Approval of N.A.V.H.

To Linda and Rennie,
with gratitude

FORTY-TWO MONTHS INTO THE TRIBULATION; THREE DAYS INTO THE GREAT TRIBULATION

The Believers

Rayford Steele, mid-forties; former 747 captain for Pan-Continental; lost wife and son in the Rapture; former pilot for Global Community Potentate Nicolae Carpathia; original member of the Tribulation Force; an international fugitive in exile; suspect in the assassination of Nicolae Carpathia; residing at new safe house, Strong Building, Chicago

Cameron ("Buck") Williams, early thirties; former senior writer for *Global Weekly;* former publisher of *Global Community Weekly* for Carpathia; original member of the Trib Force; editor of cybermagazine *The Truth;* fugitive in exile, Strong Building, Chicago

Chloe Steele Williams, early twenties; former student, Stanford University; lost mother and brother in the Rapture; daughter of Rayford; wife of Buck; mother of fourteen-month-old Kenny Bruce; CEO of the International Commodity Co-op, an underground network of believers; original Trib Force member; fugitive in exile, Strong Building, Chicago

Tsion Ben-Judah, late forties; former rabbinical scholar and Israeli statesman; revealed belief in Jesus as the Messiah on international TV—wife and two teenagers subsequently murdered; escaped to U.S.; spiritual leader and teacher of Trib Force; cyberaudience of more than a billion daily; fugitive in exile, Strong Building, Chicago

Dr. Chaim Rosenzweig, late sixties; Israeli botanist and statesman; discoverer of formula that made Israeli deserts bloom; former *Global Weekly* Man of the Year; confessed murderer of Carpathia; Strong Building, Chicago

Mac McCullum, late fifties; pilot for Carpathia; New Babylon, United Carpathian States

David Hassid, mid-twenties; high-level director for the GC; New Babylon

Annie Christopher, early twenties; Global Community corporal; Phoenix 216 cargo chief; in love with David Hassid; unaccounted for, New Babylon

Leah Rose, late thirties; former head nurse, Arthur Young Memorial Hospital, Palatine, Illinois; Strong Building, Chicago

Mr. and Mrs. Lukas ("Laslos") Miklos, mid-fifties; lignite mining magnates; Greece, United Carpathian States

Abdullah Smith, early thirties; former Jordanian fighter pilot; first officer, Phoenix 216; New Babylon

Ming Toy, twenty-two; widow; guard at the Belgium Facility for Female Rehabilitation (Buffer); on assignment at Carpathia funeral, New Babylon

Chang Wong, seventeen; Ming Toy's brother; resides in China in the United Asian States; in New Babylon for Carpathia funeral with parents, who are unaware of his faith

Professed Believer

Al B. (aka "Albie"), late forties; given name unknown; native of Al Basrah, north of Kuwait; former manager, Al Basrah Airstrip Tower; international black marketeer; told Buck Williams he had become a believer from out of the Muslim faith by studying the teachings of Tsion Ben-Judah on the Internet; mark of the believer visible on his forehead; assisting Trib Force in northern Illinois, United North American States

The Enemies

Nicolae Jetty Carpathia, thirty-six; former president of Romania; former secretary-general, United Nations; self-appointed Global Community potentate; assassinated in Jerusalem; resurrected at GC palace complex, New Babylon

Leon Fortunato, early fifties; Carpathia's right hand; GC Supreme Commander; New Babylon

The Undecided

Hattie Durham, early thirties; former Pan-Continental flight attendant; former personal assistant to Carpathia; last seen, United North American States

PROLOGUE

From The Indwelling

The announcer said, "Ladies and gentlemen of the Global Community, your Supreme Potentate, His Excellency Nicolae Carpathia."

Nicolae took one step closer to the camera, forcing it to refocus. He looked directly into the lens.

"My dear subjects," he began. "We have, together, endured quite a week, have we not? I was deeply touched by the millions who made the effort to come to New Babylon for what turned out to be, gratefully, not my funeral. The outpouring of emotion was no less encouraging to me.

"As you know and as I have said, there remain small pockets of resistance to our cause of peace and harmony. There are even those who have made a career of saying the most hurtful, blasphemous, and false statements about me, using terms for me that no person would ever want to be called.

"I believe you will agree that I proved today who I am and who I am not. You will do well to follow your heads and your hearts and continue to follow me. You know what you saw, and your eyes do not lie. I am also eager to welcome into the one-world fold any former devotees of the radical fringe who have become convinced that I am not the enemy. On the contrary, I may be the very object of the devotion of their own religion, and I pray they will not close their minds to that possibility.

"In closing let me speak directly to the opposition. I have always, without rancor or acrimony, allowed divergent views. There are those among you, however, who have referred overtly to me personally as the Antichrist and this period of history as the Tribulation. You may take the following as my personal pledge:

"If you insist on continuing with your subversive attacks on my character and on the world harmony I have worked so hard to engender, the word *tribulation* will not begin to describe what is in store for you. If the last three and a half years are your idea of tribulation, wait until you endure the Great Tribulation."

"Woe to the inhabitants of the earth and the sea! For the devil has come down to you, having great wrath, because he knows that he has a short time."

Revelation 12:12

ONE

It was midafternoon in New Babylon, and David Hassid was frantic. Annie was nowhere in sight and he had heard nothing from her, yet he could barely turn his eyes from the gigantic screens in the palace courtyard. The image of the indefatigable Nicolae Carpathia, freshly risen from three days dead, filled the screen and crackled with energy. David believed if he was within reach of the man he could be electrocuted by some demonic charge.

With the disappearance of his love fighting for his attention, David found himself drawn past the jumbo monitors and the guards and the crowds to the edge of the bier that had just hours before displayed the quite dead body of the king of the world.

Should David be able to see evidence that the man was now indwelt by Satan himself? The body, the hair, the complexion, the look were the same. But an intensity, an air of restlessness and alertness, flowed from the eyes. Though he smiled and talked softly, it was as if Nicolae could barely contain the monster within. Controlled fury, violence delayed, revenge in abeyance played at the muscles in his neck and shoulders. David half expected him to burst from his suit and then from his very skin, exposed to the world as the repulsive serpent he was.

David's attention was diverted briefly by someone next to Carpathia, and when he glanced back at the still ruggedly handsome face, he was not prepared to have caught the eye of the enemy of his soul. Nicolae knew him, of course, but the look, though it contained recognition, did not carry the usual acceptance and encouragement David was used to. That very welcoming gaze had always unnerved him, yet he preferred it over this. For this was a transparent gaze that seemed to pass through David, which nearly moved him to step forward and confess his treachery and that of every comrade in the Tribulation Force.

David reminded himself that not even Satan himself was omniscient, yet he found it difficult to accept that these eyes were not those of one who knew his every secret. He wanted to run but he dared not, and he was grateful when Nicolae turned back to the task at hand: his role as the object of the world's worship.

David hurried back to his post, but someone had appropriated his golf cart, and he found himself peeved to where he wanted to pull rank. He flipped open his phone, had trouble finding his voice, but finally barked at the motor-pool supervisor, "I had better have a vehicle delivered within 120 seconds or someone is going to find his—"

"An electric cart, sir?" the man said, his accent making David guess he was an Aussie.

"Of course!"

"They're scarce here, Director, but—"

"They must be, because someone absconded with mine!"

"But I was going to say that I would be happy to lend you mine, under the circumstances."

"The circumstances?"

"The resurrection, of course! Tell you the truth, Director Hassid, I'd love to get in line myself."

"Just bring—"

"You think I could do that, sir? I mean if I were in uniform? I know they've turned away civilians not inside the courtyard, and they're none too happy, but as an employee—"

"I don't know! I need a cart and I need it now!"

"Would you drive me to the venue before you go wherever it is you have to g—"

"Yes! Now hurry!"

"Are you thrilled or what, Director?"

"What?"

The man spoke slowly, condescendingly. "A-bout-the-res-ur-rec-tion!"

"Are you in your vehicle?" David demanded.

"Yes, sir."

"That's what I'm thrilled about."

The man was still talking when David hung up on him and called crowd control. "I'm looking for Annie Christopher," he said.

"Sector?"

"Five-three."

"Sector 53 has been cleared, Director. She may have been reassigned or relieved."

"If she were reassigned, you'd have it, no?"

"Checking."

The motor-pool chief appeared in his cart, beaming. David boarded, phone still to his ear. "Gonna see god," the man said.

"Yeah," David said. "Just a minute."

"Can you believe it? He's got to be god. Who else can he be? Saw it with my own two eyes, well, on TV anyway. Raised from the dead. I saw him dead, I know that. If I see him in person, there'll be no doubt now, will there? Eh?"

David nodded, sticking a finger in his free ear.

"I say no doubt, eh?"

"No doubt!" David shouted. "Now give me a minute!"

"Where we goin', sport?"

David craned his neck to look at the man, incredulous that he was still speaking.

"I say, where we going? Am I dropping you or you dropping me?"

"I'm dropping you! Go where you want and get out!"

"Sor-ry!"

This wasn't how David normally treated people, even ignorant ones. But he had to hear whether Annie had been reassigned, and where. "Nothing," the crowd-control dispatcher on the phone told him.

"Relieved then?" he said, relieved himself.

"Likely. Nothing in our system on her."

David thought of calling Medical Services but scolded himself for overreacting.

Motor-pool man deftly picked his way through the massive, dispersing crowd. At least most were dispersing. They looked shocked. Some were angry. They had waited hours to see the body, and now that Carpathia had arisen, they were not going to be able to see him, all because of where they happened to be in the throng.

"This is as close as I hope to get in this thing then," the man said, skidding to a stop so abruptly that David had to catch himself. "You'll bring it back round then, eh, sir?"

"Of course," David said, trying to gather himself to at least thank the man. As he slid into the driver's seat he said, "Been back to Australia since the reorganizing?"

The man furrowed his brow and pointed at David, as if to reprimand him. "Man of your station ought to be able to tell the difference between an Aussie and a New Zealander."

"My mistake," David said. "Thanks for the wheels."

As he pulled away the man shouted, "'Course we're all proud citizens of the United Pacific States now anyway!"

David tried to avoid eye contact with the many disgruntled mourners turned celebrants who tried to flag him, not for rides but for information. At times he was forced to brake to keep from running someone down, and the request was always the same. In one distinct accent or another, everyone wanted the same thing. "Any way we can still get in to see His Excellency?"

"Can't help you," David said. "Move along, please. Official business."

"Not fair! Wait all night and half the day in the blistering sun, and for what?"

But others danced in the streets, making up songs and chants about Carpathia, their new god. David glanced again at the monstrous monitors where Carpathia was shown briefly touching hands as the last several thousand were herded through. To David's left, guards fought to block hopefuls from sneaking into the courtyard. "Line's closed!" they shouted over and over.

On the screen, pilgrims swooned as they neared the bier, graced by Nicolae in his glory. Many crumbled from merely getting near him, waxing catatonic. Guards held them up to keep them moving, but when His Excellency himself spoke quietly to them and touched them, some passed out, deadweights in the guards' arms.

Over Nicolae's cooing—"Good to see you. Thank you for coming. Bless you. Bless you."—David heard Leon Fortunato. "Worship your king," he said soothingly. "Bow before his majesty. Worship the Lord Nicolae, your god."

Dissonance came from the guards stuck with the responsibility of moving the mass of quivering, jellied humanity, catching them as they collapsed in ecstasy. "Ridiculous!" they grumbled to each other, live mikes sending the cacophony of Fortunato, Carpathia, and the complainers to the ends of the PA system. "Keep moving. Come on now! There you go! Stand up! Move it along!"

David finally reached sector 53, which was, as he had been told, deserted. The crowd-control gates had toppled, and the giant number placard had been trampled.

David sat there, forearms resting on the cart's steering wheel. He shoved his uniform cap back on his head and felt the sting of the sun's UV rays. His hands looked like lobsters, and he knew he'd pay for his hours in the sun. But he could not find shade again until he found Annie.

As crowds shuffled through and then around what had been her sector, David squinted at the ground, the asphalt shimmering. Besides the ice-cream and candy wrappers and drink cups that lay motionless in the windless heat was what appeared to be residue of medical supplies. He was about to step from the cart for a closer look when an elderly couple climbed aboard and asked to be driven to the airport shuttle area.

"This is not a people mover," he said absently, having enough presence to remove the keys before leaving the vehicle.

"How rude!" the woman said.

"Come on," the man said.

David marched to sector 53 and knelt, the heat sapping his energy. In the shadows of hundreds walking by, he examined the plastic empties of bandages, gauze, ointment, even tubing. Someone had been ministered to here. It didn't have to have been Annie. It could have been anyone. Still, he had to know. He made his way back to the cart, every seat but his now full.

"Unless you need to go to Medical Services," he said, punching the number into his phone, "you're in the wrong cart."

In Chicago Rayford Steele found the Strong Building's ninth floor enough of a bonanza that he was able to push from his mind misgivings about Albie. The truth about his dark, little Middle Eastern friend would be tested soon enough. Albie was to ferry a fighter jet from Palwaukee to Kankakee, where Rayford would later pick him up in a Global Community helicopter.

Besides discovering a room full of the latest desktop and minicomputers—still in their original packaging—Rayford found a small private sleeping room adjacent to a massive executive office. It was outfitted like a luxurious hotel room, and he rushed from floor to floor to find the same next to at least four offices on every level.

"We have more amenities than we ever dreamed," he told the exhausted Tribulation Force. "Until we can blacken the windows, we'll have to get some of the beds into the corridors near the elevators where they can't be seen from the outside."

"I thought no one ever came near here," Chloe said, Kenny sleeping in her lap and Buck dozing with his head on her shoulder.

"Never know what satellite imaging shows," Rayford said. "We could be sleeping soundly while GC Security and Intelligence forces snap our pictures from the stratosphere."

"Let me get these two to bed somewhere," she said, "before I collapse."

"I've moved furniture in my day," Leah said, slowly rising. "Where are these beds and where do we put them?"

"I wish I could help," Chaim said through clenched teeth, his jaw still wired shut.

Rayford stopped him with a gesture. "If you're staying with us, sir, you answer to me. We need you and Buck as healthy as you can be."

"And I need you alert for study," Tsion said. "You made me cram for enough exams. Now you're in for the crash course of your life."

Rayford, Chloe, Leah, and Tsion spent half an hour moving beds up the elevator to makeshift quarters in an inner corridor on the twenty-fifth floor. By the time Rayford gingerly boarded the chopper balanced precariously on what served as the new roof of the tower, everyone was asleep save Tsion. The rabbi seemed to gain a second wind, and Rayford wasn't sure why.

Rayford left the instrument panel lights off and, of course, the outside lights. He fired up the rotors but waited to lift off until his eyes had adjusted to the darkness. The copter had but ten feet of clearance on each side. Little was trickier—especially to a fixed-wing expert like Rayford—than the shifting currents inside what amounted to a cavernous smokestack. Rayford had seen choppers crash in wide-open spaces after merely hovering too long in one place. Mac McCullum had tried to explain the physics of it, but Rayford had not listened closely enough to grasp it. Something about the rotors sucking up air from beneath the craft, leaving it no buoyancy. By the time the pilot realized he was dropping through dead air of his own making, he had destroyed the equipment and often killed all on board.

Rayford needed sleep as much as any of his charges, but he had to go get Albie.

There was more to that too, of course. He could have called his friend and told him to lie low till the following evening. But Albie was new to the country and would have to fend for himself outside or bluff his way into a hotel. With Carpathia resurrected and the GC naturally on heightened alert, who knew how long he could pull off impersonating a GC officer?

Anyway, Rayford had to know whether Albie was "with him or agin him," as his father used to say. He had been thrilled to see the mark of the believer on Albie's forehead, but much of what the man had done in the predawn hours confused Rayford and made him wonder. A wily, streetwise man like Albie—one who had provided so much at high risk to himself—would be the worst kind of opponent. Rayford worried that he had unwittingly led the Tribulation Force into the lair of the enemy.

As the chopper rumbled through the shaft at the top of the tower, Rayford held his breath. He had carefully set the craft as close to the middle of the space as he could, allowing him to use one corner for his guide as he rose. If he kept the whirring blades equidistant from the walls in the one corner, he should be centered until free of the building.

How vulnerable and conspicuous could a man feel? He imagined David Hassid having miscalculated, trusting old information, not realizing that the GC itself knew Chicago was safe—not off-limits due to radiation. Rayford himself had overheard Carpathia say he had not used radiation on the city, at least initially. He wondered if the GC had planted such information just to lure in the insurgents and have them where they wanted them—in one place for easy dispatch.

With his helicopter free of the tower, Rayford still dared not engage the lights. He would stay low, hopefully beneath radar. He wanted to be invisible to satellite surveillance photography as well, but heat sensing had been so refined that the dark whirlybird would glow orange on a monitor.

A chill ran up his back as he let his imagination run. Was he being followed by a half dozen craft just like his own? He wouldn't hear or see them. They could have waited nearby, even on the ground. How would he know?

Since when did he manufacture trouble?

There was enough real danger without concocting more.

Rayford set the instrument panel lights at their lowest level and quickly saw he was off course. It was an easy fix, but so much for trusting his brain, even in a ship like this. Mac had once told him that piloting a helicopter was to flying a 747 as riding a bike was to driving a sport utility vehicle. From that Rayford assumed that he would do more work by the seat of his pants than by marrying himself to the instrument panel. But neither had he planned on flying blind over a deserted megalopolis in wee-hour blackness. He had to get to Kankakee, pick up Albie, and get back to the tower before sunup. He had not a minute to spare. The last thing he wanted was to be seen over a restricted area in broad daylight. Detected in the dead of night was one thing. He would take his chances, trust his instincts. But there would be no hiding under the sun, and he would die before he would lead anyone to the new safe house.

In New Babylon frustrated supplicants had formed a new line, several thousand long, outside the Global Community Palace. GC guards traversed the length of it, telling people that the resurrected potentate would have to leave the courtyard when he had finished greeting those who happened to be in the right place at the right time.

David detoured from his route to Medical Services to hear the response of the crowd. They did not move, did not disperse. The guards, their bullhorned messages ignored, finally stopped to listen. David, looking puzzled, pulled up behind one of the jeeps, and a guard shrugged as if as dumbfounded as Director Hassid. The guard with the loudspeaker said, "Suit yourselves, but this is an exercise in futility."

"We have another idea!" shouted a man with a Hispanic accent.

"I'm listening," the guard said, as the crowd near him quieted.

"We will worship the statue!" he said, and hundreds in line cheered.

"What did he say? What did he say?" The question raced down the line in both directions.

"Did not Supreme Commander Fortunato say we should do that?" the man said.

"Where are you from, my friend?" the guard asked, admiration in his voice.

"Méjico!" the man shouted in his native tongue, and many with him exulted.

"You have the heart of the toreador!" the guard said. "Let me check on it!"

The news spread as the guard settled in his seat and talked into his phone. Suddenly he stood and gave the man a thumbs-up. "You have been cleared to worship the image of His Excellency, the risen potentate!"

The crowd cheered.

"In fact, your leaders consider it a capital idea!"

The crowd sang and chanted, edging closer and closer to the courtyard.

"Please maintain order!" the guard urged. "It will be more than an hour before you will be allowed in. But you *will* get your wish!"

David shook his head as he executed a huge U-turn and headed to the courtyard. People along the way called out to him. "Is it true? May we at least worship the statue?"

David ignored most of them, but when clusters moved in front of his speeding cart, he was forced to brake before slipping around them. Occasionally he nodded, to their delight. They ran to get in a line that already stretched more than a quarter mile. Would this day ever end?

TWO

Rayford mentally kicked himself. He had vastly underestimated the time and his ability to pick up Albie, settle on the disposition of both the fighter jet and the Gulfstream, and get back to the new safe house before sunrise. The sun was already toying with the horizon. He patted his pants pocket for his phone. He felt for it in his flight bag, his jacket, on the floor.

He wanted to swear, but since coming to his senses just days before, Rayford acknowledged that he needed a return to discipline. He had learned from an old friend in college something he had then rejected as too esoteric and way too touchy-feely. His broad-minded friend had called it his "opposite trigger" mode, and while in it, he forced himself to respond in ways diametrically opposed to how he felt. If he wanted to shout, he whispered. If he wanted to smack someone, he gently caressed his or her shoulder.

Rayford hadn't thought about that old friend or his crazy idea until the lonely, emotional flight from the Middle East to Greece and then to the United North American States. And now he decided to try it. He wanted to swear at himself for being shortsighted and for losing his phone. Instead, he surveyed his mind for an opposite response. One opposite of swearing was blessing, but whom would he bless? Another was praying.

"Lord," he began, "once again I need some help. I'm mad at myself and have few options. I'm exhausted, but I need to know what to do."

Almost instantly Rayford remembered that Albie had his phone. Albie had a phone of his own, too, but in the bustle and grabbing of various items, Rayford had entrusted his to his friend. Sometime soon he would have to get someone to rig a radio base in the safe house with a secure channel to the chopper so he could communicate directly. Meanwhile, he couldn't tell the rest of the Tribulation Force where he was or that he would not be returning until at least late that same evening.

Neither could he determine whether Albie was all right. He would have to simply land, using his alias with the tower, and hope Albie was waiting for him.

David left messages on Annie's phone and tried every other source he could think of that might know her whereabouts. Medical Services was too busy to look her up on their computers. "She wouldn't be in the system yet," he was told, "even if she were here."

"You're not swiping bar codes on the badges of employees as they are admitted?"

"They're not actually being admitted, Director. Everybody goes to triage, the living are treated, and the dead pronounced. Cataloging them is low on the priority list, but we'll eventually get everyone logged in."

"How will I know if she's there?"

"You may come look, but don't interfere and keep out of the way."

"Where's triage?"

"As far east as you can go from our main tent. We try to start 'em in the shade of three tents, but we're out of space and they're in and out of there as fast as we can move 'em."

"Mostly sunstroke?" David said.

"Mostly lightning, Director."

"Tower to GC chopper! Do you copy?"

"This is GC chopper, Kankakee," Rayford said, trying to cover that he was rattled. "My apologies. Asleep at the stick here."

"Not literally, I hope."

"No, sir."

"State your business."

"Uh, yeah, civilian under the authority of Deputy Commander Marcus Elbaz."

"Mr. Berry?"

"Roger."

"Deputy Commander Elbaz asks that we set your mind at ease about your phone."

"Roger that!"

"Cleared for landing to the south where he will meet you in Hangar 2. You can appreciate we're shorthanded here. You can handle your own securing and refueling."

Ten minutes later Rayford asked Albie

how long he thought he could keep up the ruse on the GC. "As long as your comrade Hassid is in the saddle at the palace. He's a remarkable young man, Rayford. I confess I had to hold my breath more than once here. They were tough, short of personnel as they are. I had to go through two checkpoints."

Rayford squinted. "They let me in without a second glance, and I hadn't even contacted the tower."

"That's because you're with me and a civilian."

"You convinced 'em, eh?"

"Totally. But I have to hand it to your friend. Not only does he have me on the international GC database with name, rank, and serial number, but he also has me assigned to this part of the United North American States. I'm here because I'm supposed to be here. I check out better than most of the legitimate GC personnel."

"David's good," Rayford said.

"The best. I blustered and acted impatient and pretended they would get in trouble if they detained me too long. But they were unmoved—until the second checkpoint ran me through the computer and reached

David's database. Someday he'll have to tell me how he does that. He entered all of my information, and when my papers matched with what they saw on the screen, I was gold. Then I began barking orders, telling them to pave the way for you, that we had urgent business and must be on our way."

Rayford told Albie it would be impossible to return to the safe house until dark and that he might as well carry him back to Palwaukee so he could move the Gulfstream to Kankakee.

"Would you rather have some fun?" Albie said. "You want to see if GC has torched your old safe house yet and do it for them if not?"

"Not a bad idea," Rayford said. "If they just burned it, fine, but if they start combing it for evidence, I worry what we might have left."

"They don't have the personnel for that," Albie said, moving toward the helicopter. "Fueled up?"

Rayford nodded.

"The fighter is too, ready whenever we need it." Albie slung his bag over his shoulder, dug in it for Rayford's phone, and tossed it to him.

"Three unanswered calls," Rayford muttered as they boarded the chopper. "Hope everything's all right in Chicago. When did the calls come?"

"All three about half an hour ago, one right after the other. None showed phone numbers, so I didn't think I should answer for you."

They were strapped in now, but Rayford said, "I'd better check with the safe house."

Tsion answered groggily.

"I'm sorry to wake you, Doctor," Rayford began.

"Oh, Captain Steele, it's no trouble. I only just fell asleep. Chloe's phone, it was ringing and ringing, and she was sound asleep. No one roused; they are so exhausted. I was not able to get to it in time, but when it rang again, this time I hurried and carried it to a quiet place. Rayford, it was Miss Durham!"

"You're sure?"

"Yes, and she sounded desperate. I pleaded with her to tell me where she was and reminded her that we all love her and care about her and are praying for her, but she wanted only to talk to you. She said she had tried your phone, and I told her I would try too. I tried twice to no avail. Anyway, you have her number."

"I'll call her."

"And you'll let me know."

"Tsion, get some rest. You have so much to do, setting up your computer area, teaching Chaim—"

"Oh, Rayford, I am so excited about that that I can barely contain myself. And I have so much to communicate to my audience on the computer. But you must call Miss Durham, and yes, you're right. Unless there is a compelling reason why we should know, you can tell us when you return. Frankly, I expected you by now."

"I miscalculated, Tsion. I can't return until the sky is black. But I am available by phone now."

"And you have connected with your Middle Eastern friend."

"I have."

"And is he all right, Rayford? Forgive me, but he seemed preoccupied."

"Everything's fine here, Doctor."

"He is a new believer too, correct?"

"Yes."

"And he will be staying with us?"

"That's likely."

"Then I will look forward to training him as well."

David was aghast at Medical Services. He had visited their indoor facility many times, which, despite their thinning ranks, was pristine and shipshape. What had begun as the main first-aid station, which serviced dozens of others throughout the area during the Carpathia wake, now looked like a mobile army surgical hospital.

The rest of the first-aid stations were being dismantled and leftover injured taken either to the courtyard triage center or into the indoor facility.

Row upon row of makeshift cots snaked across the courtyard. "Why aren't you moving these people inside?" David said, tugging at his stiff collar.

"Why don't you manage your area and let us manage ours," a doctor said, turning briefly from an ashen victim of the heat.

"I don't mean to criticize. It's just that—"

"It's just that we're all out here now," the doctor said. "At least most of us. The majority of the treatable cases are heatstroke and dehydration, and most of the casualties are lightning victims."

"I'm looking for—"

"I'm sorry, Director, but whoever you're looking for, you're going to have to find on your own. We don't care about their names or their nationalities. We're just trying to keep them alive. We'll deal with the paperwork later."

"I had an employee stationed at—"

"I'm sorry! It's not that I don't care, but I can't help you! Understand?"

"She would have known how to avoid sun- or heatstroke."

"Good. Now, good-bye."

"She was at sector 53."

"Well, you don't want to hear about five-three," the doctor said, turning back to his patient.

"What about it?"

"Lots of lightning victims. Big bolt there."

"Where would the victims have been taken?"

The doctor was finished talking with David. He nodded to an assistant. "Tell him."

A young man in scrubs spoke with a

French accent. "No specific place. Some came in here. Some were treated in that sector. Some inside."

David started on the cart but soon abandoned it to jog down the line of victims. This would be impossible. How could he tell who was who? Annie was in uniform, and while he was sure he could recognize her, with only shoes peeking out from sheets soaked to cool patients, he would have to check each face. And he would be interfering with the medical treatment.

As he trotted along in the heat, David reached in his belt for his water bottle and found it empty. His throat was parched, and he knew his thirst trailed by several minutes his real need for water. When had he last taken a swig? When had he eaten? When had he slept?

The huge screens showed Viv Ivins, Leon Fortunato, and Nicolae Carpathia moving the pilgrims along, cooing to them, blessing them, touching them. The waves of heat from the asphalt made David's uniform cling to him like a single, damp weight. He stopped and bent to catch his breath, but his throat felt swollen, his mouth unable to produce saliva, his windpipe constricted. *Dizzy. Annie. Lightheaded. Hot. Annie. Spinning. Thirst. Hands red.*

David pitched forward, his cap sliding off and tumbling before him. His mind told him to reach for it, but his hands stayed planted above his knees. *Break your fall! Break your fall!* But he could not. His arms would not move. His face would take the brunt of it. No, he could tuck his chin.

The top of his head smacked the pavement, the jagged asphalt digging through his hair to his scalp. He shut his eyes in anticipation of the pain, and white streaks shot past his eyes. Hands still on his knees, his seat in the air, he slowly, slowly rolled sideways and crashed onto his hip. He opened his eyes and saw his own blood trickle past his face, quickly coagulating in a pool on the baked pavement. He tried to move, to speak. Unconsciousness pursued him, and all he could think of was that he was next in a long line of victims.

"You want me to fly while you make your call?" Albie said.

"Maybe you'd better," Rayford said. They switched places as he punched in Hattie's number. She answered in a hoarse, panicked whisper on the first sound.

"Rayford, where are you?"

"I don't want to say, Hattie. Talk to me. Where are you?"

"Colorado."

"Specifically."

"Pueblo, north end, I think."

"GC has you?"

"Yes. And they're going to send me back to Buffer." Rayford was silent. "Don't leave me hanging, Rayford. We go back too far."

"Hattie, I don't know what to say."

"What?!"

"What do you want me to do?"

"Come get me! I can't go back to Belgium! I'll die there."

"What do you expect me to do?"

"The right thing, Ray."

"In other words, jeopardize my life and expose the Force to—"

Click.

Rayford couldn't tell whether she hung up because he had insulted her or because she heard someone coming. He told Albie the conversation.

"What are you going to do, my friend?"

Rayford stared at Albie in the emerging

light and shook his head. "That woman has caused us no end of grief."

"But you care for her. You've told me before."

"I have?"

"Bits and pieces. Maybe Mac told me."

"Mac doesn't know her."

"But he knows you, and you talk, no?"

Rayford nodded. "We know they let her out of Buffer, thinking she—"

"Buffer?"

"Belgium Facility for Female Rehabilitation."

"Ah, I'd better remember that."

"Anyway, we know they were hoping she would lead them to us at the gala in Jerusalem, but she—"

"Excuse me, Rayford, but do you want me to set a course over the old safe house or just head directly for Palwaukee?"

"Depends on whether I decide to go to Colorado."

"Your choice, but if I may say so, I expected you to be more decisive. I am just playacting, yet I appear more of a leader than you are. Your people admire and respect you—it's obvious."

"They shouldn't. I—"

"You've reconciled with them, Rayford. They forgave you. Now become their leader again. What are you going to do about this Hattie Durham? Decide. Tell me, tell the people in the Strong Building, and do it."

"I don't know, Albie."

"You'll never *know*. Just weigh your options, consider the pros and cons, and pull the trigger. Either way, the old safe house is fewer than ten minutes out of the way. Start with a small decision."

"Let's have a look at it."

"Good for you, Rayford."

"Don't patronize me, Albie. We're in a GC chopper. We won't look suspicious anyway."

"But you've made a decision. Now think aloud about the more important one. Are we going to Colorado?"

"I was saying, rather than lead the GC to us, she went straight there. Her family is gone, but maybe she thought she could hook up with friends in Colorado. Who knows? I couldn't even tell you whether her confounding the GC was a stroke of genius or dumb luck, but I'd lean toward the latter."

"So she may be leading *you* to *them* rather than the other way round."

Rayford turned away from Albie and looked out the window, praying silently. It hadn't been that many years since his lust for Hattie Durham had almost cost him his marriage. He took the blame for that, but since then she had been nothing but trouble. He and the others in the Tribulation Force had loved her and counseled her, provided for her, pled with her to receive Christ. But she would not be persuaded, and she pulled dangerous stunts that compromised the safety of the Force. For all he knew, she was the reason the GC had finally discovered the safe house.

Rayford's phone chirped. "Hattie?"

"I heard footsteps. They've got me in a small room in a bunker about an hour south of Colorado Springs."

"I'm a long way from there."

"Oh, thank you, Rayford. I knew I could count—"

"I haven't decided what I'm going to do, Hattie."

"Of course you have. You won't leave me here to be sent back to prison or worse. What do I have to do, promise to become a believer?"

"Not unless you mean it."

"Well, if you *don't* come for me, you can kiss that idea good-bye."

Rayford slapped his phone shut and sighed. "What an idiot!"

"Her?" Albie said. "Or you for considering what you're considering?"

"Her! This is such a transparent attempt by the GC to lure one of us out there. Once they get me, they hold me ransom for information on the rest of the Force. Who they really want, of course, is Tsion. The rest of us are irritants. He's the enemy."

"So your choice is between this Miss Durham and Tsion Ben-Judah? You want my vote?"

"It's not that easy. We want her for the kingdom, Albie. I mean, we all really do."

"And you think if you abandon her now, she'll never believe."

"She said as much."

"This may sound cold, and I admit I'm new to this, but it's her choice, isn't it? You're not making the decision for her."

"Going out there would be the dumbest thing I've ever done. They've caught her, detained her, threatened to take her back to prison, and yet they leave her with her phone. I mean, come on."

Albie scanned the horizon. "Then your decision is easy."

"I wish."

"It *is.* Either you don't go, or you consider all your resources."

"What does that mean?"

"There's one it seems you've forgotten. Maybe two."

"I'll bite."

"Assign David Hassid to find out exactly where they have her and have him send through an order from a bogus commander to keep her there until further notice. You call her back and tell her you're not coming. Make her and whoever is listening in believe it. You just show up, surprise attack, just when both she and the GC think you have abandoned her."

Rayford pursed his lips. "Maybe you ought to be in charge of the Trib Force. But surprising them doesn't guarantee success. I'll still likely be killed or detained myself."

"But you've forgotten another resource."

"I'm still listening."

"Sir? Director? Are you all right?"

"He's out."

"His eyes are open, Doctor."

"He fell on his head, Medicine Woman."

"I've asked you not to call me th—"

"Sorry. I don't know how you handled fallen braves on the reservation, but this one couldn't even break his fall. He couldn't shut his eyes if he wanted to."

"Help me get him onto—"

"There you go again, sweetie. I'm not an orderly."

"And there *you* go again, *Doc*tor! We can let him lie here and bleed to death, or I can remind you that our patients way outnumber the help."

David's tongue was swollen, and he could not maneuver it to form the word. All he wanted was water, but he knew his head required attention too.

"Spray!" the dark nurse called out, and someone tossed her a bottle. She sprayed three bursts of lukewarm water directly into David's face, and he couldn't even blink. Compared to the heat of the asphalt, which he estimated at 120 degrees, the water felt icy. A few drops reached his mouth and he panted, trying to drink them in.

The doctor and nurse gently rolled him to his back, and in his mind he was squinting against the harsh sun. Yet he knew his eyes were wide open and burning. He wanted to plead for another spray, but he felt paralyzed. The nurse mercifully laid his cap over his face, and when feeling returned, he tried not to move so as to keep the cap in place.

If he could find his voice he would plead for Annie, but he was helpless. She was probably somewhere looking for him.

When David was lifted to a canvas cot, the hat slipped off his face, but he was able to blink and was soon under the shade of a crowded tent. He had been assigned the last sliver of shadow. "Critical?" someone asked.

"No," the doctor said. "But sew that head up soon."

The first syringe that plunged into his scalp made his whole body jerk and shudder, but still he could not call out. In seconds the top of his head was numb. "You can do this?" the doctor said.

The nurse said, "It's not exactly cosmetic, is it?"

"Give him threads like a football—I don't care. He can always wear a hat."

In truth, David didn't care what his head looked like, and it was a good thing, because the nurse quickly shaved an inch on each side of the laceration, splashed more liquid on him, and began opening a huge needle.

"How bah?" David managed, his tongue lolling.

"You'll live," she said. "Strictly superficial. Tough skull. But you really yanked the flesh away from the bone. Five inches at least, laterally at the top."

"Watah?"

"Sorry."

"Little?"

She quickly removed the top of the spray bottle, which had an inch of water left in it. "Open up."

Most of it ran down David's neck, but it loosened his tongue. "Looking for Chief Christopher," he said.

"Don't know him," she said. "Now hold still."

"*Her.* Annie Christopher."

"Director, I've got about five minutes for you, and if you're lucky, I'll find an IV to re-hydrate you. But while I'm sewing, you're going to have to shut up and hold still if you don't want to look worse."

"Do you see what I see?" Albie squinted into the distance.

Rayford followed his gaze and was surprised by a gush of emotion. A black tower of smoke billowed several hundred feet in the air. "You think?" he said.

Albie nodded. "Gotta be."

"Get as close as you can," Rayford said. "That was my home for a long time."

"Will do. Now, you going to use every resource available? Or did I waste my money on this uniform and all the credentials?"

THREE

Buck awoke at noon, Chicago time, and felt twice his age. As had been true every day since the Rapture, he knew exactly where he was. In the past it was not uncommon to wake up in a foreign city and have to remind himself where he was, who he was, and what he was doing there. No more. Even when exhausted and injured and barely able to function, somehow the self-preservation flywheel kept spinning in his otherwise unengaged mind.

He had slept soundly, but at the first flutter of his eyelids and that initial glance at his watch, he knew. It all made sense in a ludicrous way. Buck stared at the wall next to an elevator in a bombed-out skyscraper in Chicago, heard muffled voices from around the corner, smelled coffee and a baby. Kenny had his own aroma, a fresh, powdery sweetness that Buck conjured when they were far apart.

But Kenny was here, barricaded from the outer hallways exposed to the windows that let in the midday sun. Buck rolled to his back and propped himself up on his elbows. Kenny had apparently given up trying to climb the makeshift barrier and sat contentedly playing with one of his loose shoelaces.

"Hey, Kenny Bruce," Buck whispered. "Come see Daddy."

Kenny's head jerked up, and then he went to all fours before righting himself and toddling to the bed. "Da-da."

Buck reached for him, and the chubby bundle climbed atop him and stretched out on his stomach and chest. Buck let his head fall back again and wrapped his arms around Kenny. The boy seldom had the patience to simply rest in his father's arms, but now he seemed almost ready to nap himself. With the baby's tiny heart beating against his own, Buck wished he could lie there forever.

"Da-da bye-bye?" Kenny said, and Buck could not stop the tears.

Rayford had made a decision, several in fact. After watching the old safe house burn to the ground, he instructed Albie to turn back to Kankakee, where they would fly the GC fighter to Colorado.

"Now you're talking, Captain," Albie said.

"Now I'm talking," Rayford groused. "Now I'm probably getting us all killed."

"You're doing the right thing."

Unable to reach David in New Babylon, Rayford left a message asking him to get back to them with Hattie's exact whereabouts. He also asked David to inform GC personnel holding her that, should their current operation fail, they should keep Hattie there until assigned personnel could come for her.

David often overrode other GC systems to send such directives in a way that they could not be traced back to him. He was the one who assigned security codes to keep such transmissions from "enemies of the Global Community," so he was also able to use the channels without detection. "As soon as you can," Rayford recorded on David's private machine, "get back to Albie and me to confirm you've paved the way for us."

Before long Rayford would have to transmit his picture, with his new look and name, to David Hassid so the young Israeli could "enlist" him in the GC Peacekeeping Forces too. Meanwhile, he and Albie would put down at what was once Peterson Air Force Base, appropriate a GC jeep David would reserve, follow his directions to this bunker, if that's what it was, and pick up the prisoner.

By the time Albie had stalled his landing until the fighter was short of fuel, Rayford had been dozing more than two hours. Albie woke him with the news that they had not yet heard back from David.

"Not good," Rayford said, placing yet another call to New Babylon. No answer. "You have a computer, Albie?"

"A subnotebook, but it's got satellite capability."

"Programmed to communicate with David?"

"If you've got his coordinates, I can make it work."

Rayford found the machine in Albie's flight bag. "Batteries are low," he said.

"Plug in to the plane's power," Albie said. "I don't do heavy-duty stuff on batteries anyway."

"Keep the power on after we land," Rayford said. "This could take a while."

Albie nodded and got on the radio to the GC outpost. "GC NB4047 to Peterson Tower."

"You ought to know we're now Carpathia Memorial, GC," came the reply.

"My mistake, tower," Albie said. "First time here in I don't know how long." He winked at Rayford, who glanced up from his computer work. Albie had never been in the States before.

"Gonna hafta take the *Memorial* out of our name, aren't we, 4047?"

"Come back?"

"He is risen."

Albie rolled his eyes at Rayford. "Yeah, I heard. That's something, eh?"

"You're supposed to reply with 'He is risen indeed.' "

Rayford pantomimed sticking his finger down his throat. Albie shook his head. "Well,

I sure believe that, tower," he said, glancing at Rayford and pointing up.

"Business here?"

"Deputy Commander with confidential orders."

"Name?"

"Marcus Elbaz."

"One moment."

"Low on fuel, tower."

"Short on people here, Commander Elbaz. Give me a minute."

"We're putting down either way," Albie told Rayford, who was busy pecking in the details that would orient Albie's computer global-positioning hardware to a satellite that would link him directly with David's computer.

"There you are, sir," the tower said. "I see you on the system."

"Roger."

"Don't have you assigned out this way, though. You been to Kankakee?"

"That's where I came from."

"And your business here?"

"Repeat, confidential orders."

"Oh, yes, sorry. Anything we can help with?"

"Refueling and a ground vehicle should have been arranged."

"As I say, sir, we don't have your disposition here. We can refuel you, no problem, with the proper authorization code. Ground transportation is scarce."

"I'll trust you to figure something out."

"We're very shorthanded and—"

"You mentioned that."

"—and frankly, sir, there's no one here near your rank."

"Then I expect whoever's in command to obey my order for transportation."

A long pause.

"I'll, uh, pass that word along, sir."

"Thank you."

"And you're cleared to land."

David awoke in the palace hospital, his head throbbing so he could barely open his eyes. He shared a room with two sleeping patients. His clothes had been removed, and he lay there in a flimsy gown, an IV in his hand, his watch on a stand next to him. Holding it before his bleary eyes was almost more than he could bear. Twenty-one hundred hours. It couldn't be!

He tried to sit up and was aware of bandages around his head and over his ears. He heard his own pulse and felt pain with every beat. It was dark outside, but a silent TV monitor showed pilgrims still in the courtyard, passing by, kneeling, bowing, worshiping, praying to the gigantic statue of Nicolae.

On David's other side was the remote control. He didn't want to wake the other patients, but the captioning system was in Arabic. He fiddled with it until it changed to English, and the captions merely represented songs piped into the courtyard as people slowly passed by the image. He stared as the camera pulled back to show the immense crowd, seemingly as big as for the funeral, snaking a mile outside the palace.

David panicked. He had been away from his phone and computer longer than he had been in months. He craned his neck looking for a phone, and the pain nearly drove him to his pillow again. He pulled a cord ostensibly connected to the nurses' station, but no one came. He knew the ratio between nurses and patients was ridiculously low, but surely they knew he was a director. That should count for something.

However they were hydrating him was working, because he had to relieve himself in a bad way. No bedpan for him. He played with the controls on the side of the bed until one railing lowered. He grimaced as he swung his legs off the side, pausing to let the throbbing subside and catch his breath.

Finally he put both hands on the edge of the bed and eased himself to the floor. The marble was incongruously cold for such a hot part of the world, but it felt good. He stood, swaying, dizzy, waiting for his equilibrium to catch up. When he felt steadier he stepped toward the bathroom, reminded by a tug at his wrist that he was still hooked to the IV. He stepped back and wiggled the metal stand on rollers away from the wall and the end of the bed, but as he dragged it with him, it caught.

A monitor cord was plugged into the wall. He tried to remove it, but it wouldn't budge from the connection or the stand. David knew there had to be some simple trick to it. Maybe it was screwed opposite of normal or you had to push to pull it, or something. All he knew was, he had to go. Painful as it might be, he yanked at the tape, which pulled hairs on his hand, then pulled the needle out with one motion. The sting brought tears to his eyes, and as the solution dripped on the floor, he made one feeble attempt to turn the stopper, then just tied the cord and headed for the bathroom.

Within seconds he heard the alarm informing the nurses' station that an IV had come loose. He opened the closet on his way back, and though his clothes were there, his phone was not. His mind nearly went blank from pain and fear. Was this the end? Would someone dial back the numbers of Trib Force members who may have tried to reach him? He could have already been discovered. Should he just find Annie and get out of there? What if she was already dead? She would want him to escape and not risk his life in a vain attempt to be sure of her.

Not a chance. He would not leave without her or without knowing for sure whether she was dead.

"What are you doing out of bed?" It was not a nurse but a female orderly.

"Bathroom," he said.

"Back to bed," she said. "What have you done with your IV?"

"I'm fine," he said.

"We have bedpans and—"

"I already went—now just—"

"Sir! Shh! I can hear you and so can everyone else on this floor. Your roommates are sleeping."

"I just need—"

"Sir, do I need to get someone in here with restraints? Now quiet down!"

"I am being quiet! Now—" Suddenly David realized the bandages over his ears made him talk louder.

"Sorry," he said. "I'm Director Hassid. I need to find—"

"Oh! *You're* the director. Are you a lightning victim?"

"Yeah, I took a bolt right through the top of my head, but here I stand."

"You don't have to—"

"Sorry. No, I just fainted in the heat, and I'm fine."

"You had surgery."

"Minor, now—"

"Sir, if you're the director, I'm supposed to tell someone when you're awake."

"Why?" And why had she asked about the lightning? Was Annie a victim, and did they somehow connect him with her? He didn't want his mind to run away with him.

"I don't know, sir. I just do what I'm told. Six nurses and two aides are handling this whole floor, and some floors have fewer staff than that, so—"

"I need to know where my phone is. I carry it with me, and it's not in my uniform. I know you're going to tell me to stay away from my uniform anyway, but—"

"On the contrary, sir. You were sponge bathed when you were brought here, and if you're ambulatory, I think you're supposed to get dressed."

"You think?" This couldn't be right. Something was wrong. David had been sure he'd have to sneak out, but now he was being given the bum's rush?

"I'll get my supervisor, but you might as well start getting dressed. Can you do it yourself?"

"Of course, but—"

"Get started then. I'll be right back. Or she will."

David had overestimated his strength. He pulled his stuff from the closet and sat in a chair to dress, but he was soon short of breath and dizzier than ever. His whole head felt afire, and it seemed his wound was oozing over both ears, but when he felt under the bandaging, he felt nothing. He didn't want to think about the first time that dressing came off.

With his uniform on and only socks and shoes to go, David opened the door wider to get light from the hall. He peered into the mirror and shuddered. Still in his mid-twenties with smooth, clear, dark skin and nearly black hair and eyes, he had often been mistaken for a teenager. Never again. When had he aged so?

His face looked thin and drawn and, yes, his color lighter. He lowered his head and peeked atop it where the bandaging evidenced blood and ooze. The outer wrapping extended over his ears and beneath his chin, reminding him of dental patients from old movies. David's head seemed to push against the tight wrapping, and when he gingerly put on his uniform cap, he knew it was more than his imagination. He couldn't be sure how thick the bandages were, but between that and the swelling of his head, his cap rode atop him as if several sizes too small. Any thought of covering the effects of his stitching to avoid attention was hopeless. Maybe he could find a bigger—much bigger—cap, but there was no way to hide the wrap that extended under his chin anyway.

The supervising nurse knocked gently and stepped in as David was pulling on his socks. She was a bottle blonde, tall and thin, about twice his age. He had to straighten up to breathe and let the pain subside every few seconds.

"Let me help you," she said, clearly Scandinavian, kneeling and putting on his socks and shoes and tying them. David was so overwhelmed he nearly wept. Could she be a Christian? He wanted to ask. Anyone with a servant spirit like that was either a believer or a candidate.

"Ma'am," he said, trying to remember to talk softly. She looked up at him and he studied her forehead, searching, hoping for the mark of the believer. None. "Thank you."

"You're welcome," she said quickly. "Happy to help and wish I could help more. If I had my way, you would be with us a couple more days at least, maybe more."

"I'd just as soon leave. I—"

"Oh, I'm sure you would. No one wants to stay, and who can blame them? All the excitement, the resurrection, and all. But the potentate has called a meeting of directors and above, his office, at 2200 hours. You are expected."

"I am?"

"When his office was told you had succumbed to the heat and had been injured and operated on, we were informed that if you were alive and ambulatory, you were to be there."

"I see."

"I'm glad someone does. You, sir, should be a patient. I wouldn't be running around so soon—"

"I was told this was superficial, minor surgery."

"Minor surgery is an operation on someone else. You've heard that, I'm sure. You know a nurse did the procedure, and good as she was, she was pressed into duty—"

"Do you know who that was? I'm pretty sure she was Native—"

"Hannah Palemoon," she said.

"I wonder if she's got my phone. It was in my—"

"I doubt it, Director. You'll find your wallet and keys and ID unmolested. We know better than to confiscate things from someone at your level."

"I appreciate that, but—"

"No one took your phone, sir. Could you have dropped it where you fell, left it in your vehicle?"

David cocked his head. Possible, but unlikely. He had not been talking on the phone when he fell, best he could remember, so it would have been in his pocket. "Where would I find Nurse Palem—"

"I told you, Director. She would not have your phone, and I'm not going to tell you where she is. We're working twenty-four on and twenty-four off here, and she's off. If she's like me, she sleeps the first twelve of those twenty-four hours off, and she ought to be allowed to."

David nodded, but he couldn't wait to get back to his computer and look her up in the personnel directory. "Ma'am, I have to find an employee I'm worried about. Name's Annie Christopher. Cargo chief of the Phoenix but assigned crowd control at sector 53 today."

"That's not good."

"So I've heard. Lightning there?"

"Bad. Several deaths and injuries. I can check to see if she's in our system. You might check the morgue."

David flinched. "I'd appreciate it if you'd check your system."

"I will, sir. Then you had better get to your quarters and relax before your meeting. You know as well as I do you're in no condition to be sitting at a table, thrilling as it may be to meet with a man who was dead this morning and is alive tonight. Follow me." She led him to the nurses' station, where she searched the computer. "No Christopher," she said, "but our entries have been hopelessly delayed."

"She would have had an employee badge," David said.

"And it should have been swiped by a wand."

"So the morgue?" he said, again trying to cover his emotion.

"Look on the bright side," she said. "Maybe she wasn't a victim at all."

That would almost be worse, David decided. Why could he not reach her, and why would she not have tried to reach him? Well, maybe she had. He had to find his phone before the meeting.

"Nothing," Rayford said. "David hasn't accessed his computer for hours, and I'm getting no answer on his phone. Now it's not even letting me leave a message, as if he's turned it off."

"Strange," Albie said. "So Pueblo doesn't even know we're coming."

"And we're not going if we don't know where it is."

"We'll find out."

"You're a resourceful guy, Albie, but—"

"I love the impossible. But you're the boss. I need your permission."

"What's your plan?"

"To find out if your new look and ID work."

"Oh, boy."

"C'mon, man. Confidence."

"The plan, Albie."

"I'll be the ranking officer down there. I blame the computer delay on all the excitement or the incompetence in New Babylon. Who can argue that? You're with me. If they demand ID, you've got it. You're no longer just a civilian helping out, though. You're a recruit, a trainee."

"Uh-huh."

"Not only do I insist on a car, but I'll get out of them the location of the bunker."

"This I've got to see."

"I love showing off."

Rayford slapped Albie's computer shut. "Tell me about it."

Kenny Bruce tried to tug Buck toward the barrier, as if knowing his dad could get him past it. But Buck was anchored to the bed. He felt as if he'd survived a plane crash. Or hadn't. It was as if his spine were compacted, every muscle, bone, joint, and tendon tender. He sat there trying to muster the strength to rise and stretch and make his way to his wife and the others.

Kenny, apparently resigned to patience, climbed onto his father's lap and put a hand on each side of his face. He looked into Buck's eyes and said, "Mama?"

"We'll see Mama in a minute, hon," Buck said. Kenny traced Buck's deep facial scars with his stubby fingers. "They don't bother you, do they, bud."

"Da-da," Kenny said. "Mama."

Presently Buck rose, lifting Kenny as he went. The boy spread his legs and settled in over Buck's hip, his arms around him, head on Buck's chest. "Wish I could take you with me everywhere I go," Buck said, limping, stiff legged, and gimpy.

"Mama, Da-da."

"Yep. We're goin', bud."

Buck prepared himself for the always embarrassing welcome saved for the last person to rise, but when he came into view of everyone else in the safe house, he was virtually ignored. Leah sat bundled in a robe, leaning back against a wall, dozing, her bleached-blonde hair with red roots wrapped in a towel. Chaim stared at the tabletop before him, his head in his hands, a straw in his coffee cup. Tsion stood beside a window, out of view from the outside just in case, head bowed, softly praying.

Chloe paced, phone pressed to her ear, tears streaming. She looked directly into Buck's eyes as if to let him know she was aware he was there, and when Kenny tried to wriggle down to get to her, Buck whispered, "Stay with Daddy a minute, hmm?"

Chloe was saying, "I understand, Zeke. . . . I know, sweetie, I know. God knows. . . . It'll be all right. We'll come get you, don't you worry. . . . Zeke, God knows. . . . It'll be after dark, but you stay strong, hear?"

She finally rang off, and everyone looked to her. "Big Zeke was busted," she said.

"Zeke Sr.?" Tsion asked. Zeke Jr. was

much bigger than his father, but still they were known as Big Zeke and Little Zeke.

She nodded. "GC goons got him this morning, cuffed him, charged him with subversion, took him away."

"How'd they miss Zeke Jr.?" Buck asked, finally letting Kenny down.

"Zeke!" Kenny said, giggling.

Chloe shrugged. "Their underground was better hidden than ours, and I don't think Little Zeke ever showed his face outside."

"Zeke!" Kenny said.

"Little Zeke coming here?" Leah said.

"Where else would he go? He says GC is staking out the place, picking up people who stop for gas."

"How's he know?"

"He's got some kind of a monitor rigged up that he used to keep track of his dad. That's how he knew Big Zeke had been arrested. He knows his dad won't give him up, but he also knows he can't stay there. He's packing."

"Yeah," Buck said, "all he'd need is for the GC to find all his files and document-making paraphernalia."

"It will be good to have him here," Tsion said. "He will be safe and can do so much for so many. Cameron, how are you feeling?"

"Better than Chaim, apparently."

The old man lifted his head and tried to smile. "I'll be OK," he mouthed through his clenched jaw. "No capers for me. Eager to study and learn."

Tsion moved away from the window. "And me with a student who cannot talk. You must listen and read. You will be an expert about our own people before you know it. God's chosen people. What a thrill to teach it. I will use the same material in my cyber-lesson, wherein I expose Carpathia as the Antichrist."

"Coming right out with it, are you?" Buck said.

"Absolutely," the rabbi said. "The gloves are off, as you Americans so like to say. There is no longer any question about him, nor should there be. I am persuaded that Leon is his false prophet, and I will say that too. Those who have ears will not be deceived. It will not be long before the Satan-indwelt beast will take out his rage against the Jews."

Chaim held up a hand. Buck could barely make out the labored, muffled question.

"And what are we to do? We are no match for him."

"You will see, my friend," Tsion said. "You will learn today not only the history of the Jews, but their future as well. God will protect his people, now and forevermore."

"I like being a believer already," Chaim managed.

"Buck," Chloe said, stepping close to embrace him, "we have to plan Zeke's rescue."

"Just what I need today, another mission."

"You slept, didn't you?"

"Like a dead man."

"Don't say that."

"Well . . ."

"It's you or me, pal," Chloe said. "If you need another day of recup—"

"I'll be ready," Buck said.

"I can help," Leah said. "I'm fit."

"Maybe the two of you, then," Chloe said. "I've got to get news to the co-op, keep everybody working together."

"We're going to need a pilot," Buck said. "Put the GC chopper down right in the middle of their stakeout, chide 'em for missing a suspect, and we arrest Zeke Jr. and bring him here. What? What's with all the looks?"

"We don't have a chopper today or

tonight, hon," Chloe said. "Probably not until tomorrow night, and we don't dare risk making Zeke wait that long."

"OK, so where's the helicopter and your dad? And Albie?"

FOUR

David hurried to his office and phoned Annie. No answer. Then he called the motor pool. The man who had originally brought him his cart was off duty, but the one he reached told him, “No, sir, no phone. Nothing was left in there. We found the cart but not you, and my boss was pretty mad until he traced you to Medical Services. You OK?”

“Fine.”

“Need the cart?”

“No.”

“Anything I can do fo—”

But David had hung up. He flipped open

his computer and saw urgent messages flashing from the code words and numbers he knew belonged to his comrades in the Tribulation Force. He would get to those when he could, but for now, before the infernal meeting, he had to get his phone back and find out where Annie was.

His watch read 2135. He searched the GC database for Personnel, Medical, Nursing, Female, under *P.* There it was: "Palemoon, Hannah L., room and extension 4223." A groggy hello greeted the fifth ring.

"Nurse Palemoon?"

"Yeah, who's this?"

"I am so sorry to be calling so late and sorry to wake you, but—"

"Hassid?"

"Yes, forgive me, but—"

"I have your phone."

"Oh, thank G—goodness! Is it on?"

"No, sir, I turned it off. Now are you coming to get it so I can get back to sleep?"

"Could I? If you don't mind terribly, I—"

"I gotta show you something anyway."

What in the world? Was he being set up? Why would she be so willing to have him come and get it? And why did she take it in the first place? To be safe, he jumped back on the computer and fired up the bugging device that would record their conversation in the corridor outside her room.

As he backed out of that program he saw the blinking signals for his urgent messages again. Looked like Rayford and Albie had been desperately trying to reach him. He didn't have time to deal with them, but what if they had heard from Annie? He had to peek.

The requests stunned him. He was way late for helping Albie and Rayford in Colorado, but his fingers flew over the keyboard anyway. His head ached, his wound oozed, and he blinked furiously. He entered the numbers to override the Peacekeeping security codes. Under his phony name as a high-level GC unit commander in New Babylon, he assigned Marcus Elbaz to Carpathia Memorial Airstrip in Colorado Springs. He also authorized him to temporarily appropriate a vehicle with which to take custody of an escapee from the Belgium Facility for Female Rehabilitation, currently incarcerated at a bunker on the north end of Pueblo. A few more keystrokes derived the exact coordinates of that facility and the name of the deputy director in charge—Pinkerton Stephens. Fortunately, Stephens was lower ranked than Deputy Commander Elbaz.

David would work on name, rank, and serial number for Rayford later, hoping the two of them could bluff their way past the GC in the meantime. It was 2150, Hannah Palemoon was waiting, and he couldn't be late for the big meeting. Healthy and in shape it would have been a challenge to get to her room, retrieve his phone, and get to Carpathia's office in time, but wounded as he was, he couldn't imagine it.

He could phone Fortunato at the last minute and explain he would be a few minutes late, coming from his hospital bed. But neither did he want to miss any of that meeting. As he locked his door and strode quickly toward the elevator, he wobbled and had to grab the wall. *Catch your breath,* he told himself. *Late is better than not there at all.*

"Give me my razor," Albie said. "It's going to be hard to pull this off if I'm out of regulation."

"You'll be on the ground in less than a minute," Rayford said.

"I have a copilot, do I not?"

Rayford pulled Albie's electric razor from his bag and took over the landing as Albie shaved and tightened his tie. When the tower confirmed the landing, Albie responded, then whipped off the headphones and put on his uniform cap. When they disembarked, Rayford was struck again how the diminutive Middle Easterner seemed taller, more commanding.

"I can point you to the refueling area so you can tank up before takeoff, Commander Elbaz."

"You can't do it for me while I'm on assignment?"

"Sorry, sir, we're shorthan—"

"I know. Carry on."

Rayford stayed a step behind Albie as they made their way to the offices, hoping that once David got him enlisted as a GC Peacekeeper, he would give him an even higher rank. How could he supervise a man who outranked him in disguise?

The officer at the desk saluted and said, "I told my chief you weren't in the computer, so you're on your own for ground transportation. If you'll give me your fueling order number, however, I can clear you for that when—"

"Excuse me?" Albie said.

"You'll have to refuel yourself, because—"

"I know all that. I need a vehicle for an important assignment, and I need it now. You expect me to rent a car?"

"Sir, I'm just telling you what my chief said. I—"

"Get him out here."

"He's a her, sir."

"I don't care if he's a gorilla. Get him, or her, out here."

The airstrip chief appeared before the deskman buzzed her. She saluted but did not smile. "Judy Hamilton at your service, Commander."

"Not enough at my service, I'm afraid."

"I can do only what I can do, sir, but I'm open to suggestions."

"Do you have a vehicle?"

"None available, sir."

"I need it for half a day, tops."

"None, sir."

"You personally?"

"Me, sir?"

Albie sighed loudly through his nose. "You understand English, Hamilton? Do-you-personally-have-a-vehicle?"

"I have not been issued GC wheels, sir."

"I didn't ask you that. How do you get to work?"

"I drive."

"Then you must have a vehicle."

"My own, yes, sir."

"That would be what *personal* means, Judy. I will be borrowing your personal vehicle this afternoon, and the Global Community will be indebted to you. In fact, we will be indebted at the rate of one Nick per mile."

She raised a brow. "The manual says half that, sir."

"I'm aware of that," Albie said. "I'll authorize it due to your cooperation."

"No demerits for stupidity, sir?"

"Only for insubordination, Hamilton, which is one way I define sarcasm."

"So you'll pay me a Nick a mile for the use of my car."

"You catch on quickly."

"No."

"No?"

"No, you'll not be using my car."

"I beg your pardon, Hamilton?"

"I have a meeting in Monument in two hours, and C-25 has been open only a week, and not all lanes. I need to leave now."

"And you believe your meeting takes precedence over that of a deputy commander?"

"It does today, sir, because of your attitude."

"You are denying me the use of your car?"

"You catch on quickly."

Albie squinted at her, reddening. "You're going on report, Hamilton. You will be disciplined."

"But surely not this afternoon. And you will be disciplined as well."

"I?" Albie said.

"How long has it been since the resurrection of the potentate, yet you greeted neither my deskman nor me with the new phrase."

"I have been busy and up for hours."

"You don't know that we greet each other with 'He is risen,' to be responded to by 'He is risen indeed'?"

"Of course, but—ma'am, I also need to know the exact location of the facility on the north end of Pueblo where—"

"You don't have full orders, sir?"

"Unfortunately not."

"Corporal, check the computer again. Let

me see what we do have on Deputy Commander Elbaz and whether we can add bluster and bullying to his profile."

"Hamilton, I—"

She silenced him with a hand.

"Hey," the deskman said, "this wasn't here before. Straight from the brass in New Babylon. Look."

Hamilton peered and blanched at the screen. Rayford let out a breath. The woman cleared her throat. "It appears everything is in order, Commander. I, uh, would like to propose a truce."

"I'm listening."

"You're cleared for a vehicle too, and we will find you one, though I will be happy to use the jeep if you still care to use my car."

"You would let me?"

"I will not only let you use the car, but I will also agree not to report your breach of protocol if you will keep between us your opinion of my insubordination."

Buck and Chloe left the baby in Leah's care while Tsion and Chaim studied. The couple made their way to the basement of the tower, where Buck had parked the Land Rover among many other vehicles.

"We can be grateful this place had the ritzy clientele it did," Chloe said. "Look at these rigs."

Buck had to smile at the difference between them and the filthy, banged-up Rover, which wasn't so old. He smacked a palm atop it, and it echoed throughout the parking garage. "Ol' Bessie saw us through a lot, didn't she?"

Chloe shook her head. *"She?* You men and your penchant for attributing female characteristics to your cars."

Buck leaned back against a pillar and beckoned Chloe to him. He enveloped her. "Think about it," he said. "I couldn't pay the car, or women, a higher compliment."

"Keep digging. You'll need a backhoe in a minute."

"Not if you think about it."

She leaned back and cocked her head, pointing to her temple. "Hmm, let's see if ol' Charley and I can figger this out. Callin' mah brain by a man's name is the biggest compliment I can pay it and men."

"C'mon," Buck said. "Think what that car's been through with us. It got us through traffic when the war broke out. Kept you alive when you sailed it into a tree, no less. Rode with me into a crevice in the earth and back out again, not to mention up, over, and through every obstacle."

"You're right," she said. "No man could have done that."

"You and Charley figger that out all by yourselves?"

"Yep. And wanna know what else? I think a Humvee is the way to go this time."

"We got one?"

"Two. Down around the corner near the luxury cars."

She pulled him to a darker area of the underground structure. "All the spaces are numbered, and they coincide with the key Peg-Board in the attendant's shack. There's hardly a car in here with less than half a tank of gas, and most of 'em are full."

"People must have been prepared."

"Some were listening to the rumors of war, apparently."

Buck tapped her head. "Thank you, Charley." He surveyed the selection of vehicles—dozens of them, mostly new—and let out a low whistle. "When God blesses, he blesses." But Chloe had grown quiet. "Whatcha thinking?" he said.

She pursed her lips and buried her hands

in her jacket pockets. "About what fun we would have had if we'd been lovers at any other time in history."

He nodded. "We wouldn't have been believers."

"Someone might have gotten to us. Look at us. This is the most fun I've had in ages. It's like we're in a free car dealership and it's our turn to pick. We've got a beautiful baby and a free sitter, and all we have to do is decide what model and color car we want."

She rested against a white Hummer and Buck joined her. She shook her head. "We're older than our years, wounded, scarred, scared. It won't be long before our days will be spent looking for ways to just stay alive. I worry about you all the time. It's bad enough living now, but I couldn't go on without you."

"Yes, you could."

"I wouldn't want to. Would you, without me? Maybe I shouldn't ask."

"No, Chlo', I know what you mean. We have a cause, a mission, and everything seems crystal clear. But I wouldn't want to go on without you either. I *would.* I'd *have* to. For Kenny. For God. For the rest of the Force. Like Tsion says, for the kingdom.

You'd have been the best thing that ever happened to me even if you weren't my whole life. But you are. Let's watch out for each other, keep each other alive. We've got only three and a half years to go, but I want to make it. Don't you?"

"'Course."

She turned and held him tightly for a long minute, and they kissed fiercely.

When David finally mince-stepped his way down the fourth floor of the employee residence tower, he found room 4223 open a crack, a sliver of light peeking out. He was about to knock when a dark hand poking out the end of a quilted robe thrust his phone out at him.

"Thanks, ma'am," he said. "I've got to run."

"Ma'am?!" Nurse Palemoon said. "I can't be *that* much older'n you, boy. How old *are* you?"

"Why?"

She opened the door and leaned wearily against the jamb. Her hair was in a ponytail, and her eyes looked sleepy behind puffy cheeks. David was surprised how short she was. "I'm not even thirty yet," she said, "so quit with the ma'am, all right?"

"Fair enough. Listen, I'm late for a meeting. I wanted to thank you, and—"

"I said I wanted to show you something."

"So you did. What? And why did you take my phone?"

"Well, that's sort of what I wanted to show you."

David didn't want to be rude, but what was this game? She just stood there, arms folded, gazing at him with raised brows. "OK," he said. "What?"

She didn't move. *Oh, brother,* he thought. *She's not trying to make a move on me. Please!*

He slipped the phone in his pocket and gestured with both palms raised. "Oh!" she said. "You're in the dark."

I sure am.

She straightened and flipped a switch just inside the door. The tiny light above her door illuminated them both. She matched his gesture and he stopped breathing. *You've* got *to be kidding!* Plain as the nose on her face, the mark was clear on her forehead.

"Check it," she said. "I wouldn't blame you. I *know* yours is real. I rubbed it with alcohol."

David looked up and down the hall, asked

her to forgive him, licked his thumb, and pressed it against her forehead as she leaned in to him. He looked both ways one more time and leaned down to embrace her briefly. "Sister," he whispered. "I am glad to see you! I didn't know we had *any*body in Medical."

"I don't know of anyone else," she said. "But as soon as I saw your mark and knew your rank, I thought of your phone."

"You're brilliant," he said.

"You're welcome. I'll be back in touch."

"I'm sure you will."

"And thanks, Nurse P—"

"Hannah," she said. "Please, David."

On his way back to the elevator he checked his phone. There were several messages, none from Annie. He would visit the morgue only as a last resort. He speed-dialed the Supreme Commander's office and reached Sandra, the assistant Carpathia and Fortunato had shared.

"Glad to hear you're up and about," she said. "They're expecting you. I'll tell them you'll be a few minutes."

Assuming that because David had finally gotten Albie's clearance into the system he might also have passed along the location of the Pueblo bunker, Rayford jogged to the fighter to grab Albie's computer on their way out.

"This used to be an interstate," he said, driving Judy Hamilton's nondescript minivan south on C-25. "Until everything got renamed for St. Nick."

Albie was accessing data. "It's here," Albie said. "The interchanges and exits are still under construction, so watch for a hard left into Pueblo. I'll tell you from there. *Humph.* Pinkerton Stephens. There's a handle for you. The man we want to see there."

"Heard of him?"

Albie shook his head. "Ask me tomorrow."

A few minutes later they passed the Quonset-hut-style building deep off a side road. Rayford said, "Question. Why not come in here with a GC jeep—complete the image?"

"Surprise. You told Ms. Durham in no uncertain terms you were not coming, knowing they were listening. They're not expecting anyone. Let them wonder who's pulling in. I show up in uniform, outranking everyone; they don't recognize the civilian.

They'll worry more about impressing us than making up a story. Anyway, I don't want to transport this woman in an open jeep, do you?"

Rayford shook his head. "You really think we'll surprise 'em?"

"Only briefly. The gate guard will let them know brass is coming."

Rayford popped a U-turn and headed for the entrance. The guard at the gate asked him to state his business. "Just chauffeuring the deputy commander here."

The guard stooped to get a look at Albie, then saluted. "An appointment with whom, sir?"

"Stephens, and I'm late, if you don't mind."

"Sign here, please."

Rayford signed "Marvin Berry," and they were waved on.

As they entered the front office, a woman at the desk was listening to a strange voice over the intercom. It was high-pitched and nasal, and Rayford couldn't tell if it came from a man or a woman. "A deputy commander to see me?" the voice said.

"Yes, Mr. Stephens. I checked the name with the GC database and the only Marvin

Berry employed by us is not in Peacekeeping. He's an elderly fisherman in Canada."

"I smell a rat," the voice said.

So it's a man, but what's the matter with him? Rayford wondered.

"One moment, sir," the woman said, standing when she noticed the deputy commander behind Rayford. "Is your name Berry?"

"Berry's my driver," Albie barked. "Look up Elbaz on your computer. None of my family knows how to fish."

"Mystery solved, Mr. Stephens," the woman announced over the intercom. "The gate guard had the driver sign."

"Incompetent!" Stephens's weird voice sang into the squawk box. "Send him in!"

"The guard?"

"The deputy commander!"

She pointed to the first door on the left down a short hallway, but when Rayford moved to follow, she said, "Only the deputy commander, please."

"He's with me," Albie said. "I'll clear it with the boss."

"Oh, I don't know."

"I do," Albie said. He stopped at the door and knocked.

"Come in," came the disembodied voice.

"Come in?" Albie repeated in a whisper. "Is he going to be embarrassed when he realizes he didn't open the door to a superior officer."

Albie pushed the door open, stepped in, and hesitated, causing Rayford to bump into him. "Sorry," Rayford mumbled. He could not see Stephens, but he heard the whine of an electric motor.

"Forgive the lack of protocol," came the voice as Stephens's wheelchair rolled into view. Rayford was taken aback. The man had one leg, the other a stump just above the knee; his right hand had small protrusions in place of fingers, and the other hand, though whole, had clearly suffered severe burns. "I'd stand, but then, I can't."

"Understood," Albie said, hesitantly shaking the man's partial hand.

Rayford did the same, and they followed Stephens's gesture to two chairs that filled the small office. What was it about the face? Stephens's neck was permanently red and scarred, as were his cheekbones and ears. He was clearly wearing a toupee. Except for the lips, the middle of his face—chin, nose, eye sockets, and the center of his forehead—seemed all of one piece, the color of a plastic hearing aid.

"Don't know you, Elbaz," Stephens said, almost like a man with no tongue or no nose. "You, Berry, you look familiar. You GC?"

"No, sir."

"I'm here on business," Albie said. "I don't have a hard copy of my orders, but—"

"Excuse me, Deputy Commander, but I'll get to you. You got a minute?"

"Well, sure, but—"

"Just give me a minute. I mean, I know you outrank me and all, but unless you're in an unusual hurry, bear with me. Your story checks out. I'll give you all the help I can on whatever you need. Now, Berry, were you *ever* GC?"

Rayford, disconcerted by the wasted body and the voice, hesitated. "No, uh, no, sir. Not Peacekeeping anyway."

"But something."

"I didn't mean to say that."

"But you did. You were GC connected some way, weren't you? You look familiar. I know you or of you, or I'll bet I know a friend of yours."

Albie gave Rayford a look, and Rayford

quit talking. Regardless of the question, Rayford merely stared at the man, racking his brain. Where would he have run into a Pinkerton Stephens, and how could he forget him if he had?

"I was a whole man then, Mr. Berry. If that's your real name."

Rayford grew more uncomfortable by the second. Had they been set up? Would he ever get out of here? And what of Hattie? Albie seemed to have stiffened and was no more comfortable than he.

Stephens cocked his head for one more lingering glance at Rayford, then turned to Albie. "Now then, Deputy Commander Elbaz. What might be your business with me?"

"I've been assigned to take custody of your prisoner, sir."

"And who told you I had a prisoner?"

"Top brass, sir. Said the subject was uncooperative, that some plan or mission failed, and that we were to return her to Buffer."

"Buffer? What's that?"

"You know what that is, Stephens, if you are who you say you are."

"Doesn't make sense that half a man

would be in a leadership role in the GC?" Stephens said.

"I didn't say that."

"But it doesn't add up, does it?"

"Can't say it does."

"Never saw another like me in the ranks, have you, Elbaz?"

"No, sir, I haven't."

"Well, I'm legit whether you like it or not, and you're going to have to deal with me."

"Happy to, sir, and when you check me out, you'll see that everything is in order, and—"

"Did I say I was housing a prisoner here, Deputy Commander?"

"No, sir, but I know you are."

"You know I am."

"Yes, sir."

"Buffer is a female rehab facility, sir. Were you under the impression I had a female incarcerated here?"

Albie nodded.

"Does this look like a detention center to you?"

"They take different forms during different times."

"Indeed they do. Is there a reason, sir, why you did not greet me with the new protocol?"

"I've been having trouble remembering that, Mr. Stephens."

"Indeed? Do you realize, sir, that you have a smudge on your forehead?"

Albie jerked. Rayford felt a chill. A GC Peacekeeper could see Albie's mark? Things tumbled into place so fast that Rayford could barely keep up. How much had been compromised? Albie knew everything!

"I do?" Albie said innocently. He swiped at his forehead with his palm.

"There, that's better," Stephens said.

Albie slowly moved his hand until it rested on his side arm. If only Rayford had one.

"Gentlemen," Stephens enunciated carefully past his awful sound, "if you'll do me the kindness of following me, I'd like us to start over in a new room. This time we'll begin with the proper protocol—what do you say?"

He rolled past Rayford and Albie, reached for the door, swung it open, and sped through before it slammed on him. Albie rose and grabbed it, and Rayford followed him down the hall. Albie unsnapped the strap that held the 9 mm in its holster. Rayford wondered if he had time to peel off and get out the front door to the van before Albie knew he was gone. He hesitated, hoping the whir of the chair would cover him if he made the decision.

But Albie turned and motioned Rayford to walk in front of him, behind the fast-moving chair. Even if he could escape, Hattie was history. He had no choice but to stay and play it out.

FIVE

Buck settled on the white Hummer, confirmed it had a full tank, checked the tires, found the keys, checked the engine, and fired it up.

"What shall we name her?" Chloe said.

"This is a big, ol' muscle car," he said. "It's got Chloe written all over it."

It would be hours before dark, and they would be in touch with Zeke frequently to discover what he knew about the positioning of the GC stakeout. They were looking for rebels who gassed up at his dad's station, not expecting Zeke Jr. to even be there. But could Buck get him out of there without their seeing?

Kenny was down for a nap, and Leah was reading when they returned. "Tsion said you could join him and Chaim," she said. "And Chloe was going to involve me in the co-op stuff."

"I've got to start communicating with everyone," Chloe said, setting up her computer as Leah pulled up a chair. Buck moved up one floor to Tsion's hideaway.

What a spot he had set up for himself. In a room just big enough for a U-shaped desk, Tsion had what amounted to a cockpit, where he was within arm's length of whatever he needed. With his computer before him and his commentaries and Bible on a ledge above, he was ready. Buck was struck by how few books he had brought with him, but Dr. Ben-Judah explained that most of what he needed had been scanned onto his massive hard drive.

Chaim sat in a comfortable chair looking less than comfortable. He had been hurt worse than Buck in the plane crash, yet he sat weeping tears of apparent joy, as Tsion rushed to teach him.

"Much of this you have heard from your youth, Chaim," the rabbi said, "but now that God has opened your eyes and you know Jesus is the Messiah, you will be amazed at how it all comes together for you and makes sense."

Chaim rocked and wept and nodded. "I see," he said over and over. "I see."

Buck sat transfixed, hearing in a gush much of what he had learned over the past three-plus years from Tsion's daily cyber-messages. At times the rabbi himself would be overcome and have to stop and exult, "Chaim, you don't know how we prayed for you, again and again, that God would open your eyes. Do you need a break, my brother?"

Chaim shook his head but held up a hand, trying to make himself understood despite the wired-shut jaw. "God is opening my eyes to so many things," he managed. "Cameron, come close. I must ask you something."

Buck looked at Tsion, who nodded, and he pulled his chair closer to Chaim's. "I always wondered why you had not come to Nicolae's first meeting with his new leadership team at the United Nations. Remember?"

"Of course."

"Forgive me for spitting on you, Cameron, but I cannot speak another way just now."

"Don't give it a second thought."

"I could not fathom it! The privilege of a lifetime, the opportunity no self-respecting journalist could miss. You were invited. I invited you! You said you would come, and yet you did not. It was the talk of New York. You were demoted because of it. Why? Why did you not come?"

"I was there, Chaim."

"No one saw you there! Nicolae was disappointed, enraged. Everyone asked about you. Your boss, what was his name?"

"Steve Plank."

"Mr. Plank could not believe it! Hattie Durham was there! You were the one who introduced her to Carpathia, and yet you were not there when she expected you."

"I was there, Chaim."

"I was there too, Cameron. Your place at the table was empty."

Buck was about to say again that he was there, but he suddenly realized what was happening and why Chaim would bring this up again after so long. "Your eyes truly are being opened, aren't they, Chaim?"

The old man put a quivering hand on Buck's knee. "I could not understand it. It made no sense. Jonathan Stonagal had embarrassed Nicolae by going after you. Nicolae shamed him into committing suicide, and he killed Joshua Todd-Cothran in the process."

Buck wanted to say he had seen it and that was not the way it had happened, but he waited.

"None of it made sense," Rosenzweig whined. "None of it. But the eyes don't lie. Stonagal grabbed the gun from the security guard, shot himself and his colleague with him."

"No, Chaim," Buck whispered. "The eyes don't lie. But the Antichrist does."

Rosenzweig began to shiver until his whole body shook. He pressed his hands against his tender face to stop the quivering of his lips. "Why were you not there, Cameron?"

"Why would I not have been there, sir? What could have kept me away?"

"I cannot imagine!"

"Neither could I."

"Then why? Why?"

Buck did not respond. He had quit trying

to convince the old man. "I was assigned to be there; my boss expected me to go."

"Yes, yes!"

"It was the mother of all cover stories for the largest circulation magazine in history. It was the apex of my career. Would I have thrown that away?"

Rosenzweig shook his head, tears falling, hands trembling. "You would not."

"Of course I wouldn't. Who would?"

"Maybe you had come to believe Nicolae was Antichrist and you didn't want to be exposed to him?"

"By then I knew, yes, or I thought I did. I would not have gone in there without the protection of God."

"And you did not have it?"

"I had it."

"And so why not go? You would have been the only one there with God's hand upon you."

Buck merely nodded. Rosenzweig's eyes cleared, and it appeared he was studying something a thousand miles away. His pupils darted back and forth. "You were there!"

"Yes, I was."

"You were there, weren't you, Cameron?"

"I was, sir."

"And you saw it all!"

"I saw everything."

"But you did not see what the rest of us saw."

"I saw what really happened. I saw the truth."

Chaim's hands fluttered beside his head, and through clenched teeth he described what he had once seen and what he now saw anew. "Nicolae! Nicolae murdered those men! He made Stonagal kneel before him, stuck the weapon in the man's ear, and killed the both of them with one shot!"

"That's what happened."

"But Nicolae told us what we had seen, told us what we would remember, and our perception became our reality!"

Chaim turned around and knelt, resting his fragile head in his hands, elbows on the seat of his chair. "Oh, God, oh, God," he prayed, "open my eyes. Help me to always see the truth, your truth. Don't let me be led by a madman, deceived by a liar. Thank you, Jehovah God."

Slowly he stood and embraced Buck, then turned to face Tsion. "Truly Nicolae is

Antichrist," he said. "He must be stopped. I want to do whatever I have to do."

Tsion smiled ruefully. "May I remind you that you already tried?"

"I certainly did, but not for the reasons I would try today."

"If you think you know the depths of the depravity of the man," Tsion said, "wait till we get to what he has in mind for God's chosen people."

Chaim sat and reached for a pad of paper. "Skip to that, Tsion. Please."

"In due time, my friend. Just a few thousand more years to go."

Despite his pain, David was rested. He could have used more, but he had slept the sleep of the drugged, and his mind—at least—felt refreshed. Unfortunately, that made it hard for him to separate his dread over Annie from his wariness over the indwelt Carpathia. He had been in the presence of evil many times, but never in the company of Satan himself. He breathed a prayer for Annie, thanks for Nurse Palemoon, for Tsion who had taught him that Satan—though more powerful than any human—was no match for the Lord God. "He is not omniscient," Tsion had taught. "Not omnipresent. Deceiving, persuasive, controlling, beguiling, possessive, oppressive, yes, but greater is he that is in you than he that is in the world."

"They're waiting for you," Sandra told him. "Apparently the risen potentate did not want you to miss a thing."

"Well, good then."

"And with your arrival, I leave. And that's good too. Long day."

"You and me both."

"Feeling all right? Heard you took a tumble."

"Better."

"Good night, Director Hassid. And, oh yes. He is risen."

David stared at her and was struck by the plainness of her forehead compared to that of the beautiful, dark sister he had just met. "He is risen indeed," he said, meaning just what he said.

He knocked and entered and was dazed when not only Carpathia and Fortunato stood, but all the other managers too. "My beloved David," Carpathia began, "how good that you were up to joining us."

"Thank you," David said as Intelligence

Director Jim Hickman pushed out a chair for him.

"Yes," Hickman said. "How good it is!" He beamed, peeking at Carpathia as if to see whether he had pleased the boss. The potentate pursed his lips and squinted, ignoring Hickman. To David it appeared purposeful. Hickman was Fortunato's choice, and Carpathia had scarcely hidden his opinion of the man as a buffoon.

The team of two dozen, plus Nicolae and Leon, sat around a huge mahogany table in Nicolae's office, the first time David had been there for this size of a meeting. David felt a dark foreboding as he sat and was shaken to see a well-worn Bible on the table in front of Nicolae. Everyone else sat when David did, but Carpathia remained standing. The man seemed energized, his breath coming quickly in great gasps that whistled through his teeth. It was as if he were a football player caged in the locker room before kickoff of a championship game.

"Gentlemen and ladies," he began, "I have a new lease on life!"

The room exploded with laughter, and when it waned, Nicolae was still laughing.

"Trust me, there is *nothing* like waking from the dead!"

The others nodded and smiled. David was aware of Security Chief Walter Moon's gaze, so he offered a cursory nod.

"Oh, I was dead, people, lest anyone wonder." They shook their heads. "Mr. Fortunato, we should publish photographs from the autopsy, the coroner's report, the rising itself. There will always be skeptics, but anyone who was there knows the truth."

"We know," several said.

David felt evil emanating so pervasively from Carpathia that he sat rigid and worried he might faint. Suddenly Nicolae faced him. "Director Hassid, you were there."

"I was, sir."

"You had a good view?"

"Perfect, sir."

"You saw me rise from the dead."

"I'll never deny it."

Carpathia chuckled warmly. He strode to his desk and stood behind the huge, stuffed, red leather chair. He caressed it, then massaged it deeply. "It is as if I am seeing this for the first time," he said to twenty-four pairs of admiring eyes. "Leon, what is directly above my office?"

"Why, nothing, sir. We are on eighteen, the top floor."

"No utility room, no elevator-maintenance area?"

"Nothing, sir."

"I want more room, Leon. Are you taking notes?"

"Yes, sir."

"What do you have so far?"

"Autopsy photos, coroner's report, the rising."

"Add the expansion of my office. I want it twice as high, with a transparent ceiling that exposes me to the heavens."

"Consider it done, Excellency."

"How soon?" Carpathia said. "Who would know that?" Fortunato pointed at the construction director, who waved a tentative hand. "Yes, sir," Nicolae pressed, "and may I assume this would be top priority?"

"You bet your life," the man said, and Carpathia nearly collapsed in laughter.

"Let me tell you something, Director. I know you must displace me for a few days because of the mess it will be to raze and raise this ceiling. But I want this done as fast as humanly possible, and do you know why?"

"I have an idea, sir."

"Do you?"

The man nodded.

"By all means, let us hear it!"

"Because I don't believe you are human anymore, and you could do it faster than my team on its best day."

"Only God bestows such wisdom, Director."

"I believe I am in his presence, Potentate."

Nicolae smiled. "I believe you are too." He turned and gestured to all. "When I lay there dead for three days, my spirit was so strong and powerful that I knew, I knew, I knew my time would come. When death had enjoyed victory over me long enough, I willed myself to live again. I raised myself, people. I raised myself back to life."

A murmur filled the room as the men and women approved aloud and pressed their hands together as if praying to him or worshiping him.

Nicolae picked up the Bible in what seemed to David a loving manner. "You may wonder what this is doing here," he said. He opened it and let it plop spine first onto the table. "This is the playbook of those who oppose me. This is the holy book of those who do not recognize me and who will not, despite what they saw with their own eyes." He slammed a fist onto the book. "This holds the lies about the chosen people of God and the supreme lie that there is one above me."

His team, save one, murmured disapproval.

Carpathia stood back from the end of the table and folded his arms, legs spread. "We shall use their very blueprint to bring them to their knees. The Jews who worship their coming Messiah in their own Holy Land, in their beloved city where they deigned slay me. I shall return there triumphant, and they will have one opportunity to repent and see the light.

"And the Judah-ites, who believe Messiah already came and went, who believe Jesus is their Savior—and whom I see nowhere; do you?—also trace their heritage to Jerusalem. If they want to see the true and living god, let them journey there, for that is where I shall soon be. If the sacred temple is the residence of the most high God, then the most high god shall reside there, high on the throne.

"In the city where they slew me, they shall see me, high and lifted up."

Many directors raised fists of victory and encouragement.

"Now, some plans. As I have left no doubt in any thinking person's mind about who I am, I no longer feel the need for a buffer between my team and me. While my dear comrade, Supreme Commander Leon Fortunato, has ably assisted me since first I came to power, I have need of him now in another crucial role, one he has already accepted with enthusiasm. What was once nobly attempted and ultimately failed shall now be consummated in success and victory.

"The Enigma Babylon One World Faith failed because, despite its lofty goal of unifying the world's religions, it worshiped no god but itself. It was devoted to unity, yet that was never achieved. Its god was nebulous and impersonal. But with Leon Fortunato as Most High Reverend Father of Carpathianism, the devout of the world finally have a personal god whose might and power and glory have been demonstrated in the raising, *of himself,* from the dead!"

Many applauded and Carpathia motioned to Leon to rise and speak as he himself backed away but remained standing.

"I am deeply humbled by this assignment," Leon said, moving to Nicolae, dropping to his knees, and kissing the potentate's hands. He rose and moved back to the head of the table. "Let me clarify, not that His Excellency needs any help from a mere mortal, that the very name of the new religion was my idea. It was no stroke of brilliance. What else could we call a faith in which the object of our worship is His Excellency?

"The outpouring of emotion from the citizens this very day spurred the idea that we should reproduce the image of His Excellency, the great statue, and erect it in all the major cities throughout the world. Plans have already been sent out, and each city is required to have the image constructed. They will be only a quarter of the size of the original, which as you know, is four times life-size. It doesn't take a scientist to figure out, then, that the replicas will be exactly life-size.

"While our beloved potentate lay dead, he imbued me with power to call fire from the sky to kill those who would oppose him. He blessed me with the power to give speech to the statue so we could hear his own heart. This confirmed in me the desire to serve him as my god for the rest of my days, and I shall do that for as long as Nicolae Carpathia gives me breath."

"Thank you, my beloved servant," Nicolae said as Leon sat. "Now, blessed comrades, I have written assignments for one and all. These were prepared just before my demise and now will make more sense than ever to you. First, one of my oldest and dearest friends, a woman closer to me than a relative, shall explain something to you. Ms. Ivins, if you would come."

Viv Ivins, prim and proper, her blue-gray hair piled atop her head, made her way to the head of the table and embraced Nicolae. As she passed out file folders with each director's name inscribed on them, Nicolae said, "Many of you know that Ms. Ivins helped raise me. Indeed for many years I believed she was my aunt—we were that close. She has been working on a project that will help me put in place certain unfortunately necessary controls on the citizenry. Most people are devoted to me—we know that. Many who were not or who were undecided are now decidedly with us, and, you will agree, for good reason.

"But there are those factions, primarily the two that I have already mentioned, who are not loyal. Perhaps now they have seen the error of their ways and will henceforth be loyal. If so, they will have no trouble with the safeguards I feel must be initiated. I am asking those loyal to the Global Community, specifically to me and to the unified faith, to willingly bear a mark of loyalty."

Walter Moon stood. "Sir, I beg of you, allow me to be the first to bear your mark."

"Let us not get ahead of ourselves, brother," Nicolae said. "You may just get your wish, and while I am touched by your sentiment, how do you know that I will not brand you with an iron like a head of cattle?"

Moon spread his hands on the table and bowed his head. "As you, my lord, are my witness, I would endure it and bear it with endless pride."

"My, my," Nicolae said, "if Director Moon's sentiment is shared by the populace, we shall need no enforcement measures, shall we?"

David peeked at his packet and fanned the pages until his eye fell on a startling word. "Guillotines?" he said aloud before he could stop himself.

"Now we *are* ahead of ourselves," Nicolae said. "Needless to say, such would be a last resort and I pray it will never be needed."

"I would gladly offer my head," Moon rhapsodized, "if I should be so foolish as to deny my lord."

Nicolae turned to David. "You are responsible for technical purchasing, correct?"

David nodded.

"I do not imagine we have an adequate supply of immediate-response mechanisms for the reluctant. We must study the expected need and be prepared. As I have said, my loftiest dream is that not one would refuse the loyalty mark. Ms. Ivins, please."

"The first page of your folders," she began, in a precise and articulate tone with a hint of her native Romanian dialect, "long before you reach the guillotines—" she paused for the chuckling, in which David did not join—"is a listing of the ten world regions and a corresponding number. It is the product of a mathematical equation that identifies those regions and their relationships to His Excellency the Potentate. The loyalty mark, which I shall explain in detail, shall begin with these numbers, thus identifying the home region of every citizen. The subsequent numbers, embedded on a biochip inserted under the skin, will further identify the person to the point where every one shall be unique."

Suddenly, as if in a trance, Leon rose and began to speak. "Every man, woman, and child, regardless of their station in life, shall receive this mark on their right hands or on their foreheads. Those who neglect to get the mark when it is made available will not be allowed to buy or sell until such time as they receive it. Those who overtly refuse shall be put to death, and every marked loyal citizen shall be deputized with the right and the responsibility to report such a one. The mark shall consist of the name of His Excellency or the prescribed number."

With that, Leon dropped heavily into his chair. Viv Ivins smiled benevolently and said, "Why, thank you, Reverend," which caused all, including Leon, to laugh.

David was afraid his crashing heart and shaking hands would make him conspicuous. What if someone got the bright idea to apply the mark to the inner circle that very night? He might be in heaven before Annie knew he was dead.

"We have settled on the technology," Viv

continued. "The miniature biochip with the suffix numbers embedded in it can be inserted as painlessly as a vaccination in a matter of seconds. Citizens may choose either location, and visible will be a thin, half-inch scar, and to its immediate left, in six-point black ink—impossible to remove under penalty of law—the number that designates the home region of the individual. That number may be included in the embedded chip, should the person prefer that one of the variations of the name of the potentate appear on their flesh."

"Variations?" someone asked.

"Yes. Most, we assume, will prefer the understated numbers next to the thin scar. But they may also choose from the small initials—no bigger than the numbers—*NJC.* The first or last name may be used, including one version of *Nicolae* that would virtually cover the left side of the forehead."

"For the most loyal," Nicolae said with a grin. "Someone like, oh, say, Director Hickman, for instance."

Hickman blushed but called out, "Sign me up, Viv!"

"The beauty of the embedded chip is twofold," she continued. "First, it leaves the visible evidence of loyalty to the potentate, and second, it serves as a method of payment and receipting for buying and selling. Eye-level scanners will allow customers and merchants to merely pass by and be billed or receipted."

Several whistles of admiration sounded. David's head throbbed. He raised his hand.

"Director Hassid," Viv said.

"What are you looking at in the way of timing?"

"Worried that your head won't take any more invasion just now?" she said, smiling.

"I had an IV in the hand too."

"Not to worry," she said. "While the potentate and the former Supreme Commander see value in employees serving as examples to the world, you will have thirty days, beginning tomorrow, to fulfill your obligation."

"I'll do it tonight," someone said, "and I'm not even Hickman!"

A month, David thought. *A month to get out of Dodge.* What would become of him and Annie and Mac and Abdullah? And Hannah Palemoon?

Viv said that over the next few days she would be sure each director knew his or her part in the rollout of images of Carpathia and the application of the mark of loyalty. Meanwhile, she said, "His Excellency has a closing comment."

"Thank you, Viv," Nicolae said. "Allow me to tell you just one story of a family I met today, and you know I met thousands. We have such a nucleus of loyal citizenry! This was a beautifully loyal Asian family named Wong."

David fought to maintain his composure.

"Their daughter already works for us at Buffer in Brussels. The parents are well-to-do and great supporters of the Global Community. The father was quite proud of his family and of his record of loyalty. But I was most impressed with the seventeen-year-old son, Chang. Here is a boy who, according to his father, loves me and everything about the world as we see it today. He wants nothing more than to work for me here at the palace, and though he has another year of high school, would rather bring his talents our way.

"And such talents! I will arrange for the completion of his schooling here, because he is a genius! He can program any computer, analyze and fix any procedural or operational or systems problem. And this is not just a proud father talking. He showed me documents, grades, letters of recommendation.

This kind of boy is our future, and our future has never looked brighter."

That boy, David thought, *would die before he took the mark.*

SIX

As Rayford followed the wheelchair down the hall, barely able to breathe, his mind reeled with his mistakes. Were it somehow possible to extricate himself from this, he would be the most decisive leader the Tribulation Force could imagine.

They repaired to an office even smaller than the original. Pinkerton Stephens opened the door and neatly pivoted his chair so he could hold it open and leave room for Rayford and Albie to enter. He pointed Rayford to a steel gray chair near the wall, facing a desk of the same color and material. Albie sat to Rayford's left.

Stephens let the door shut and locked it, breathed something nasally about the room being secure and not bugged, then steered himself to the other side of the desk, plowing a standard chair out of the way. He maneuvered his wheelchair up to and under the desk, leaned forward and rested his elbows atop it, and folded his hand and a half under his chin.

Part of Rayford could hardly bear to look at the man; another part could not take his eyes off him. "Now then," Stephens began slowly, "Deputy Commander Elbaz—if that's your real name—you may restrap your side arm and keep your hand off it. We're both on the same team, and you have nothing to fear. As for you, Mr. Berry, while you may be out of uniform and likely using an alias yourself, neither do you have anything to fear. You are about to be pleasantly surprised to find that the three of us are on the same team."

Rayford wanted to say, "I doubt it," but feared he would emit no sound if he tried.

"Shall we start over, gentlemen?" Stephens said.

If only . . . , Rayford thought.

"Mr. Elbaz, as the superior officer, I believe it falls to you to begin our session with the proper protocol."

"He is risen," Albie said, miserably in Rayford's opinion.

"Who is risen indeed?" Stephens responded, and Rayford attributed the mispronunciation to the man's malady, whatever it was. Albie just stared at Stephens. Rayford noticed that while Albie had taken his hand off his gun, he had not fastened the strap. Rayford wondered if he could grab the gun, kill them both, and get away with Hattie.

"Commander Elbaz, you have business here, and I will let you get to it after I satisfy the curiosity on both your parts. I realize that I am difficult to look at, that you both have to be wondering what happened to me, and that as hard as I have worked on my speech, I am difficult to understand. Have either of you ever seen someone with most of his face missing?"

Both shook their heads, and Stephens placed his good thumb beneath his chin. "Once I remove my prosthesis, I will be unable to be understood at all, and so I will not attempt to speak."

Snap!

Rayford flinched as Stephens unsnapped the plastic covering under his chin.

Snap! Snap!

As he continued, it became clear that the prosthesis was all one piece that substituted for most of his chin, nose, eye sockets, and forehead. It was held in place by metal fasteners embedded in what was left of the original facial bones. Stephens kept it in place with his stub-fingered hand and said, "Prepare yourselves; I won't make you look long."

Albie held up a hand. "Mr. Stephens, this is unnecessary. We have business here, yes, and I don't see the need to—"

He stopped when Stephens pulled the piece away from his face, revealing a monstrous cavity. Only what was left of his lips hinted at anything human, and Rayford fought to keep from covering his own eyes. The man had no nose and his entire eyeballs were exposed. Through gaps in his forehead, Rayford believed he could see through to the brain.

Rayford could breathe again when Stephens refastened the appliance. "Forgive me, gentlemen," he said, "but just as I assumed, neither of you really saw what I wanted you to see."

"And what was that?" Albie said, clearly shaken.

"Something that explains what I see on your faces."

"I'm lost," Rayford said.

"Oh, but you're not," Stephens said with a twisted smile. "You once were lost, but now you're found. Would you like me to remove the prosthesis again and—"

"No," Rayford and Albie said in unison. And Albie added, "Just get to the point."

Pinkerton folded his hands beneath his chin again, and his eyes seemed to bore into Albie. "How did I respond when you said, 'He is risen'?"

Albie seemed to have regained his voice and composure. "Sounded like you said, 'Who is risen indeed?' "

"That's what I said. What's your answer?"

Albie shifted and cleared his throat. "I believe the protocol is that I say, 'He is risen,' and that you respond, 'He is risen indeed.' "

"Fair enough, but my question remains. Who is risen indeed?"

So, Rayford concluded, *somehow he's*

onto me. And yet he sat silent, knowing a moment of truth had arrived and waiting to see what would come of it.

"Humor me one more time, Commander."

Albie sighed and glanced at Rayford. Albie's phony mark sure looked real. "He is risen," Albie muttered.

"Who is risen indeed?" Stephens said, forcing another smile through the misshapen lips.

"Oh, for Pete's sake!" Albie said. "I'm tired of this game."

"Christ!" Stephens whispered excitedly. "Come on, brothers! The answer to the question is 'Christ!' Christ is risen indeed! I see the marks of the believer on both your foreheads! You missed mine for the horror of the rest of my face. Now look!"

He unfastened the prosthesis from the top this time and merely peeled it back. Rayford and Albie leaned forward, and there, amidst the gore, the mark was clear. As Stephens reapplied the piece, Rayford turned and grabbed Albie's head in both hands. He cupped the back with his left hand and rubbed the forehead hard with his right.

"Satisfied?" Albie said, smiling.

Rayford felt like jelly. He flopped back in his chair, panting and unable to move.

"So who are you anyway?" Stephens said.

Rayford leaned forward, "I'm—"

"Oh, I know who you are. I knew almost immediately, though I like the new look. But who's this character?"

Albie introduced himself.

Stephens leaned forward and shook his hand. He nodded to Rayford. "I've got Mr. Steele completely dumbfounded, don't I?"

"That's an understatement," Rayford said.

"You and I both worked for Carpathia at the same time, Rayford, and before that your son-in-law worked for me."

"Steve Plank?"

"In the flesh, or what's left of it. Crushed, chopped up, burned, and left for dead by the wrath of the Lamb earthquake. I'd been on the edge for weeks, reading Buck's stuff, realizing things about Carpathia. I decided that if Buck and other believers were right about a global earthquake, I was in at the sound of the first tremor. I was praying the prayer as the building came down."

Rayford shook his head. "But why the ruse—why work for the GC again?"

"It came to me in the hospital. No one, including me, knew who I was. When my memory returned, I made up a name and a history. That was twenty-one months ago, and all through a year of therapy and rehab, I had time to think about where I wanted to land. I wanted to take Carpathia down from the inside."

"But why not tell anyone? Everyone thought you were dead."

"The best secrets are kept between two people, providing one of them is dead. One of the most shameless stunts Carpathia pulled was how he treated Hattie Durham. I got myself into the Peacekeeping Force and kept my eye on her till I tracked her out here. I prayed this day would come. I'll follow orders, obey the rules, do my job, and you'll rescue her."

David panicked. After sitting through the surreal performance by Carpathia, Fortunato, and Viv Ivins, he was in line to leave with the others. But Carpathia stood by the door, accepting embraces, handshakes, kisses, and bowing from each director. The shameless Hickman fell to his knees and wrapped his arms around Nicolae's knees, weeping loudly. The potentate rolled his eyes and gave Fortunato a look that would have put a wart on a gravestone.

When he was about sixth in line, David prayed desperately. What was he to do? In the flesh he wanted to fake whatever he had to fake in order to not be found out and jeopardize the rest of the Force. But he could not, would not, bow the knee to Antichrist. It was impossible that his breach of etiquette would go unnoticed. From what he could tell, it appeared he would be the only director who did not gush over the resurrected leader.

"God, help me!" he prayed silently. Was this the end? Should he merely bolt now and hope for the best? Or shake Carpathia's hand and say something neutral: "Glad you're feeling better after that dying thing"? "Welcome back"?

Except for his obvious disgust with Hickman, Carpathia oozed graciousness and humility as his people poured on the sugar. "Oh, thank you. I am grateful for your partnership and support. Great days ahead. Yes. Yes."

Now second in line, David was nauseated. Literally. His tender scalp vibrated against the bandages with every beat of his heart. He tried to pray, tried to be sensitive to what God wanted him to do. But as the director in front of him finally pulled away from a long embrace of the potentate, David stood there blankly.

Carpathia spread his arms and said, "David, my beloved David."

David could not move and sensed the turning heads of those nearby. Carpathia looked puzzled, seeming to beckon him. David said, "Pothen—potenth—Exshell—" and pitched forward. His last image before crashing to the floor, head banging the marble, was that he had vomited all over Carpathia.

"How you doing, Zeke?" Buck said.

He pictured the all-black-wearing, flabby forger huddled underground at his dad's one-pump filling station in ravaged Des Plaines. "I'm OK," came the whispered reply. "I been watchin' TV to keep from gettin' bored, and I got all kinds of food down here. Kinda dark though. And 'course there's nothing on but all this Carpathia junk."

"Have you been keeping an eye on the GC?"

"Yeah, every time I hear a car I scoot over to my monitor and watch what they do. Some of these people aren't even our real customers. They just see the pump and stop in. Then the GC car swings over from across the road and parks right in front of 'em."

"A jeep?"

"No, it's a little four door, a dark compact."

"Good."

"Why's that good, Mr. Williams?"

"Because when I come for you, I'm going to be in a white Hummer, and it'll squash a compact like a bug."

"It's not a VW, sir. It's—"

"That was just an expression, Zeke."

"Oh, I getcha."

"So they don't pull up in front *and* behind the car?"

"No, there's only one GC car over there. I looked."

"You did?"

"Yeah. I know I shouldn't've, but I was real bored, so I sneaked up the stairs where I was still in the dark and could see across the way. You know this road never really got rebuilt. They threw some asphalt on it a little over a year ago, but there was no real base, so it went to potholes and now it's just chunks of pavement. We don't get much traffic."

"You don't think the GC knows you're there, do you?"

"Nope, and I'm real sure they don't know there's a basement. There didn't use to be. Dad and I dug it ourselves."

"Where's the debris?"

"Out back, through the door at the back of the service bay."

"Hmm, never noticed it. How close are the secret stairs to the underground?"

"Maybe ten feet. It's kinda hidden in the corner."

"So if I was to drive to the back of the station, I'd see a door right about in the middle of the building, a door you could get to by sneaking up the stairs and moving about ten feet along the back wall."

"Yeah."

"So if you knew exactly when I was coming, you could sneak out the back without the GC stakeout guys seeing you."

"They'd probably see you, though."

"I'll worry about that. We don't want them to know you were ever in the underground. You come out and crawl in the back and I'll have a blanket you can hide under."

"I'll have a lot of my stuff."

"That's OK. If they see me and stop me, I'll bluff my way out of it, but I'm going to try to do it in a way where they won't even know I'm there."

A beep told Buck he had another call. It was Rayford. "Zeke, let me call you back. It could be a while, so be packed." He pushed the button. "Buck here."

"Buck, you're not going to believe who I just prayed with."

"Hattie?"

"No, you'd never guess."

David awoke in the palace hospital during the wee hours to someone caressing his hand.

"Don't speak," she whispered. It was Nurse Palemoon. "You're a celebrity."

"I am?"

"Shh. It's all over the palace that you blew chunks on Carpathia."

David was on an IV again. He felt better. "Did you change my dressing?"

"Yes, now be quiet."

"I thought you were off duty."

"So did I, but I was yanked in here because I was the one who had stitched you up, and you know no doctor was going to be dragged out of bed."

"Hannah, I've got to get out of here."

"No, you should have been with us a few days anyway, and now you've got the chance."

"I can't and neither can you." He quickly whispered what he had learned at the meeting. "We've got to be out of here before thirty days from today or be prepared for the consequences."

"I'm prepared, David. Aren't you?"

"You know what I mean. I've got to find my fiancée and my pilots, and if you know of any other believers—"

"Fiancée? You're attached?"

"The Phoenix cargo chief, Annie Christopher."

"I don't know what to tell you, David. If she were here, she'd be in the system by now."

"Would you check again for me? And see if you can get Mac McCullum and Abdullah Smith to visit me."

"That's quite an alias, Albie," Plank said. "You want me to report that a Deputy Commander Elbaz came in here with the proper credentials and that I followed the letter of the law?"

"I'm so visible on the GC database, no one will even question it," Albie said. "They'll probably wonder why they haven't met me yet."

"And soon enough," Rayford said, "I'll be enlisted and we'll make sure Albie reports to me. I just worry about compromising our inside guy, the one who sets this stuff up for us."

"How will they trace it to him or even to the palace?" Albie said.

"I don't know. Maybe he's precluded that, but we'll have to let him know what's happening."

Plank led them out the door and down the hall, past the receptionist and into the cell area. "I heard a noise back there a minute ago," Mrs. Garner called out from the desk.

"Trouble?"

"Somethin' banging, that's all."

Plank led the men to Hattie's door and knocked but heard no response. "Ma'am," he called out, "GC personnel are here to transport you back to Buffer." He winked at Rayford and Albie. "May I come in, ma'am?"

Plank fished for his key ring, unlocked the

door, and pushed it open about an inch until it met resistance. Albie and Rayford stepped forward to help, but Plank said, "I got this."

He backed up his chair, then threw it forward, bashing into the door and pushing past the bed that had been wedged against it. "Oh, no!" he said, and Rayford stepped over him, driving his shoulder into the door to force his way in.

The room was dark, but when he flipped the light switch, sparks startled him from the ceiling where the fixture had been. Light from the hall showed the fixture now on the floor, knotted at the end of a sheet. The other end was tight around Hattie's neck, and she lay there twitching.

"Tried to hang herself from a flimsy light," Plank said, as Albie leaped past him and slid up to Hattie on his knees. He and Rayford dug and tore at the sheet until it came loose. Rayford gently turned her on her back, and she flopped like a dead woman. As his eyes grew accustomed to the dark, he saw that hers were open, pupils dilated.

"She was moving!" Albie whispered, grabbing her belt and lifting her hips off the floor. Rayford plugged her nose, forced her mouth open, and clamped his mouth over hers. Her tiny frame rose and fell as he breathed into her, and Albie applied pressure to help her breathe out.

"Shut the door," Albie told Plank.

"You don't need the light?"

"Shut it!" he whispered desperately. "We're going to save this girl, but nobody but us is going to know it."

Plank steered his chair to push the bed out of the way, then shut the door.

"She's got a pulse," Albie said. "You OK, Ray? Want me to take over?"

Rayford shook his head and continued until Hattie began to cough. Finally she gulped in huge breaths and blew them out. Rayford sat heavily on the floor, his back against the wall. Hattie cried and swore. "I can't even kill myself," she hissed. "Why didn't you let me die? I can't go back to Buffer!"

She collapsed in tears and lay rocking on the floor on her knees and elbows.

"She doesn't recognize anybody," Albie said.

Hattie looked up, squinting. Rayford leaned over and turned on a small lamp. "No, I don't," she said, peering at Albie and glancing at Rayford. "I know Commander Pinkerton here, but who are you losers?"

Albie pointed to Rayford. "He saved your life. I'm just his loser friend."

Hattie sat in the middle of the floor, her knees pulled up, hands clasped around them. And she swore again.

"You're not going to Buffer, Hattie," Rayford said finally, and it was clear she recognized his voice.

"What?" she said, wonder in her voice.

"Yeah, it's me," Rayford said. "There are no secrets in this room."

"You came?" she squealed, scrambling to him and trying to embrace him.

He held her away. She looked at Plank. "But . . ."

"We're all in this together," Rayford said wearily.

"I almost killed myself," Hattie said.

"Actually," Albie said, "you did."

"What?"

"You're dead."

"What are you talking about?"

"You want out of here? You want the GC off your back? You go out of here dead."

"What are you saying?"

"You called your old friend to rescue you. He refused. You were despondent. When you gave up hope and were convinced you were going to Buffer, you lost all hope, wrote a note, and hung yourself. We came to get you, discovered you too late, and what could we do? Report the suicide and dispose of the body."

"I *did* write a note," she said. "See?" She pointed to a slip of paper that had fallen off the bed.

Rayford picked it up and read it under the lamp. "Thanks for nothing, old FRIENDS!!!" she had written. "I vowed never to go back to Buffer, and I meant it. You can't win them all."

"Sign it," Rayford said.

Hattie massaged her neck and tried to clear her throat. She found her pen and signed the note.

"How long can you hold your breath?" Albie asked.

"Not long enough to kill myself, apparently."

"We're going to wheel you out of here under a sheet, and you're going to have to look dead when we load you on the plane too. Can you pull that off?"

"I'll do whatever I have to." She looked at Plank. "You're in on this too?"

"The less you know, the better," he said.

He glanced at Albie, then Rayford. "She never needs to know, far as I'm concerned." They nodded.

Plank told them to leave the sheet the way it was, with the light fixture still embedded in one end. "Use the other sheet from the bed to cover her, and do it now."

Rayford ripped the sheet from the bed, and Hattie lay on the bare mattress. He floated the sheet atop her and let it settle. Plank opened the door. "Mrs. Garner!" he called, "we've had a tragedy here!"

"Oh my—"

"No, don't come! Just stay where you are. The prisoner hanged herself, and the GC will dispose of the remains."

"Oh, Commander! I—is that what I heard?"

"Possibly."

"Could I have done something? Should I have?"

"There's nothing you could have done, ma'am. Let's let these men do their work. Bring the gurney from Utility."

"I don't have to look, do I, sir?"

"I'll handle it. Just get it for me. I'll dictate a report later."

Despite her ashen countenance and

protestations, Rayford noticed that Mrs. Garner watched the "body" until it was loaded into the minivan. He was amazed at Hattie's ability to look motionless under that sheet.

Plank agreed to call ahead to the former Carpathia Memorial Airstrip to clear the way for Deputy Commander Elbaz and his driver to pull Judy Hamilton's vehicle right up to their fighter jet in order to load a body for transport. No, they would not need any assistance and would appreciate as little fuss as possible over it.

Hattie slipped back under the sheet a few miles from the airstrip, and though curious eyes peered through the windows, Rayford and Albie carried her aboard without arousing undue suspicion.

SEVEN

Buck pulled the Hummer out of the garage under the Strong Building after dark, lights off. He had spent the afternoon rigging up a special connection to the brake lights and backup lights. Once in regular traffic outside Chicago, he didn't want to risk getting stopped for malfunctioning rear lights, but neither did he want those lights coming on when he braked at Zeke's place.

Zeke himself was an expert at this and walked Buck through it by phone. It would be great when Zeke was tucked away at the new safe house, available to help with just those kinds of details. The brake lights were now disengaged, so with his lights on or off, Buck would have to manually illuminate them when applying the brake. A thin wire led from the back, through the backseat and up to the driver's side. If he could just remember to use it.

No one knew how frequently, if ever, the GC invested the time, equipment, and manpower to overfly the quarantined city their own databases told them was heavily radioactive. It didn't make sense that anyone would be near the place. If the readings were true—which David Hassid and the Tribulation Force knew was not the case—no one could live there long.

Still, Rayford's plan was to come and go in his helicopter from the tower in the dark of night. And Buck, or anyone else coming or going, would do the same from the garage. It was tricky going, because no light sources—outside the Strong Building—were engaged in the city. Unless the moon was bright, seeing anything in the dark was almost impossible on what used to be those miles of city streets.

Buck pulled away slowly, the gigantic Hummer propelling itself easily over the jagged terrain. He wanted to get used to the vehicle, the largest he had ever driven. It was surprisingly comfortable, predictably powerful, and—to his delight—amazingly quiet. He had feared it would sound like a tank.

Driving around Chicago in the dark was no way to familiarize himself with the car. He needed open road and the confidence that no one was paying attention. Half an hour later he hit the city limits and took the deserted frontage road that would deliver him into the suburbs without detection. He turned on his lights and set the manual brake light switch where he could reach it with his left hand.

Near Park Ridge a rebuilt section actually had a few miles of new pavement and a couple of working traffic lights. The rest of northern Illinois seemed to have regressed to the earliest days of the automobile. Cars made their own trails through rubble, and rain sometimes made those routes impassable.

Buck saw a couple of GC squad cars, but traffic was light. When he felt safe, he tested the power of the Hummer and practiced several turns at varying speeds. The faster he went and the sharper he turned, the more violently his body was pressed against the safety belt. But it seemed nothing would make the Hummer tip. Buck found a deserted area where he was sure no one could see him and tried a couple of fast turns even on inclines. The Hummer seemed to ask for more. With its superwide stance, its weight, and its power, it had unmatched maneuverability. Buck felt as if he were starring in a commercial.

He floored the vehicle, got it up to near eighty on packed dirt, slammed on the brakes, and turned the wheel. The antilock system kept him from skidding or even hinting at going over. He couldn't wait to compete with whatever toy the GC was using in its stakeout in Des Plaines.

Buck had to calm himself. The idea was to pick up Zeke undetected. He considered stopping at the station like a normal customer and ramming the GC as they came to investigate. But they had phones and radios and a communications network that would hem him in. If he could find a way to approach the station from the back, lights out, they might never see him, even after he pulled away with his quarry.

His phone chirped. It was Zeke. "You close by?" the young man said.

"Not far. What's up?"

"We're gonna hafta torch this place."

"Why?"

"Once they figure they've busted every rebel that used to gas up here, they're going to torch it anyway, right?"

"Maybe," Buck said. "So why not let them?"

"They might search it first."

"And find what?"

"The underground, of course. I can't even think about gettin' all the stuff outta here that could give my dad away."

"What more can they do to him?"

"All they got him on now is sellin' gas without GC approval. They fine him or make him sit a month or two. If they find out me and him was runnin' a rebel forgery biz outta here, he becomes an enemy of the state."

"Good thinking." Buck never failed to be amazed at the street wisdom of the unlikely looking Zeke. Who would have guessed that the former druggie-biker-tattoo artist would be the best phony credentials man in the business?

"And remember, Mr. Williams. We were feedin' people outta here too. Groceries, you name it. Well, you know. You bought a bunch of 'em. OK, here's what I'm thinkin'. I rig up a timer to a sparking device. You know, it ain't the gas that burns anyway."

"I'm sorry?" Buck felt stupid. He had been a globe-trotting journalist, and a virtual illiterate was trying to tell him gasoline fires aren't what they seem?

"Yeah, it's not the gas that burns. When I was workin' above ground, helpin' Dad in the station when it was legal and all, I used to toss my cigarettes in a bucket of gas we kept in the service bay."

"No, you didn't."

"I swear."

"Lit cigarettes?"

"Swear to—I mean, honest. That was how we put 'em out. They'd hiss like you was tossin' 'em into a bucket o' water."

"I'm confused."

"We kept gas in there to clean our hands on. Cuts grease, you know. Like if you just did an axle job and now you gotta go fill a tank or write on a credit card receipt or something."

"I mean I'm confused about how you

could throw a cigarette into a container of gasoline."

"Lots of people don't know that or don't believe it."

"How'd you keep from blowing yourselves to kingdom come?"

"Well, if the bucket of gas was fresh, you had to wait awhile. If you saw any of that shimmerin' of the fumes over it, like when you first pour it in there, or when you're fillin' your tank, well, you don't want any open flame of any kind near that."

"But once it sat and the, uh, shimmering fumes were gone?"

"Then we tossed our cigarette butts in there."

"So, it's the fumes."

"Yeah, it's the fumes what burns."

"I get it. So, your thoughts?"

"See, Mr. Williams, it works the same in an engine. Like a fuel-injected engine shoots a fine spray of gas into the cylinders and the spark plugs spark and burn it, but they're not burning the spray."

"The spray is emitting fumes and that's what's, in essence, exploding in the cylinder," Buck said.

"Now you've got it."

"Good. I'm heading your way, so cut to the chase."

"OK. I moved two huge boxes of stuff out by the pile of dirt in the back, and I got one big canvas bag. All my files, my equipment, everything is there. Even had room for some food."

"We have plenty of food, Zeke."

"Never have enough food. Anyway, the stuff's out there waitin'. I figure if you don't get seen comin', I can be waitin' for ya and load my stuff in there real quick before I jump in."

"Sounds like a plan. Back to the torching."

"Yeah. I've got auto parts down here. I cut a feed from the pipe that leads to the storage tank, which runs right by the wall we dug out here, and I hook a fuel injector to it. When I leave, I turn the spigot, the gas runs through the fuel injector and starts sprayin' gasoline."

"And pretty soon the underground is filled with gas."

"Fumes."

"Right. And you, what, toss a match down the stairs on your way out to the car?"

Zeke laughed.

"Shh."

"Yeah, they can't hear me. But no, tossing a flame down here then would blow me all the way to Chicago. Save you a trip, eh?"

"So how do you ignite it?"

"Put a spark plug on a timer. Give myself five minutes or so, just in case. At the right time, kaboom."

"Kaboom."

"Bingo."

"Zeke, even if I agreed, you'd never have time to rig that all up. I'm not ten minutes away."

"I figured you'd agree."

"And so—?"

"It's all done."

"You're kiddin' me."

"Nope. If you're ten minutes away, I'll set the timer for fifteen, and when I leave I'll open the spigot."

"Hoo, boy, you're resourceful."

"I know how to do stuff."

"You sure do, but do me a favor."

"Name it."

"Set the timer for five, but don't start it until after you've turned the spigot on your way out. Deal?"

"Deal."

"Oh, and one more thing. Make sure I'm there before you open that spigot."

"Oh, yeah, right. That would be important."

"Kaboom, Zeke."

"Bingo."

"Call you when I get there."

"Her name is not in our system, David," Nurse Palemoon said. He tried to sit up and she shushed him. "That doesn't have to mean the worst."

"How can you say that? The sun is coming up, and I haven't heard from her. She'd communicate with me if she could!"

"David, you must calm down. This room is empty but not secure. Your friends are on their way, but you can't trust anyone else."

"Tell me about it. Hannah, you have got to get me out of here. I can't stay here another few days. There is so much I have do before leaving New Babylon."

"I can supply you with extra meds and dressings and try to make sure you're set, but you're going to be sore."

"I'm not worried about that. Will you—" His throat caught and he couldn't say it. "Ah, would you—"

"You want me to check the morgue?" She said it with such compassion that he nearly broke down.

He nodded.

"I'll be right back. If your friends get here while I'm gone, remind them there are ears everywhere."

Rayford and Albie and their human cargo from Colorado put down at a tiny airstrip near Bozeman, Montana, rather than try to get back to Kankakee without sleep. Albie bluffed and blustered the tiny GC contingent at the strip, who bought his story of transporting a criminal and let the three of them borrow a jeep to get into town.

Such as it was. Bozeman had been left with few amenities, but one was a nearly deserted motel where they rented two rooms. "I don't guess we have to worry about you bolting," Rayford told Hattie.

"Compared to Buffer," she said, "the new safe house sounds like heaven."

"You'll be in for the pitches of your life," he said. "There are more of us, and you're going to be our prime target."

"I might just listen for once," she said.

"Don't say that lightly."

"I don't say anything lightly anymore."

Hattie had a million questions about Pinkerton Stephens, but Rayford and Albie told her only that "he is one of us." Then she wanted Albie's story, and he told of becoming a believer after a lifetime as a Muslim. "You know who I mean when I mention Tsion Ben-Judah then?" he said.

"Do I know?" she said. "I know him personally. Talk about a man who loves the unlovable . . ."

"Are you speaking of yourself, young lady?"

She snorted and nodded. "Who else?"

"Let me tell you something. I was unlovable. I was no kind of husband or father. My whole family is dead now. I was a criminal, and the only people who cared about me paid me well to get what they needed for illegal acts. I began to justify my existence when my black marketing was used to oppose the new evil world ruler. But I would not have called him Antichrist, would not even have known the term. I was in the same business when the world was merely chaotic, not so evil. My god was cash, and I knew how to get it.

"When Mac and Rayford needed my

services, I took some comfort in the fact that they seemed to be good people. I was no longer just helping criminals. I watched them, listened to them. They were outlaws in the eyes of the Global Community, but to me that was a badge of honor.

"When all the predictions Mac and Rayford had told me began coming true, I could not admit to them I was intrigued. More than that, I was scared. If this were all true, then I was an outsider. I was not a believer. I began monitoring the Internet messages of Dr. Ben-Judah without telling my friends. I was full of pride still. What struck me hardest was that Dr. Ben-Judah made it so clear that God was the lover of sinners. Oh, I knew I was that. I just could hardly accept that anyone would love me.

"I downloaded a Bible to my computer and would switch back and forth between it and Dr. Ben-Judah. I was able to see where he was getting his information, but his insights! Those had to come from God alone. What I was learning went against everything I had ever heard or been taught. My first prayer was so childish that I would never have prayed it aloud in front of another living soul.

"I told God I knew I was a sinner and that I wanted to believe that he loved me and would forgive me. I told him that the Western religion—for that is what it sounded like to me—was so foreign to me that I did not know if I could ever understand it. But I said to the Lord, 'If you are really the true and living God, please make it plain to me.' I told him I was sorry for my whole life and that he was my only hope. That was all. I felt nothing, maybe a little foolish. But I slept that night as I had not slept in years.

"Oh, do not misunderstand me. I was *not* sure I had gotten through to God. I was *not* sure that he was, in fact, who Dr. Ben-Judah and the others believed him to be. But I knew I had done all I could. I had been honest with myself and honest with him, and if he was who I hoped he was, he would have heard me. That was the best I could expect."

Albie sat back and inhaled deeply.

"That's it?" Hattie said. "That's all?"

He smiled. "I thought I would pause and see if I had bored you to sleep yet."

"You two are the ones who were up all night. Tell me what happened."

"Well, I awoke the next morning with a feeling of expectancy. I didn't know what to make of it. Before I could even eat, I felt a deep hunger and thirsting—there is no other word for it—for the Bible. I believed with my whole being that it was the Word of God, and I had to read it. I pulled it up on my computer and read and read and read and read. I cannot tell you how it filled me. I understood it! I wanted more of it! I could not get enough. Only after midday, when I was weak from hunger, did I realize I had not eaten yet.

"I thanked God over and over for his Word, for his truth, for answering my prayer and revealing himself to me. Occasionally I would break from my Bible reading and check to see if Dr. Ben-Judah had posted anything new. He had not, but I followed some of his links to a site that walked the reader through what the rabbi calls the sinner's prayer. I prayed it, but I realized that it was what I had already done. I was a believer, a child of God, a forgiven, loved sinner."

Hattie appeared unable to speak, but Rayford had seen her this way before. Many had told her their stories of coming to faith. She knew the truth and the way. She simply had never accepted the life.

"There is a reason I wanted to tell you that story," Albie said. "Not just because I want to persuade you, which I do. Those among us who have found the truth long for everyone else to have it. But it was because of what you said about yourself. You said Dr. Ben-Judah was one who loved the unlovable. He does, of course. This is a Christlike quality, a Jesus characteristic. But then you referred to yourself as unlovable, and I identified with you.

"But more than that, Ms. Durham, if I may use a phrase of Dr. Ben-Judah's. Often he will say that this or that truth 'gives the lie' to certain false claims. Have you heard him say that, and do you know what it means?"

She nodded.

"Well, it applies to you, dear woman. I have just met you, and yet God has given me a love for you. Rayford and his family and friends speak often of you and their love for you. That gives the lie to your claim that you are unlovable."

"They shouldn't love me," she said, just above a whisper.

"Of course they shouldn't. You know yourself. You know your selfishness, your sin. God should not love us either, and yet he does. And it is only because of him that we can love each other. There is no human explanation for it."

Rayford sat praying silently, desperately, for Hattie. Was it possible she was one who had for so long rejected Christ that God had turned her over to her own stubbornness? Was she unable to see the truth, to change her mind? If that were true, why did God plague Rayford and his friends with such a concern for her?

Suddenly she rose and stepped to Rayford. She bent and kissed the top of his head. She turned and did the same to Albie, cupping his face in her hands. "Don't worry about me tonight," she said. "I'll be here in the morning."

"You have no reason not to be," Albie said. "You are not really in our custody. In fact, you are dead."

"Anyway," Rayford said, standing and stretching, "where would you bolt to? Where would you be safer than where we're taking you?"

"Thanks for saving my life," she said as she turned to head for her room.

When she shut the door, Rayford said, "I just hope this wasn't for nothing."

They heard her door open and shut and her moving about in her room.

"It wasn't," Albie said.

Rayford was bone weary, but as he disrobed for bed he thought he heard something over the sound of Albie's shower. From the adjoining room he thought he heard voices. He moved closer to the wall. Not voices, just one. Crying. Sobbing. Wailing. Hattie, muffled, apparently with her face buried in a pillow or blanket.

As he drifted off to sleep half an hour later in the bed across from Albie's, Hattie's laments still wafted through the wall. Rayford heard Albie turn and pat his pillow, then settle back. "God," the little man whispered, "save that girl."

Buck drove straight past the little filling station, pretending to not notice the GC stakeout car amidst a small grove of trees across the road. He didn't even slow, so as not to attract attention. If he had to guess, he thought just two GC guards were in the car.

He phoned Zeke. "Any more activity?"

"Nope. Was that you what just passed? Nice rig."

"I'm going to circle way around and see if

I can come in from the back with my lights off. Might take ten minutes. I'll call you when I'm in position."

Buck drove until he couldn't see even the outline of the station in his rearview mirror, assuming the GC could no longer see him either. He cut his lights and took a right, slowly feeling his way over rough ground. He was a couple of miles from the station, and he wanted to be sure he didn't find a hidden fence or culvert that would mess up the Hummer.

At one point, after taking two more rights and thus heading in the general direction of the back of the station, he felt the vehicle dip and hoped he hadn't found a hole too deep to pull out of. When the front grille hit something solid, he hit the brakes and briefly turned on the headlights. He shut them off again quickly, hoping the GC hadn't seen anything in the distance. Buck saw that he needed to back up and swing left around a five-foot-high or so mound of dirt and boards.

He wanted to turn on his brights and be able to see if anything else obstructed his path to the back of the station, but he didn't dare. By the time he could make out the shape of the place, he slowed to just a few miles an hour and crept along in the uneven dirt, bouncing, jostling, and—he hoped—not sending up too much dust. It was a starry night, and if the GC noticed anything blocking the sky, they were sure to come nosing around the back.

Buck phoned Zeke.

"I hear you," Zeke said.

"You *hear* me? From inside? That can't be good."

"That's what I was thinking. You ready for me?"

"Better come quick. Carrying anything?"

"Yeah, one more bag. Figured I might as well not leave anything I could bring."

"Good thinking. Come on."

"Gotta open the spigot and turn on the timer."

"For how long?"

"Five minutes."

"Anything on the monitor?"

"They're just sittin'."

"Good. Let's go."

Buck knew he could come back the way he came, and though the ride would be pretty rugged, he estimated he could do as much as 40 mph. But in case the GC could hear the Hummer as well as Zeke could, he jumped out and started loading the car to save time.

The inside light stayed dark as he opened the door to get out, and he left it open. He opened the back door on the far side and crept around to start lifting. The first box was almost too heavy, and it was all he could do to not cry out under the weight. He heard Zeke coming up the stairs.

Buck lugged the box onto the backseat from the car door farthest from the station's back door, feeling every sore fiber from his recent ordeal. When he got back around the car to grab the other box, figuring Zeke could load the bag he was carrying and the one on the ground at the same time, he nearly ran into the young man, startling him.

Zeke grunted. Buck tried to shush him, but Zeke dropped his bag and lurched back inside, slamming the door. Buck heard him lumbering down the stairs. Now they were making way too much noise.

Buck yanked open the station door and called out desperately, as quietly as he could, "Zeke, it's just me! C'mon, man! Now!"

"Oh, man!" Zeke hollered. "I thought it

was them! The timer's goin', the gas is spittin'. And they're comin', Buck! I can see 'em on the monitor!"

Buck turned and opened the back door nearest the station. He picked up the bag that had been waiting and the one Zeke had dropped and hurled them across the backseat. He left the door open and jumped behind the wheel, slamming his door and putting the Hummer in gear. Zeke barreled out and dove into the backseat, knocking one of the bags out the other side, where Buck had left the door open.

Buck floored the accelerator, but Zeke yelled, "We can't leave that bag! It's got lots of stuff we need!"

The door had started to close when Buck took off, but when he hit the brakes, it swung the other way and creaked against the hinges. "Get it!" he screamed, and Zeke scrambled over the stuff and out onto the ground, his foot dragging a bag out too. And here came the GC mobile around the station in front of Buck.

"Go! Go!" Zeke yelled, forcing himself into the backseat with both heavy bags tucked under his arms.

The door was still open, but Buck had to

move. He gunned the engine and slammed into the GC car, driving it back against the station as his back door shut. The guards had weapons out and appeared to be reaching for door handles. Buck knew he couldn't outrace bullets, so he threw the Hummer into Reverse, floored it, and the monstrous vehicle climbed the hill of debris near the door.

Buck stopped at the top as they teetered some twelve feet above their pursuers. He shifted into Drive, and when the GC saw the vehicle start to move, they lowered their weapons and dove out of the way. The Hummer dropped almost vertically, ramming the hood of the little car and blowing both of its front tires. The engine gushed water and steam, and Buck could tell he had rendered the GC vehicle useless.

Rather than look for the guards, he merely backed up six feet, whipped the wheel right, and sped off into the night. Zeke had somehow gotten the door shut, but neither he nor Buck had time to buckle in. As the Hummer lurched across the plains at high speed, both men were thrown around like rag dolls, their heads hitting the ceiling, their shoulders banging the doors.

Buck skidded to a stop.

"What?" Zeke demanded.

"Buckle up!"

They both did and off he flew again. Fewer than five minutes later, as Buck found a route that would lead them back to Chicago, the sky behind them went from night to day in a massive orange ball of flame. A few seconds later the sound and the shock rocked the car anew. Buck, high from the adrenaline, knew how close they had come to dying.

Zeke, laughing like a child, kept turning in his seat and looking back at the flaming horizon. "Well," he said, cackling, "so much for that job!"

EIGHT

Mac and Abdullah sat sullenly in David's hospital room, whispering. "Thirty days?" Mac said over and over. "Hard to believe."

"No way of staying around here," Abdullah said. "Not that I'll miss it. Well, in some ways I will."

"I know I will," David said, coming to full attention whenever he heard footsteps in the corridor. "So much we can do from the inside that we'll never be able to pull off from the outside."

Mac let out a sigh that made him sound old and tired. "David, this may sound like I'm kissin' up to the boss, but you know I wouldn't kiss up to you if you were the potentate. But we both know you can do anything technologically. Get yerself healthy and do whatever you got to do to keep tabs on this place from anywhere in the world. Isn't that doable?"

"Theoretically," David said. "But it won't be easy."

"Somehow you've got this place bugged, sliced, and diced. Why can't you access computers here the way you did that buildin' in Chicago where we're all likely gonna wind up?"

David shrugged. "It's possible. I can't imagine psyching myself up to get it done. Not without Annie." David caught the glance between Mac and Abdullah. "What?" he said. "You know something you're not telling me?"

Mac shook his head. "We're just as worried as you. Makes no sense. No way she wouldn't let you know where she was, if she could." He paused and a twinkle played at his eyes. "Unless she locked herself in that utility room again."

David laughed in spite of himself. Annie was one of the most disciplined, buttoned-down employees he'd ever had, but one out-of-character stunt she pulled would hang over her head as long as she lived.

The way Hannah Palemoon knocked at the half-open door told David way more than he wanted to know. A sob rose in his throat. Mac stood and David nodded to him.

"Come in," Mac said.

David tried to ignore the small, corrugated box in Hannah's hands and desperately searched her face for some trace of optimism. She approached slowly and set the box near David's feet. "I am so sorry," she said, and David collapsed inside.

His pain, his fatigue melted away, overwhelmed by grief and loss too great to bear. He groaned and drew his fists up under his chin, turning from his friends, rolling onto his side, drawing his knees up, and folding in on himself.

"Lightning?" The question forced its way past his constricted throat.

"Yes," Hannah whispered. "There would have been no pain or suffering."

Grateful for that, David thought. *At least not for her.*

"David," Mac said huskily, "me and Smitty will be right outside—"

"I'd appreciate it if you could stay," David managed, and he heard them sit again.

"I have a few of her personal effects," Hannah said. David tried to sit up, feeling the cursed dizziness. "It's just her purse and phone, jewelry, and shoes."

David finally sat up and put the box between his knees. His breath caught at the charred smell. The phone had melted in spots. One shoe had scorched holes in the heel and toe.

"I have to see her," he said.

"I wouldn't recommend it," Hannah said.

"David, no," Mac urged.

"I have to! She's not really gone and never will be unless I know for sure. This is her stuff, but did you see her, Hannah?"

The nurse nodded.

"But you didn't know her. Had you ever seen her before?"

She shook her head. "Not that I know of. But, David, I don't know how to say this. If the woman in the morgue were my best friend, I wouldn't recognize her."

The sobs returned and David pushed the box toward the end of the bed, shaking his head, his fingers pressed lightly against his temples, tender and fiery to the touch. "You know she was my first love?"

No one responded.

"I had dated before, but—" he pressed a hand over his lips—"the love of my life."

Mac stood and asked Abdullah to shut the door. He pulled the hanging curtain around the bed so the four of them were cocooned in the dim white light. Mac lay a hand gently on David's shoulder. Abdullah reached for a knee. Hannah gripped David's sheet-covered foot.

"God," Mac whispered, "we're long past asking why things happen. We know we're on borrowed time and that we belong to you. We don't understand this. We don't like it. And it's hard for us to accept. We thank you that Annie didn't suffer," and here his voice broke and became barely audible. "We envy her because she's with you, but we miss her already, and a part of David that can never be replaced has been ripped away. We still trust you, still believe in you, and want to serve you for as long as you'll let us. We just ask that you'll come alongside David now, unlike you ever have before, and help him to heal, to carry on, to do your work."

Mac could not continue. Abdullah said, "We pray in the name of Jesus."

"Thank you," David said, and he turned away from them again. "Please don't go yet." As he lay there, his friends still by the bed inside the curtain, he realized that there would be no formal funeral for Annie and that even if there was—because she was an employee—he would have to conduct himself as a somber superior, not as a grieving lover. When he was forced to separate himself from this place, he didn't want it to reflect upon her and call into suspicion everyone she knew or spent time with.

He heard the drape being opened again. Hannah put the box under the head of the bed, and Mac and Abdullah returned to their chairs. "You need sleep," Hannah said. "You want me to get you something?"

He shook his head. "I'm sorry, Hannah, but I really have to see her. Can you unhook me and help me down there?"

She looked as if about to refuse him, but he saw the light of an idea come to her eyes. "You're sure?" she said.

"Absolutely."

"It won't be easy."

"And this is?"

"I'll get a wheelchair and I'll pull the IV along with us."

Zeke was wearing his trademark getup when Buck presented him to the Tribulation Force at the new safe house and introduced him to Tsion. "When the boss gets back, we'll make you a full-fledged member," Buck said. "But meanwhile, find yourself some privacy and appropriate whatever you need to settle in, make yourself at home, and become part of the family."

"By all means," Tsion said, embracing the fleshy young man. In thick-soled, square-toed, black motorcycle boots, black jeans, black T-shirt under black leather vest, Zeke was a stark contrast to the sweatered, corduroyed rabbi, standing there in his Hush-Puppies. "Welcome and God bless you."

Zeke was awkward and shy, and while he shook hands all around and lightly returned hugs, he stared at the ground and mumbled replies. Soon enough, however, he was exploring, unpacking, moving a bed, setting up his stuff. An hour later he returned to the central meeting place near the elevators. "This place is really uptown," he said.

"Literally," Leah said, clearly bemused by

the man who had once changed her entire look and given her a new identity.

Zeke stared at her, and Buck got the impression he didn't know what she meant but was afraid to admit it. As if to cover his embarrassment and change the subject, Zeke dug in both back pockets and one vest pocket for huge rolls of twenty-Nick bills, which he slapped noisily on the table. "I intend to earn my keep," he said. "Put this here in the pot."

"You might want to wait until it's official," Buck said. "Rayford will be here tomorrow night and—"

"Oh, it's all right. Consider it a donation, even if I get voted out or blackballed or whatever."

"I don't see that happening," Chloe said, burping the sleeping Kenny Bruce on her shoulder.

"Oh, man!" Zeke said quietly, noticing the baby. He approached slowly and reached carefully toward Kenny's back. "Can I?"

"You may," Chloe said. "Your hands clean?"

Zeke stopped and turned his hands before his eyes. "They have to be for my kinda work. Can't smudge the new IDs, you know.

They look dirty, 'cause I work on engines and stuff, but they're just stained."

He bent at the knees before Chloe and gently put his meaty hand on Kenny's back. His fingers nearly stretched from shoulder to tiny shoulder. Zeke lightly touched the boy's feathery hair.

"Sit and you can hold him," Chloe said, as the others watched. Buck was especially amused by Chaim, whose eyes filled.

"Want a turn?" Buck whispered.

"It's been so long," Chaim whispered, trying to make himself understood. "It would be a privilege."

Somehow Kenny slept through everyone's turn, even Tsion's. He was last and quickly passed Kenny back to Chloe, as he was overcome. "My children were teenagers when they . . . when they . . . but the memories . . ."

"We need to identify a body," Hannah Palemoon said, pushing David's wheelchair and pulling his IV to the desk just inside the morgue.

"Sign in," a bored older woman said.

"Forget it," Hannah said. "The system is behind by several days. Nobody'll ever check anyway."

The woman made a face. "Less work for me," she said. "I'm just filling in."

David's heart raced as Hannah pushed him past rows and rows of bodies as far as the eye could see—on gurneys, in lateral refrigerators, and sheet-wrapped head to toe, shoulder to shoulder on the floor. "She's not one of these, is she?"

"Next room, around the corner."

Hannah steered him to the foot end of a covered body on a bed. He took a deep, quavery breath. Hannah lifted the sheet from one foot and peered at the toe tag to make sure she had the right corpse. "You're sure you want to do this?"

He nodded, though now not so sure.

She showed him the tag thin-wired to the big toe. It bore Annie's name and rank and serial number all right, plus date of birth and date of death. The foot was swollen and discolored, but no doubt hers. David reached to envelop it with both hands and was struck by the cold stiffness.

It was the other foot whose shoe had showed lightning damage. David began pulling the sheet from it, ignoring Hannah when she cleared her throat and said, "Uh, David . . ."

He recoiled at the damage. The heel was split wide and the big toe mangled. He covered her feet and dropped his head. "You're sure she never felt that?"

"Positive."

"Fortunato was given the power to call down fire from heaven on those who didn't worship the image."

"I know."

"I could have easily been struck."

"Me too."

"Why her?"

Hannah did not answer. David tried to wheel himself between beds to the other end of the body. His IV stretched. "Let me," Hannah said, and she pushed him slowly. When he reached for the sheet, Hannah reached over his shoulder and put a hand on his forearm. "You may want to look only at her face," she said. "There was severe cranial trauma."

He hesitated.

"And David? For some reason no one closed her eyes. I tried, but with time and rigor mortis . . . well, a mortician will have to do that."

He nodded, panting. His head throbbed, and when he was able to control his breathing again, David lifted the sheet and brought it down to her neck, careful not to look. With another deep breath, his eyes traveled to hers.

For an instant it didn't look like Annie. Her eyes were fixed on something a million miles away, her face bloated and purple. Burns on her ears and neck evidenced where her necklace and earrings had been.

He sat staring at her for so long that Hannah finally said, "OK?"

David shook his head. "I want to stand."

"You shouldn't."

"Help me."

She pushed the IV stand around the chair so it was next to him. "Use that to brace yourself. If the room starts to spin, sit again."

"Starts?"

She locked the wheels and put a hand on his back, guiding as he rose. He pushed with his left hand on the arm of the chair and pulled with his right on the stand. Finally, up and wobbly, Hannah's hand still on his back, David cupped Annie's cheek with his free hand. Despite the cool rigidity, he imagined she could feel his caress. In spite of himself, he leaned over her until he could see past where a tuft of hair had been pushed up in front. Behind that was a silver dollar-sized hole that exposed her brain.

David shook his head and carefully sat again. He didn't want to think what a lightning bolt through her body would have done to vital organs. He now believed Hannah that Annie never would have known what hit her.

Hannah pulled David's chair and left him at the foot of the bed. He sat with his head in his hands, unable to produce more tears. He heard Hannah rearranging the sheet and carefully re-covering Annie, almost as if she were still alive, and it struck him as sweet and thoughtful.

As she wheeled him out, he whispered his thanks.

"I wish I had known her," Hannah said.

Rayford had briefed Buck and Chloe and Tsion the night before, so when a phone woke him at dawn in Montana, he assumed it was one of them. As he reached to answer, however, it was not his cell but the room phone. He had not given out that number, so who would be calling? The desk? Was someone onto them? Should he identify himself as Rayford Steele or Marvin Berry?

Neither, he decided. “Hello?”

“Ray,” Hattie said, “it’s me. I’m awake, I’m up, I’m starved, and I want to get going. You?”

He groaned and glanced at the other bed. Albie was sound asleep. “You’re a little too chipper for me,” he said. “I’m asleep, I’m in bed, I’m not hungry, and there’s no sense leaving so early that we get to Kankakee before dark. We can’t go to the safe house until after that anyway.”

“Oh, Rayford! C’mon! I’m bored. And I’m dead, remember? I need a new identity, but I’m as free as I’ve been in years, thanks to you! How ’bout some breakfast?”

“We can’t be too obvious or public.”

“Are you going to go back to sleep, really?”

“Back? I never woke up.”

“Seriously.”

“No, I probably won’t. Someone in the next room is up banging around anyway.”

She knocked on the wall. “And I’ll keep banging until I get company for breakfast.”

“All right, dead girl. Give me twenty minutes.”

“I’ll be outside your door in fifteen.”

“Then you’ll be waiting five.”

Rayford was glad his showering and dressing hadn't wakened Albie. He peeked out the window and saw nothing and no one. Out the peephole in the door he saw Hattie stretching in the sun, just beyond the shadow caused by the second-floor walkway. He peeked through the curtain. The place was otherwise deserted.

Rayford stepped out, and Hattie nearly lunged at him. "Let me see, let me see!" she said, staring at him. "I can see yours!" she said. "That means you can see mine! Can you?"

His eyes were still adjusting to the sun, but as she pulled him out of the shadow by the door, it hit him. His knees buckled and he almost fell. "Oh, Hattie!" he said, reaching for her. She leaped into his arms and squeezed him around the neck so hard he finally had to push her away so he could breathe.

"Does mine look like yours?" she said.

He laughed. "How would I know? We can't see our own. But yours looks like every other one I've seen. This is worth waking Albie for."

"Is he decent?"

"Sure. Why?"

"Let me."

Rayford unlocked the door and Hattie burst in. "Albie, wake up, sleepyhead!"

He didn't stir.

She sat on the bed next to him and bounced. He groaned.

"C'mon, Albie! The day is young!"

"What?" he said, sitting up. "What's wrong?"

"Nothing will ever be wrong again!" she said, taking his face in her hands and pointing his bleary eyes toward her. "I'm just showing off my mark!"

NINE

Buck awoke at dawn and made the rounds, checking on everyone. He smiled at Zeke's domain and was grateful it was private. Zeke had worked until after midnight arranging his area, getting his computer and other equipment set up. Zeke snored loudly, but when Buck peeked in, he found Zeke on the floor next to his bed. *Each to his own.*

Leah's door was shut and locked. She had been up late on a call from Ming Toy, who had returned to Buffer frantic about her parents' staying in New Babylon until her brother could find a position with the GC.

Chloe had been on her computer until after Kenny was in bed, coordinating the international co-op. She urged the tens of thousands of members to watch for Tsion's next missive, wherein he planned to discuss the importance of their readiness when the buying/selling edict would go into effect. He would also be asking volunteer pilots and drivers to bring small planes and vehicles into Israel for a secret mission.

The only other two Trib Force members were awake and working. Chaim was hunched over a stack of books, several of them open, assigned by Tsion. He looked up with twinkling eyes when Buck poked his head in. Buck seemed to understand his constricted speech better than the others.

"Miss Rose, the redhead," Chaim said.

"Leah."

"Yes, she is a trained nurse, you know."

Buck nodded.

"She tells me she can remove the wires when I am ready. Well, I am more than ready. A man my age cannot lose this much weight this fast. And I want to be able to speak clearly!"

"How is everything else?"

"On my body, you mean? I am an old man. I've survived a plane crash. I should complain? Cameron, this building is a gift from God! What a luxury! If we have to live in exile, this is where to live. And what young Tsion has given me to read, well . . . I call him young because he was once my student, but you knew that. There are times, Cameron, when the Scriptures are like an ugly mirror to me, showing me again and again my bankrupt soul. But then I rejoice at the redemption, *my* redemption! The story of God, the history of his people, it is all coming alive to me before my eyes."

"Did you remember to eat?"

"I don't eat. I drink. Agh! But yes, thank you for asking. I am now drinking in the truth of God."

"Carry on."

"Oh, I will! Tsion was looking for you, by the way. Did he find you?"

"No. I'm on my way to him now."

Buck moved up a floor and found Dr. Ben-Judah with his fingers flying over the computer keyboard. He didn't want to disturb him, but the rabbi must have heard him. Without looking up or slowing, he said, "Cameron, is that you? So much to do. I shall be busy all the day, I fear. Dark as the days are, my joy is complete. Prophecy comes alive by the minute. Did you see what Master Zeke did for me? A precious lad!"

Buck looked again. Tsion had not only a main computer but also two laptops networked to it on each side. "No more switching back and forth between programs," Tsion sang out. "Bibles on one, commentaries on the other. And I am writing to my people in the middle!"

"Glad to get back to it?"

"You cannot imagine."

"Don't let me slow you."

"No, no! Come in, Cameron. I need you." He finally stopped and hit the Print command. Pages began piling in the printer output tray. Tsion swiveled in his chair. "Sit, please! You must be my first reader today."

"I'd be honored, but—"

"First, tell me. What news from our brothers and sisters in the field?"

"We know little. We haven't heard from David Hassid, except secondhand through Rayford, since the Carpathia resurrection."

"And what did you hear then?"

"Only that Ray and Albie had trouble raising him. They needed him to pave the way for a scheme they were pulling, trying to get

Hattie Durham back from the GC. At the last minute he must have gotten their messages, because the stuff came through and the mission was accomplished."

Tsion nodded, pursing his lips. "Praise the Lord," he said quietly. "She is coming back to us then?"

"Tonight. We expect Ray and Albie and Hattie after dark."

"I will pray for their safety. And we must continue to pray for her, of course. God has given me such a weight of care for that woman."

Buck shook his head. "Me too, Tsion. But if ever there seemed a lost cause . . ."

"Lost cause? Cameron, Cameron! You and I were lost causes! All of us were. Who was a less likely candidate than Chaim? We pleaded and pleaded with him, but who would have believed he would eventually come into the kingdom? Certainly not I. Don't give up on Miss Durham."

"Oh, I haven't."

"With God, all things are possible. Have you taken a close look at this young man you brought home last night?"

"Zeke? Oh, yeah."

"Clearly this was not a churchgoing boy.

He is so delightful, so bright! Shy, bashful, uneducated. Almost illiterate. But what a sweet, gentle spirit! What a servant's heart! And, oh, what a mind! It would take him the next three and a half years to read one of the many books Chaim will finish by tomorrow, and yet he has proclivities for this technical stuff that I could not learn in a lifetime."

Buck smacked his palms on his thighs and began to rise. "Don't let me keep you."

"Oh, you're not! My mouth is keeping me from it. If you are not too busy today, I could use your help."

Buck sat back down, and Tsion handed him a sheaf of papers from the printer. "I have many pages to go, but I need a first impression. I will not transmit these until I know they are right."

"They are always right, Tsion. But I'd love to get the first look at them."

"Then begin! I will try to stay ahead of you. And if I start talking again, feel free to become parental with me."

That'll be the day, Buck thought. He tapped the papers even and settled back to read. Every so often Tsion printed out the next several pages, and Buck idly pulled them from the printer as he read, sitting, standing, pacing. All the while he thanked God for the gift of Tsion Ben-Judah and his incredible mind.

To: The beloved tribulation saints scattered to the four corners of the earth, believers in the one true Jehovah God and his matchless Son, Jesus the Christ, our Savior and Lord

From: Your servant, Tsion Ben-Judah, blessed by the Lord with the responsibility and unspeakable privilege of teaching you, under the authority of his Holy Spirit, from the Bible, the very Word of God

Re: The dawn of the Great Tribulation

My dear brothers and sisters in Christ,

As is so often true when I sit to write to you, I come in both joy and sorrow, with delight but also soberness of spirit. Forgive me for the delay since last I communicated with you, and thank you each and every one for the expressions of concern for my welfare. My comrades and I are safe and sound and praising the Lord for a new base of operations. And I always want to remember to also thank God for the miracle of technology that allows me to write to you all over the world.

Though I have met few of you personally and look forward to that one day, either in the millennial kingdom or in heaven, I feel deeply that family bonds have been created by our regularly sharing the deep riches of Scripture through this medium. Thank you for your continued prayers that I will remain faithful and true to my calling and healthy enough to continue for as long as the Father himself gives me breath.

I ask that all of you who have volunteered to translate these words into languages not supported by the built-in conversion programs begin to do that immediately. As I have been unable to write to you for several days, I anticipate that this will be a longer than usual communiqué. Also, as always, in those areas where computers or power sources are scarce and this message is reproduced as hard copy, I ask that those responsible feel free to do so free of charge with no credit necessary, but that every word be printed as it appears here.

Glory to God for news that we have long since passed the one-billion mark in readership. We know that there are many more brothers and sisters in the faith who are without computers or the ability to read these words. And while the current world system would, and does, deny these figures, we believe them to be true. Hundreds of thousands join us every day, and we pray you will tell more and more about our family.

We have been through so much together. I say this without boasting but with glory to God Almighty: As I have endeavored to rightly divide the Word of Truth to you, God has proven himself the author over and over. For centuries scholars have puzzled over the mysterious prophetic passages in the Bible, and at one time I was one of those puzzled ones. The language seemed obscure, the message deep and elusive, the meanings apparently figurative and symbolic. Yet when I began an incisive and thorough examination of these passages with an open mind and heart, it was as if God revealed something to me that freed my intellect.

I had discovered, strictly from an academic approach, that nearly 30 percent of the Bible (Old and New Testaments together) consisted of prophetic passages. I could not understand why God would include these if he intended them to be other than understandable to his children.

While the messianic prophecies were fairly straightforward and, indeed, led me to believe in Jesus as their unique fulfillment, I prayed earnestly that God would reveal to me the key to the rest of the predictive passages. This he did in a most understated way. He simply impressed upon me to take the words as literally as I took any others from the Bible, unless the context and the wording itself indicated otherwise.

In other words, I had always taken at its word a passage such as, "Love your neighbor as yourself," or "Do unto others as you would have them do unto you." Why then, could I not take just as straightforwardly a verse which said that John the Revelator saw a pale horse? Yes, I understood that the horse stood for something. And yet, the Bible said that John saw it. I took that literally, along with all the other prophetic statements (unless they used phrases such as "like unto" or others that made it clear they were symbolic).

My dear friends, the Scriptures opened

to me in a way I never dreamed possible. That is how I knew the great Seal Judgments and Trumpet Judgments were coming, how I was able to interpret what form they might take, and even in what sequence they would occur.

That is how I know that the Bowl Judgments are yet to come, and that they will be exponentially worse than all those that came before. That is how I knew that these plagues and trials were more than just judgments on an unholy and unbelieving world. That is how I knew that this whole period of history is also one more evidence of the long-suffering, lovingkindness, and mercy of God himself.

Believers, we have turned a corner. Skeptics—and I know many of you drop in here now and then to see what we zealots are up to—we have passed the point of gentility. Up to now, while I have been forthright about the Scriptures, I have been somewhat circumspect about the current rulers of this world.

No more. As every prophecy in the Bible has so far come to pass, as the leader of this world has preached peace while wielding a sword, as he died by the sword and was resurrected as the Scriptures foretold, and as his right-hand man has been imbued with similar evil power, there can be no more doubt:

Nicolae Carpathia, the so-called Excellency and Supreme Potentate of the Global Community, is both anti-Christian and Antichrist himself. And the Bible says the resurrected Antichrist is literally indwelt by Satan himself. Leon Fortunato, who had an image of Antichrist erected and now forces one and all to worship it or face their own peril, is Antichrist's false prophet. As the Bible predicted, he has power to give utterance to the image and to call down fire from heaven to destroy those who refuse to worship it.

What's next? Consider this clear prophetic passage in Revelation 13:11-18: "Then I saw another beast coming up out of the earth, and he had two horns like a lamb and spoke like a dragon. And he exercises all the authority of the first beast in his presence, and causes the earth and those who dwell in it to worship the first beast, whose deadly wound was healed. He performs great signs, so that he even makes fire come down from heaven on the earth in the sight of men. And he deceives those who dwell on the earth by those signs which he was granted to do in the sight of the beast, telling those who dwell on the earth to make an image to the beast who was wounded by the sword and lived. He was granted power to give breath to the image of the beast, that the image of the beast should both speak and cause as many as would not worship the image of the beast to be killed. He causes all, both small and great, rich and poor, free and slave, to receive a mark on their right hand or on their foreheads, and that no one may buy or sell except one who has the mark or the name of the beast, or the number of his name.

"Here is wisdom. Let him who has understanding calculate the number of the beast, for it is the number of a man: His number is 666."

It won't be long before everyone will be forced to bow the knee to Carpathia or his image, to bear his name or number on their forehead or right hand, or face the consequences.

Those consequences? Those of us without what the Bible calls the mark of the beast will not be allowed to legally buy or sell. If we publicly refuse to accept the mark of the beast, we will be beheaded. While it is the greatest desire of my life to live to see the Glorious Appearing of my Lord and Savior Jesus the Christ at the end of the Great Tribulation (a few days short of three and a half years from now), what greater cause could there ever be for which to give one's life?

Many, millions of us, will be required to do just that. While it conjures in us age-old self-preservation instincts and we worry that at that hour we will be found lacking courage, loyalty, and faithfulness, let me reassure you. The God who calls you to the ultimate sacrifice will also give you the power to endure it. No one can receive the mark of the beast by accident. It is a once-and-for-all decision that will forever condemn you to eternity without God.

While many will be called to live in secret, to support one another through private markets, some will find themselves caught, singled out, dragged into a public beheading, to which the only antidote is a rejection of Christ and a taking of the mark of the beast.

If you are already a believer, you will not be able to turn your back on Christ, praise God. If you are undecided and don't want to follow the crowd, what will you do when faced with the mark or the loss of your head? I plead with you today to believe, to receive Christ, to envelop yourself with protection from on high.

We are entering into the bloodiest season in the history of the world. Those who take the mark of the beast will suffer affliction at the hand of God. Those who refuse it will be martyred for his blessed cause. Never has the choice been so stark, so plain.

God himself gave name to this three-and-a-half-year period. Matthew 24:21-22 records Jesus saying, "For then there will be great tribulation, such as has not been since the beginning of the world until this time, no, nor ever shall be. And unless those days were shortened, no flesh would be saved; but for the elect's [that's you and me, believer] sake those days will be shortened."

In all God's dealings with mankind, this is the shortest period on record, and yet more Scripture is devoted to it than any other period except the life of Christ. While the Hebrew prophets referred to this as a time of "vengeance of our God" for the slaughter of the prophets and saints over the centuries, it is also a time of mercy. God goes to extreme measures to compress the decision-making time for men and women before the coming of Christ to set up his earthly kingdom.

Despite that this is clearly the most awful time in history, I still say it is also a merciful act of God to give as many souls as possible an opportunity to put their faith in Christ. Oh, people, we are the army of God with a massive job to do in a short time. May we do it with willingness and eagerness, and the courage that comes only from him. There are countless lost souls in need of saving, and we have the truth.

It may be hard to recognize God's mercy when his wrath is also intensifying. Woe to those who believe the lie that God is only "love." Yes, he is love. And his gift of Jesus as the sacrifice for our sin is the greatest evidence of this. But the Bible also says God is "holy, holy, holy." He is righteous and a God of justice, and it is not in his nature to allow sin to go unpunished or unpaid for.

We are engaged in a great worldwide battle with Satan himself for the souls of men and women. Do not think that I lightly advance to the front lines with this truth, not understanding the power of the evil one. But I have placed my faith and trust in the God who sits high above the heavens, in the God who is above all other gods, and among whom there is none like him.

Scripture is clear that you can test both prophet and prophecy. I make no claim of being a prophet, but I believe the prophecies. If they are not true and don't come to pass, then I am a liar and the Bible is bogus, and we are all utterly without hope. But if the Bible is true, next on the agenda is the ceremonial desecration of the temple in Jerusalem by Antichrist himself. This is a prediction made by Daniel, Jesus, Paul, and John.

My brothers and sisters of Jewish blood, which I proudly share, will cringe to know that this desecration shall include the sacrificing of a pig on the sacred altar. It also includes blasphemy against God, profanity, derogatory statements about God and Messiah, and a denial of his resurrection.

If you are Jewish and have not yet been persuaded that Jesus the Christ of Nazareth is Messiah and you have been deceived by the lies of Nicolae Carpathia, perhaps your mind will be changed when he breaks his covenant with Israel and withdraws his guarantee of her safety.

But he shows no favoritism. Besides reviling the Jews, he will slaughter believers in Jesus.

If this does not happen, label me a heretic or mad and look elsewhere than the Holy Scriptures for hope.

Thank you for your patience and for the blessed privilege of communicating with you again. Let me leave you on a note of hope. My next message will concern the difference between the Book of Life, and what those mean to you and me. Until then, you may rest assured that if you are a believer and have placed your hope and trust in the work of Jesus Christ alone for the forgiveness of sins and for life everlasting, your name is Lamb's Book of Life.

And it can never be erased.

Until we meet again, I bless you in the name of Jesus. May he bless you and keep you and make his face to shine upon you, and give you peace.

When Buck looked up from reading, his eyes moist, he was surprised to see that Tsion had slipped out without his knowledge. Despite the length of the rabbi's message, Buck knew that if the rest of the constituency was as thirsty for the truth as he was, they would welcome it and hang on every word. And a difference between the Book of Life and the Lamb's Book of Life? He had never heard of such a thing and couldn't wait to learn more.

He stood and stretched, the pages still in his hand. As he left he saw a note on the door. "Cameron, I welcome any suggestions. If you think it acceptable, feel free to hit Enter to post it on the Web site."

It may have seemed a small thing, a utilitarian task. But to Buck it was a monumental honor. He hurried to Tsion's computer, brushed the cordless mouse to clear the screen saver, and with great relish hit the key that broadcast Tsion's words to a global audience.

* * *

Rayford offered to give Albie a break and pilot the fighter back to Palwaukee. His friend had done the bulk of the "flying and the lying," as they called it, and both could be grueling. Deceiving the enemy was tightrope work, and until David Hassid was able to get Rayford a phony rank, ID, and uniform, Albie was always in the hot seat.

It worked out best this way, though, because Hattie would have worn Rayford out during the flight, had he been free to listen. He heard most of it anyway, of course, but he was glad for the busyness of flying so he didn't have to maintain eye contact and match her energy.

He was thrilled beyond words for her and couldn't wait to see the faces of the rest of the Tribulation Force later that evening. More than that, he was happy for the whole Force. More than once, he, and he knew the others too, had given up hope for Hattie.

Albie was too new a believer to counsel her much, but she asked him to tell her again and again about the hunger for the Bible God had seemed to plant in his heart. "I don't know if that's what I have yet," she said, "but I'm sure curious. Do you have a Bible I can read?"

Rayford's was packed away somewhere at the safe house, and Albie said he did not have one. But then he remembered. "I have one on my hard drive!"

"Oh, good," she said, until he fired it up and she discovered it was in his native language. "Now my understanding *that* would be a miracle!" He tried his decoding conversion software on it, but it didn't support his language.

"Something to look forward to this evening," he said.

"Among other things. You know, Albie, I owe a lot of those people some serious apologies."

"Yes?"

"Oh, yes. I'll hardly know where to begin. If you only knew."

"There was a time," he said, "when I would have been most curious. Captain Steele can attest that there is something in the black marketeer akin to a pathological gossip. We are quiet and do not say much, but oh, how we love to listen. But do you know, I would rather not hear of the offenses you may have committed against those who love you so much."

"I don't care to talk about them either."

"You can hope that your new brothers and sisters won't either. A wise man once counseled me that apologies must be specific, but now that I am a believer, I am not sure I agree. If your friends know that you are sorry, deeply remorseful, and that you mean it when you apologize, I expect they will forgive you."

"Without making me rehash everything so they'll know I know what I did?"

Albie cocked his head and appeared to be thinking. "That doesn't sound like a born-again response, as Dr. Ben-Judah would call it. Does it?"

She shook her head. "That would be like rubbing it in."

Rayford's phone rang. The area code was Colorado. "Yeah," he said.

"Ah, Mr. Berry?" It was the unmistakable voice of Steve Plank.

"That's me."

"Are you maintaining my anonymity with the dear departed?"

"I am indeed, Mr. Stephens. I'm assuming we're on a secure connection?"

"Absolutely."

"Then I am happy to tell you that she

has come back from the dead, both physically and spiritually."

Silence.

"Did you catch that, Pinkerton?"

"I'm speechless, and that's new for me. Are you serious?"

"Roger."

"Wow! Better still keep my confidence, but pass along my best and a big welcome to the family."

"Will do."

"I have good news for you too. I reported to the brass the unfortunate incident in the detention area, and they said to just dispose of the body and send in the paperwork. I asked 'em where I was supposed to do that—with the body, I mean—and they said they'd just as soon not know. I guess there's more'n enough corpses to deal with everywhere so we luck out on this one."

"You know the irony, don't you, Pink?"

"Tell me."

"The GC pretended she was dead once too."

"I remember that. She must be the woman with nine lives."

"Well, three anyway. And now she has all she needs."

"Amen and roger that. Keep in touch."

When they arrived within airspace of Kankakee, Albie got on the radio to talk to the tower. He identified himself as Commander Elbaz and asked permission to load a body into his chopper for "proper disposition."

"We have no extra personnel to help with that, Commander."

"Just as well. We're not totally sure of the cause of death or any potential contagions."

"It's you and Mr. Berry and the deceased?"

"Roger, and the paperwork has been filed with International."

"Consider yourselves processed. Oh, stand by, Commander. I've been reminded that a shipment has arrived for you from New Babylon."

"A shipment?"

"It's stamped Confidential and Top Secret. About half a skid. I'd say two hundred pounds."

"Can it be delivered to the chopper?"

"We'll see what we can do. If we've got

a free man and a forklift, what say we load her for ya?"

"Obliged."

Half an hour later, as Rayford and Albie carried Hattie to the chopper under a sheet, she whispered, "Anyone around?"

"No, but hush," Rayford said.

"I need a new identity. This is really getting old."

"Shut up or I drop you," Albie said.

"You wouldn't."

He pretended to let his end slip, and she cried out. "You two are gonna get us busted," Rayford said.

Once she was loaded, Rayford told her to stay out of sight until they were airborne. He got behind the controls again because he knew the way and Albie had not performed a landing inside a bombed-out skyscraper before.

Before Rayford lifted off, Albie turned and reached over the hidden Hattie and began unfastening the skid and boxes until he found a gross of black spray paint cans. The snapping of plastic fasteners and wrap made Hattie ask, "What in the world are you doing?"

"Just clearing the trapdoor so Rayford can eject you if you don't behave."

A full day had passed in New Babylon, and David felt well enough to leave the hospital. Hannah came to change his dressing. "How are we doing?" she asked, peering into his eyes.

"Nurses all use the collective *we*, don't they?"

"We're trained in it."

"Physically I feel a hundred percent better."

"You'll still have to take it easy."

"I've got a desk job, Hannah."

"You also have a ton of stuff to do fast. Pace yourself."

"I don't feel like doing it anyway."

"Do it for Annie."

"Touché."

With his new bandage in place, she put her hands gently over his ears. "I wasn't trying to be mean, David. I mean it. I know your heart is broken. But if you wait for that pain to go away before doing what you have to do, it'll be time to get out of here."

He nodded miserably.

"You're going to be OK, David," she said.

"That sounds trite now, but just knowing you a little makes me certain."

He wasn't so sure, but she was trying to help.

"I've been thinking," she added.

Uh-oh. "Glad somebody's up to that."

"I knew I wanted to be a nurse when I was a veterinarian's aide in high school."

He raised his eyebrows. "I'm expecting some joke about me as a patient."

"No jokes. It's just that one of the things our office offered was the injection of biochips into pets so they could always be found and identified."

"Yeah?"

"Isn't that what you said the GC is going to do to everybody?"

He nodded.

"And I'm sort of an expert in that, and now you know it."

"Guess I'm still too medicated, Hannah. Spell it out for me."

"Aren't they going to need to train people in how to do this and send experts here and there to supervise it?"

He shrugged. "Probably, sure. What? It looks like a plum job, a way to see the world? You want a letter of recommendation?"

She sighed. "If you weren't hurting, I'd smack you. Give me some credit. You think I'd want to teach people how to apply the mark of the beast? Or that I'd want to watch while they do it? I'm looking for a way we can all get out of here without making it obvious why we left. You want to be among Carpathia's top ten most wanted?"

"No."

"No, so you get in there with Viv Ivins and offer the services of your pilots and even a nurse you know who has some background in this stuff. Get us sent somewhere to get the ball rolling, whatever. You're the one with the creativity. I'm just shooting wild here."

"No, keep going. I'm sorry. I'm listening now."

"You get us all on the same plane, maybe a big expensive one, because the bigger the lie, the more people want to believe it. Crash it somewhere, like the middle of an ocean, where it would be more trouble than it's worth to confirm we're all dead. We hook up with the rest of your friends, but we're not constantly looking over our shoulders for GC."

"I like it."

"You're not just saying that?"

"I wouldn't. It's a stroke of genius."

"Well, it's a thought."

"A great thought. Let me run it past Mac and Abdullah. They're good at finding holes in schemes and—"

"I already did. They liked it too."

"Anything left for me, or can you keep everybody in the palace healthy and stitched up and do my job too?"

She bit her lip. "I was just trying to help."

"And you did."

"But we both know I can't do your job. Nobody can. So I mean it when I say you have to channel your grief into productivity and do it for Annie. It's the only way to make any sense out of this. Mac tells me the Tribulation Force sees you as second in importance only to Dr. Ben-Judah."

"Oh, come on."

"David! Think about it. Look what you've done here. It doesn't have to fizzle when we all leave if you can figure a way to keep it going from anywhere."

When Buck's phone rang, he assumed it would be Rayford, telling him he and Albie and Hattie were close. But it was Mac McCullum.

"Hey, Mac!" he said, holding up a hand to quiet the others. Buck had to sit when he heard the news. "Oh, no. No. That's awful. . . . Oh, man . . . how's he doing? . . . Tell him we're with him, will you?" Buck's face contorted and he couldn't control his tears. "Thanks for letting us know, Mac."

Chloe rushed to him. "What, Buck? What's happened?"

TEN

"Excuse me, Rayford," Hattie said, a hand on each of his shoulders as he directed the chopper over Chicago toward the Strong Building. Albie was dozing.

Rayford slipped off one headphone so he could hear her, and she let her hands slip to the top of his chair. "I'm worried about how I'm going to be received."

"Are you joking? I can think of three who will be overjoyed."

"I've been terrible to them."

"That was before."

"But I should apologize. I don't even know where to begin with you. Planting that stuff about Amanda. Making you all wonder about her."

"But you admitted that, Hattie."

"I don't remember apologizing for it. That seems so weak compared to what I did."

"I won't say it wasn't an awful time for me," he said. "But let's put it behind us."

"You can do that?"

"Not by myself."

"Chloe really lost patience with me."

"With me too, Hattie. And I deserved it."

"She forgave you?"

"Of course. Love forgives all."

Hattie fell silent, but Rayford felt the pressure of her hands on the back of his chair. "Love forgives all," she repeated, as if mulling it over.

"That's from the Bible, you know. First Corinthians 13."

"I didn't know," she said. "But I hope to learn fast."

"Want another one? I'm doing this from memory, but there's a verse in the New Testament—more than one, I think—that quotes Jesus. He basically says that if we forgive others, God will forgive us, but if we don't forgive others, neither will God forgive us."

Hattie laughed. "That puts us over a barrel, doesn't it? Like we don't have a choice."

"Pretty much."

"You think I should find that verse and memorize it so I can quote it to them when I get there? Tell them they'd better forgive me, if they know what's good for them?"

Rayford turned and raised an eyebrow at her.

"I'm kidding," she said. "But, um, you think they all know that verse?"

"You can bet Tsion does. Probably in a dozen languages."

She sat quiet awhile. Rayford pointed out the Strong Building in the distance and rapped lightly on Albie's knee with his knuckles. "You might want to be awake for this, friend."

"I'm nervous," Hattie said. "I was all psyched up, but now I don't know."

"Give them some credit," Rayford said. "You'll see." He hit the button on his phone to call Buck and handed it to Hattie. "Tell Buck the next sound he hears will be us."

Buck had told Chloe the news about Annie, then gathered everyone in the safe house to tell them. None had met her, of course, but

Tsion, Buck, Chloe, and Leah had had enough interaction with David that they felt they knew Annie. Chaim and Zeke were brought up to speed; then they all prayed for David and Mac and Abdullah. Zeke asked if they would mind praying for his father too.

"I don't know 'xactly where they took him, but I know Dad, and he ain't gonna be co-operative."

"David says they're going to try out the mark on prisoners first," Buck said.

"Dad would die first."

"That might be the price."

"Ten to one he'd take a couple of 'em with him," Zeke said.

Buck's phone rang, and he was grateful when Chloe reached for it.

"Hattie?" she said. "Where are you guys? . . . That close? See you in a few then. . . . Yeah, we heard Dad and Albie found a, um, friend on the inside. You ought to be grateful for all the time and expense and effort that went into—well, I don't know if you realize how risky that was. And investing Dad and Albie's time and an aircraft—I mean—it's not like you did anything to deserve it. I'm not trying to be mean, I'm just saying . . . don't start the waterworks with me, Hattie. We go back too far. For all we know the old safe house is ashes now because of—Yeah, we can talk about it when you get here. . . . Of course I still care about you, but you may not find all of us as soft as my dad. There's a delicate balance here and a lot more people than before. Even in a place as huge as this, it's not easy living together, especially with people who have a history of putting *their* needs ahead of everybody el—OK, all right. We'll see you in a minute."

Hattie clapped the phone shut and slapped it into Rayford's hand. "I take it that wasn't Buck," he said.

"She hates me!" Hattie said. "This is a bad idea. You should have left me there, let them take me back to Buffer and take my chances. I might not have lasted, but at least I'd be in heaven."

"Should we have let you kill yourself too? Then where would you be?"

"Chloe didn't sound like she's going to forgive me. Ah, I don't blame her. I deserve it."

Rayford felt Hattie sit back and she muttered something.

"Can't hear you," he said, maneuvering toward the building.

"I said she probably only said what I would have if the shoe was on the other foot."

Hannah Palemoon had dressed David's wound differently, applying a tight-fitting bandage that adhered to the shaved part of his head and did not touch his hair. It aided the stitches in keeping his scalp together for fast healing, she told him, and he didn't need the layers of gauze covering his ears and extending under his chin anymore. He felt almost normal except for the residual pain—much less—and the itching he knew he had to ignore. The best he could do was to gently press around the edges of the bandage, but as the stitches would not be removed for at least another two days, he had to be careful.

Still, his cap fit again. He stopped by his quarters for a fresh uniform, checked the mirror, and realized how incongruous he looked. His youthful, Israeli features and dark complexion went well with the tailored, form-fitting garb of the senior GC staff. But as he studied his visage, he wondered if any of the Nazis he'd seen in history books hated the swastika on their snappy uniforms as much as he hated the insignia of the Global Community. How he would love abandoning the whole look. And it wouldn't be long.

He stopped with his hand on the inside door handle. Though he was better, he still felt the fatigue of one whose body was trying to heal itself. Part of him wanted to stretch out on the bed and not move for twelve hours, to simply lie there in his grief and embrace the gnawing emptiness. David found some solace in Hannah's insistence that Annie would not have suffered even for a split second. But why couldn't the power that obliterated her nervous system and baked her vital organs also destroy the longing in him she could now never fulfill? No lightning bolt of any magnitude could extinguish a love so pure.

He bowed his head and prayed for strength. If he had, say, two months, he might have allowed himself the luxury of another day or two to take the hardest edge off his pain. But even the time he had was not really enough for all he had to do. *For Annie,* he told himself as he headed for his office. And he would remind himself of that every few minutes for as long as it took to keep himself going.

His relegating Annie to a sacred, protected part of his mind was not helped when he encountered Viv Ivins in the corridor outside his office. "I need to see you," she said in her crisp, delicate voice and Romanian accent. "My office or yours?"

He was so glad she had not begun with the obligatory "He is risen," which he and Mac and Abdullah and Hannah had decided they would respond to with "He is risen indeed," privately knowing they were referring to Christ. Perhaps Vivian eschewed the formality because technically she was outside the hierarchy. She did not even wear a uniform, though her light blue, dark blue, black, charcoal, and gray suits were uniform enough. She wore sensible shoes, and her blue-gray hair was teased into a helmetlike ball.

Giving David the option of meeting with her in his own office was unusual, for while Ms. Ivins bore no official title, everyone knew she was akin to the boss's daughter, or, in this case, the boss's aunt. She was not a blood relative, as far as anyone knew, but Carpathia himself made it plain that she was as close to him as anyone in the world. She had been a dear family friend and had, from almost the beginning, helped his late parents raise their only child.

She did not overtly lord it over anyone that she had clout without title. There was simply an unspoken knowledge between her and everyone. What she wanted she got. What she said went. Her word was as good as Carpathia's, and so she didn't have to assert herself. She employed her understood power in the same way everyone else accepted it.

"Please," David said, "come in." He enjoyed the brass of having someone so close to Carpathia sitting in his office, not six feet from the computer he used to subvert the potentate's efforts.

His assistant greeted him with a concerned look as he passed. David merely said, "Good morning," but she slowed him with, "Are you all right?"

"Better, Tiffany, thanks," he said.

When she noticed his visitor, she lurched to her feet. "Ms. Ivins," she said.

Viv merely nodded. David held the door for her, and once she was inside and he shut it, she stood waiting for him to pull out a chair for her. He imagined saying, "Is your arm broken?" But there was almost as much feminist power in her expecting his chivalry as there would have been in her not doing so.

"I heard you say you were feeling better," she said, opening a folder in her lap and pulling a pencil from behind her ear. "So I won't belabor that. I trust you're able to get past your unfortunate incident with His Excellency?"

"Throwing up on the leader of the world, you mean?" he said, eliciting a grimace from her. "Except that such news travels fast and I doubt there is an employee in New Babylon not aware of it, yes, I try not to dwell on it."

"Senior management understands," she said.

He wanted to ask if they understood that barfing on the big boss was actually an answer to a desperate prayer to be spared from pretending to worship him.

Viv made a tiny check mark after her first listed item. David wondered what she might have written there as the discussion point. Regurgitation?

"Now then," she said, "a few more items. First, your new immediate superior will be James Hickman."

"My area will report to Intelligence?"

"No, Jim has been promoted to Supreme Commander to replace Reverend Fortunato."

David mused that having had *Intelligence* in Hickman's previous title was similar to Fortunato now having *Reverend* in his. "Surely this was Leon's, er, Commander Fortunato's choice, not the potentate's."

David detected the hint of a smile, but Viv wouldn't take the bait. "So Jim will be relocating to Leon's old office?" he said.

"Please don't get ahead of me, Mr. Hassid. And I would urge you to use titles or at the very least *Mister* when you refer to personnel at such levels. You shall be expected to refer to Mr. Hickman as Supreme Commander and Mr. Fortunato as Reverend or Most High Reverend."

Do I get a vote? David wondered. He might rather have vomited on Leon than call him Most High anything. He bit his tongue to keep from asking Viv, er, Ms. Ivins, whether it had been Hickman's groveling that won him his promotion. Or perhaps that performance was in gratitude for a move that had already been put in place.

"And no," Viv continued, "the new Supreme Commander will not be moving into Reverend Fortunato's old office. Mr. Hickman will be sharing space with His Excellency's assistant."

"*Real*-ly," David said. "Seems Sandra's kind of cramped as it is."

"How shall I put this? Though Mr. Hickman will have the same title Mr. Fortunato had, the job may not have quite the same range of influence."

"Meaning?"

Viv appeared frustrated, as if she were seldom asked to be more precise. "Mr. Hassid, it should be obvious to everyone that a leader whose deity has been publicly affirmed would not have need for the same level of assistance he may have in the past. Mr. Fortunato was, in essence, the chief operating officer to His Excellency's chief executive officer. Mr. Hickman's role will be more that of facilitator."

Like sergeant at arms or town crier? David wanted to say.

"And, of course, you are aware of Reverend Fortunato's new duties."

More than you are. But False Prophet *may not look right on the business card.* "Refresh me."

"He will be the spiritual head of the Global Community, directing homage to the object of our worship."

David nodded. To cover any unconscious look that might have given him away, he said, "And, what, ah, is to become of Leon's, excuse me, Reverend Fortunato's old office?"

"It will become part of the potentate's new quarters."

"Oh! I knew he wanted to expand upward. But out as well?"

"Yes, it should be magnificent. One of the benefits, so far anyway, of his resurrected body is that he is apparently immune to the need for sleep. Busy twenty-four hours a day, he needs variety in his work environment."

"Uh-huh." *That's all we need. Satan with no downtime.*

"The potentate's new office will be spectacular, Director Hassid. It will encompass both his and Mr. Fortunato's old spaces, as well as the conference room, and above the ten-foot walls will extend another thirty feet of windows to a clear roof."

"Sounds impressive, all right."

"I'm sure you will have your share of audiences with him," she said, "though you will more often meet with the new Supreme Commander."

"If I were the potentate, I would want an office large enough to allow plenty of distance between him and me."

"I don't understand."

"You know, the throwing up thing."

"Oh, yes. I get it. Amusing." But she did not appear amused.

"Will Mr. Hickman have a meeting area, or will we have to keep our voices down so as not to disturb the potentate's assistant?"

"I'm sure between the two of you, you'll be able to work something out. For instance, meeting here. Oh, my, look at the time. I have several other appointments, so you'll forgive me if I plunge ahead."

No, time's up. Get out. "Certainly, Ms. Ivins. I understand."

"During your incapacity, we were unable to wait on several important issues. We needed to get orders placed for several technical purchases that involve international shipping and manufacture."

David had to concentrate to keep from making a face. He knew exactly what she was talking about, and he had hoped he could stall such requisitions and frustrate the potentate's efforts.

"Technical purchases?" he said.

"Biochip injectors. And, of course, loyalty enforcement facilitators."

Loyalty enforcement facilitators!? Why not just call them cranium and trunk separators? "Guillotines, you mean?"

That made her wince. "Director, please. That has such an eighteenth-century sound to it, and you can understand why we want to avoid any language that bespeaks violence or conjures images of beheading and the like."

And the like? "Begging your pardon, ma'am, but do we not assume that people will recognize the guillotines, or loyalty enforcement facilitators, for what they are? What else might they be used for, halving cabbages?"

"I don't find that the least bit amusing."

"I don't either, but let's call a blade a blade. People see a heavy, angled, razor-sharp edge waiting to be triggered from the top of a grooved track, with a head-shaped yoke at the bottom over a handy basket, and my guess is they'll have a clue what it's about."

Ms. Ivins shifted in her chair, made another check mark on her list, and said, "I shouldn't put it so crassly. But my guess, no my sincere belief, is that these will hardly, if ever, be used at all."

"You really think so?"

"Absolutely. They shall merely serve as a tangible symbol for the seriousness of the exercise."

"In other words, willingly express your loyalty or we chop your head off."

"That will not need to be said."

"I should guess not."

"But, Mr. Hassid, I wager that only the most unusually hard cases, so few and far between that they will be newsworthy for their uniqueness, will result in complete consummation of the enforcement."

I'd hate to see incomplete consummation of the enforcement. "You're confident, then, that all opposition has been eradicated."

"Of course," she said. "Who in their right mind could see the resurrection of a man dead three days and not believe in him as God?"

Rayford did not get the reception he expected, and Chloe hurried to him to explain it. He was staggered by the news of Annie. The three sat, stunned as the rest, and most, it appeared, avoided eye contact with Hattie.

"What do we hear from David?" Rayford said. "Is he all right?"

"We heard from Mac," Buck said. "Worse is that David collapsed from heat exhaustion or sunstroke or something, and that just delayed his finding out about Annie."

Rayford sat shaking his head. He knew more and more of this would be their lot, but it never seemed to get easier.

"Not everybody knows everyone else here," he said finally, and made cursory, subdued introductions.

"'Scuse me," Zeke said, "but is it OK if I ask a dumb question?"

"Anything," Rayford said.

"No offense, lady," he said to Hattie, "but I didn't expect to see a mark on you."

Tsion stood, lips trembling, and approached her. "Is it true, dear one?" he said, putting his hands on her shoulders. "Let me look at you."

Hattie nodded, her eyes darting to Buck and Chloe, who stared, wide eyed.

Tsion embraced her, weeping. "Praise God, praise God," he said. "Lord, you take one away and send one anew." He opened his eyes. "So, tell us. When? How? What happened?"

"Not twenty-four hours ago," she said. "It wasn't just one thing, but all of you caring about me, loving me, pleading with me, praying for me. If you have not heard Albie's story, though, make sure you do soon."

She leaned close and whispered in Tsion's ear.

"Certainly," he said. "Chaim, Zeke, Albie, Leah, let's let our new sister have a few moments with the Steele family, shall we? There will be plenty of time for getting acquainted."

The others rose and followed Tsion as if they understood, though Zeke looked puzzled. When it was just the four of them, Hattie stood as Rayford, Buck, and Chloe sat. "I'm so happy for you," Chloe said, "and I mean it even if I sound stunned. I am. I wish you'd told me on the phone before I went off on you."

"No, Chloe, I deserved that. And I don't

blame any of you for being shocked. I'm a little shocked myself. But I have so much to explain. Well, not to explain, because who can explain rottenness? But to apologize for it. I was so awful to you, all of you at different times. I don't know how you could ever forgive me."

"Hattie," Chloe said, "it's all right. You don't have to—"

"Yes, I do. And Chloe, one thing you need to know is that something you said to me a long time ago never left me. I couldn't get it out of my mind, though I tried over and over. It was when I visited you at Loretta's house and I accused you all of just trying to change my mind about an abortion and of only really loving me if I bought into the whole package and agreed with everything you said. Remember?"

Chloe nodded.

Hattie continued. "Even though you were so much younger than me, you told me that you all wanted to love me the way God loved me, and that was whether I agreed with you or not. No matter what I did or what I decided, you would love me because that was the way God loved you, even when you were dead in your sins."

"I don't remember being that articulate," Chloe said, her eyes filling.

"Well," Hattie said, "you were right. God loved me at my lowest. And to think I almost killed myself before he finally got to me."

"They don't know that story," Rayford reminded her. And she told them everything, from the time the GC in Colorado apprehended her to that very moment.

"I was so worried that you would never forgive me," she concluded.

Chloe stood to embrace her. Then Buck did. "You've never forgiven me for something that was worse than anything you ever pulled, Hattie."

"What?"

"I introduced you to Nicolae Carpathia."

She nodded, smiling through tears. "That *was* pretty bad," she said. "But how could you know? He fooled almost everybody at first. I wish I'd never laid eyes on him, but I also wouldn't trade a thing about my life now. It all pointed to today."

David was antsy. He wanted Viv Ivins to leave so he could get started on his real chores. She rattled on about Fortunato.

"He'll move into Peter Mathews's old office, but nothing will be the same there. There's no Enigma Babylon One World Faith anymore, because there's no enigma. We know whom to worship now, don't we, Mr. Hassid?"

"We sure do," he said.

"Now," she said, "there is one more item. You're aware that you lost an employee the other day?" She flipped a page in her notebook and read, " 'Single, white, female, twenty-two, almost twenty-three, Angel Rich Christopher.' Rich is apparently a family name."

David held his breath and nodded.

"Lightning victim," Viv added. "One of several."

"I was aware of that, yes."

"I just wanted to tell you that if you were planning any sort of memorial, I'd advise against it."

"I'm sorry?"

"We have simply lost too many employees to make it practical to give them all their moments, if you will."

David was offended, especially for Annie. "I, uh, have attended other such ceremonies. They have been short but appropriate."

"Well, this one would not be appropriate. Understood?"

"No."

"No?"

"I'm sorry, I don't understand. Why would it not be appropriate to remember a co-worker who—"

"If you would think about it for just a moment, you would likely understand."

"Save me the time, please."

"Well, Mr. Hassid, Miss Christopher was apparently struck by lightning when the now Reverend Fortunato was calling down fire from heaven on those who refused to recognize His Excellency the Potentate as the true and living God."

"You're saying her death proves she was subversive. That Fortunato killed her."

"God killed her, Director. Call it subversive or whatever you will, it is obvious to all who were present—and I know you were—that only skeptics suffered for their unbelief that day."

David pursed his lips and scratched his head. "If we are not memorializing employees who did not recognize Nicolae Carpathia as deity, I understand and will comply."

"I thought you would, sir." She rose and waited for David to open the door for her. "Good day to you, Director. You know I am always available, should you need anything at all."

"Well, there is one more thing."

"Name it."

"The biochip injectors you mentioned. Are they similar to the type used for inserting the same into household pets?"

"I believe they are, with certain modifications."

"One of the nurses who attended me happened to mention that she got her start in medicine as a veterinarian's assistant. I wonder if she has any experience with that kind of technology that might be helpful to us."

"Good thinking. Give me her name and I'll check it out."

"I don't recall offhand," he said. "But it should be easy enough to find out. I'll call you with it."

As soon as Viv was gone, David phoned Hannah. "I'll be giving your name to Viv Ivins. Expect a call."

"Got it."

He told her of the prohibition against even

a moment of silence in his department for Annie.

"That's perfect," she said. "David, she would wear that like a badge of honor. If being honored made it appear she was a Carpathia loyalist, you'd have to answer to her in heaven someday."

ELEVEN

For the next several days in the safe house, Rayford quietly observed the group dynamics and took notes. Tsion and Chaim spent most of their time studying. Leah seemed bored with helping Chloe with the international co-op, and while she got acquainted with Hattie, Hattie was getting on everyone's nerves. Everyone's except Zeke's. He mostly kept to himself and didn't appear affected by personal idiosyncrasies.

Rayford asked Tsion to lead the group in a brief Bible study each day, and they prayed together. Everyone was also expected to log on to Tsion's daily cybermessage. Each took a turn spray painting the insides of exposed windows until all the floors they were using were invisible to the outside, even with lights on.

A week after Rayford had brought Hattie into the safe house, he called a meeting to officially insert Chaim, Zeke, Albie, and Hattie into the Tribulation Force. They watched the Internet and television for information on when and how the mark of loyalty would be administered. And Buck was back in full swing with his *The Truth* cyberzine. With his international contacts and his ability to write stories that had a ring of authenticity without exposing believers in high places, Buck's was the most popular site on the Net, except for Tsion's. Through contacts Chloe lined up in the co-op, Buck enlisted underground printers all over the world who risked their lives publishing *The Truth* and Tsion's messages for those without access to computers.

Hattie evolved from a hesitant newcomer to the vivacious, excited believer she had been that first morning in Bozeman. Rayford enjoyed her spirit, and it seemed Tsion did too. The others' eyes seemed to glaze over each time she exulted over something anew. Something had to give. The Trib Force had plenty of space and privacy, but even in a massive skyscraper, cabin fever set in.

Fresh air was a problem. The building ventilation system worked fine, but other than the occasional slightly opened window that brought in crisp, fall breezes, everyone longed for time outdoors in the daylight. Too risky, Rayford told them, and even Kenny Bruce was taken out only after dark.

One by one his comrades came to Rayford in private, and while they carefully avoided bad-mouthing each other, all had similar requests. Each wanted an assignment, something away from the safe house. They wanted to be proactive, not waiting for Nicolae and the GC to be the only ones on the offensive.

All but Zeke, that is, who seemed content with his role. He inventoried the tools and supplies necessary to outfit the best forgery and phony identification operation possible. "I'm not a book readin' kind of a guy," he told Rayford, "but I can see what's coming."

"You can?"

Zeke nodded. "Dr. Ben-Judah is training Chaim what's-his-name to go back to Israel. That means I gotta work on a new ID for him, and not just on paper. He's gotta look like somebody else, because everybody knows him all over the world."

Rayford could only nod.

"You can't change a guy's height and weight, and I'm no plastic surgeon. But there's things you can do. He's got that Einstein hair thing goin' now, and he shaves. I'd bald him and dye his eyebrows dark. Then have him grow a big bushy beard or maybe muttonchops and a mustache, and make them dark too. He'll look younger and kinda hip, but mostly he won't look like himself. We gotta get rid of the glasses or change 'em drastically. Then I'd give him colored contacts. If he can get along without a prescription, I got plenty he can choose from."

"Uh-huh," Rayford said. "Zeke, what makes you think he's going back to Israel?"

"Oh, he isn't? Well, my mistake then. I just figured."

"I'm not saying you're wrong. I just wondered why you figured that."

"I don't know. Somebody's got to go, and

you guys have never wanted to risk Dr. Ben-Judah."

"Somebody's got to go to Israel? Why?"

Zeke furrowed his brow. "I don't know. You can tell me if I'm wrong 'cause a lot of time I am, but Dad says I've got intuition. I try to figure out Zion's messages each day, but like I say, readin's not my thing. I don't think I ever read a book all the way through, except maybe a parts manual and then only over about six years. But Zion makes those daily message things pretty easy to understand for a smart guy. I'm sayin' he's smart, not me. Most smart guys think they're explainin' something, but they're the only ones who understand it. You know what I mean?"

"Sure."

"Well, what I'm gettin' from Zion lately is that Carpathia is up to somethin'. And it has to do with Jerusalem. Zion says the Bible says the Antichrist is not only gonna pull a fast one on the Jews, he's also gonna brag about it right in their own temple and defile it somehow and break his promise."

"I think you've pretty much got that down, Zeke. How does Chaim play into it?"

"Zion says God's preparin' a safe place for the Jews to run off to, but they got to have a leader. Zion can lead 'em on the Net, but they need somebody there, somebody they can see. He's gotta be Jewish. He's gotta be a believer. He's gotta be popular or at least be able to get people to follow him. And he's gotta know a lot of stuff. The only person that's gonna know more than Zion pretty soon will be Chaim. And no way I think *Zion's* goin' over there."

"It's just as dangerous for Chaim, isn't it, Zeke?"

"Well, I don't know who'd be worse in Carpathia's mind, the guy who's tellin' the whole world Carpathia's the devil himself or the guy what ran a sword through his brain. But the fact is, we—I mean us believers—could probably get along without Chaim if we had to. But we're in trouble without Zion."

Zeke looked troubled for having said it.

Rayford stood and paced. "Well, Zeke, your dad's right about your intuition. You've hit this nail on the head."

"Then I'm gonna be asked to help send him over there as, what's his new name?"

"Tobias Rogoff."

"Right. As him?"

"You are."

"Don't you think a lot of people will recognize his voice and his body type? People notice hands too. I might have to work on that."

"Yes, there will be people who know right away who he is. And if David is right that there is tape showing him murdering Carpathia, I can see the GC showing that to the world. But Carpathia himself has already pardoned his attacker."

"But Carpathia also said he can't control what other citizens might do to the guy, so Chaim would be livin' on borrowed time, don't you think?"

"If he can get to the safe haven with the Jews, I think he will be supernaturally protected."

"That would be cool."

"You said you weren't a plastic surgeon. Are there less invasive ways to change someone's appearance?"

Zeke nodded. "There's dental gizmos."

"Appliances."

"Right. I used one on Leah, and I've got plenty more. We can really change the look of a man's teeth and jaw."

"How about one whose jaw is wired shut?"

"Even better. Leah's going to take out those wires soon. I think we can make him look like somebody else. Then he has to dress different than he ever has, maybe walk different. I can get him to do that just by adding a little somethin' to one of his shoes. I'll be ready when he is."

David dealt with his grief by working every waking moment and then crashing hard till he had no choice but to sleep. He assigned Mac and Abdullah the task of planning their disappearance, as conceived by Hannah. Meanwhile, he planted far and wide in the complex access numbers that would allow him, with the right keystrokes, to hack into the system and monitor the goings-on as fully as he was able to do now, at least for as long as the current system was used.

David found listening in on Nicolae and Leon and Hickman almost addictive, but he also enjoyed hearing what Security Chief Walter Moon had to say. While it was unlikely Moon would become a believer, who could know for sure? If he did, it would have to be before the initiation of the mark on employees, because, as Tsion taught, Scripture was clear that that was a once-and-for-all decision. But Moon, from what David could gather, shared openly with both his assistant and his most trusted subordinate that he believed he had been overlooked for the role of Supreme Commander. He spent most of his time swearing, ironically, "on a stack of Bibles," that he wouldn't have taken the job if it had been offered. But the opposite was so obviously and patently true that even his confidants felt free to tell him, "Of course you would have, and it should have gone to you."

David daydreamed of having Moon on his side, a grouser within the palace who had the potential for subversion.

The new intelligence director, replacing Jim Hickman, was a Pakistani named Suhail Akbar. A devout Carpathia supporter, he was a behind-the-scenes kind of guy, quiet and slow to voice an opinion but with a rsum that far outstripped his former superior's for experience and training. David feared he was bright enough to be a problem. *Bright* was not an adjective ever applied to Hickman.

"It is crucial," David e-mailed Mac one afternoon following a heavy day of hacking and setup for a future of the same, "that we leave no room for questioning our loyalty to the GC and to Carpathia specifically. I challenge the brass occasionally for the very purpose of keeping them from suspecting me, and I believe they do suspect those who seem blindly loyal. I want them to ask themselves, Why would Hassid challenge us and yet stay and serve so capably if he is not simply trying to make the place the best it can be?

"Mac, we have to plan ahead, plant the problem that will explain our demise and cost the GC some plum pieces of equipment. I wouldn't mind seeing the plane go down with a few million Nicks' worth of biochip injectors and even loyalty enforcement facilitators. Wonder if guillotines are listed that way in the top end head-chopping paraphernalia catalogs? Sorry for the gallows humor; it's no laughing matter. Praise God he can make glorified bodies even of those saints who have been dismembered, cremated, or lightning struck.

"At the risk of insulting your intelligence, I must caution against even considering wasting the Phoenix 216. Much as I would love to tweak Carpathia's nose with the loss of his precious ride, we have way too much invested in the bugging system, which I am now able to access even from outside the plane. For whatever time God allows us the freedom to listen in, I can imagine no greater source of information. I have developed a program that can even track the position of the craft via satellite. It is always fun and enlightening, isn't it, when Nicolae thinks he's in a wholly secure environment and lets his hair down? The bluster and posturing among his people is one thing, but to hear him cackle and admit to his most trusted aides the very things he denies everywhere else, well, that's when it's worth it.

"Speaking of that, he has a meeting scheduled with Hickman, Moon, Akbar, and Fortunato that I plan to tape. If you think his go-rounds with just Leon were hilarious, wait till you hear this. I'll upload it to you. Remember the unique secure code for all this privileged information and secure transmissions. Should anyone, yourself included, try to access these files with the wrong code, I have programmed in a bug so nasty that it really should be called a monster.

This is a creature that ignores the software programs and attacks the hardware.

"If I hadn't developed it myself, I wouldn't have believed it. This thing will literally intercept the impulses being relayed from point to point in the processor, carry them to the power source, whether battery or AC, and draw the current into the motherboard itself. If there were an incendiary device in there, I could get a computer to literally blow up in a hacker's face. Given that all that is in there is plastic and metal, the best I can do is produce a lot of heat, smoke, and some melting. Regardless, the victim computer is irreparable after that.

"More later, confrere. I'll look for something concrete from you and Abdullah within forty-eight hours. Meanwhile, it's less obvious and risky for you to have occasion to run into Hannah than for me to. Keep her warm and courageous as a compatriot and assure her that we will get out in time and have productive years left to devote to the cause of the kingdom."

Rayford, who had been kept up-to-date by David once he was up and around again, worried about the calendar. He had been noodling the most effective roles for each member of the Force, and the prospect of a sudden infusion of four members displaced from the palace had both its up- and downsides. Were he to bring them all to Chicago, he would add to the base of operations two pilots, a nurse, and one of the world's greatest computer geniuses. Clearly he had the room, but he wondered if having virtually everybody in one place was the most efficient use of resources.

Not just for their own psyches but also for the sake of the two-pronged overall mission—stymieing Carpathia where possible and winning as many people to the kingdom as they could—it might make more sense to spread the talent around the globe. Hattie and Leah were restless and eager for assignments. Chloe was resigned to staying, because of Kenny and the work of the co-op, but Buck needed live exposure to what was going on to make his cyberzine as effective as it could be.

Rayford and Albie needed all the pilots they could get, but planes weren't plentiful either. If he and the insightful if inarticulate Zeke were right about what Tsion was up to, thousands of pilots and planes would have to be recruited from around the world to airlift Jewish believers to safety. Veteran pilots like Mac and Abdullah could help make that happen.

But in an instant in the middle of the night, Rayford went from thinking he had more than two more weeks to think and plan how to best make use of the New Babylon contingent to realizing he had to act quickly. Time was a luxury he never had enough of, but an emergency threw everything into turmoil.

Rayford's phone rang, but no one was there. He checked the readout. A message from Lukas (Laslos) Miklos. "Have been found out," it read. "Pastor and my wife detained, among others. Pray please. Help please."

The underground church in Ptolemaïs was the largest in Greece and likely the largest in the United Carpathian States. Up to now the local GC presence had not been a problem. The Greek believers had been careful, Rayford knew from personal experience, but even they feared GC Security and Intelligence sources could not look the other way much longer. Part of the reason they felt they had been ignored was that local GC leadership believed Carpathia wanted the region that bore his name to have the lowest reported incidence of insurgence of the ten global supercommunities.

Whatever public relations sensitivities Carpathia had exhibited before his assassination, since his resurrection his emphasis had been on enforcement. Apparently, Rayford deduced, the new Carpathia would rather eradicate the opposition within his own duchy than pretend it didn't exist. Rayford would ask David to check into the situation and see what would be served by a Trib Force party showing its face over there.

Rayford had known Mrs. Miklos to be a quiet, deeply spiritual woman. But Laslos had told him she was also opinionated, stubborn, and brave. She was not the type to back down if confronted over the exercise of her beliefs by those in authority. Rayford imagined the GC storming a meeting and Mrs. Miklos resisting and even putting up a fuss rather than allowing her pastor, Demetrius Demeter, to be taken into custody.

But Rayford didn't want his imagination to run away with him. He would find out what he could from David and perhaps take a run over there with Albie. Or perhaps with Buck. He hated the idea of leaving the Trib Force without so much as a helicopter pilot.

David was keying in his coordinates to listen to Carpathia's meeting with Hickman and the others when he got a call from Rayford regarding a GC vs. underground church skirmish in Greece. "I'll let you know what I find out," he told Rayford. David phoned Walter Moon, but before Walter answered, David was surprised to be paged to Hickman's office.

His office? Hickman shared space with Carpathia's assistant. And didn't Hickman have a meeting with Carpathia soon? David hung up and called Hickman. The assistant, Sandra, answered. "Hassid here. Was I just paged?"

"Yes, sir. The Supreme Commander would like you to meet with him in the conference room, eighteenth floor."

David found a mess. Though the workday was moments from being over and Sandra was packing up to leave, workmen still jammed the area. Drills, saws, hammers, dust, scaffolds, ladders, materials everywhere.

"They're not going to relocate you while they're working?" David said.

"Apparently not," Sandra said, and she marched off.

Hickman opened the door to a conference room that was not long for this world and waved David in. "Hurry and let me get this door closed, Hassid. Less sawdust."

The new Supreme Commander, a Western version of Fortunato with even less class, offered a fleshy hand and shook David's enthusiastically. "Yeah, hey, how ya doin'? He is risen, huh?"

"Huh," David said, and when Hickman shot him a double take, he added, "Indeed."

Hickman appeared nervous and in a hurry. David thought he could pry information from him by playing dumb. "So, just about the end of your day, hmm? How's it been, sharing space with—"

"Never mind that," Hickman said, sitting and letting his generous belly push past his unbuttoned uniform jacket. "Got a meeting coming up with the big guys, and I'd rather not go in there unprepared."

That'll be the day, David thought. "How can I help?" he said.

"We all up-to-date, up to snuff, on track, on target, on course?"

David shook his head, amazed. "All of the above, I guess. What are we talking about?"

Hickman grabbed a dog-eared pad and riffled through a couple of pages. "Guillotines, syringes?"

"You mean loyalty enforcement facilitators and biochip injectors?"

"Yeah, thanks!" Hickman said, scribbling. "I *knew* Viv had some special names for those. You know, Hassid, basically I was a cop. I'm honored and everything, but I gotta prove to His Majesty, ah, His Excellency, that I can handle this. That I'm not in over my head."

"You feel you are?"

"What I feel is that my loyalty and my devotion to the potentate will make up for any lack of experience I've had at this level of management. Now where are we on these things? What can I tell him?"

"That we're on track, on pace."

"Good. I can count on you then."

"Oh, can you ever, J—, er, Supreme Commander."

"Ah, you can call me Commander when

it's just you and me. Keep it formal in public, of course."

"Of course."

"By the way, do you purchase livestock too?"

"You mean foodstuffs? No, that would be Food Services."

"No, this is live. I don't need food. I need a live animal."

"Still not my area, I'm afraid. Rolling stock, avionics, computers, communications hardware. That's my game."

"Who's going to help me procure a pig?"

"A pig, sir?"

"Huge and live, Hassid."

"I have no idea."

Hickman stared at him, apparently not accepting the dodge.

"I could look into it," David said. "But—"

"I knew I could count on you, David. Good man. Let me know first thing in the morning, 'cause the word I get is that the big man is going to assign me that today."

"Oh, you haven't even heard from him about it yet?"

"No, this is what you'd call a heads-up from a colleague who cares."

"Really?"

"Oh, yeah. Guy like me tends to accumulate friends all up and down the corporate ladder. Buddy told me today he was in on a meeting with Fortunato and Carp—oh, forgive me! I know better'n that. I should never use those names, especially in front of a subordinate. I'm gonna direct you to disregard that, Hassid, as your superior officer."

"Jury will disregard, sir."

"Yeah, good. Anyhow, this guy's in a meeting with His Excellency and the Most High Reverend, and he says they're agitated—you know what that means? Exercised, I guess you'd say."

"Understood, Commander."

"They're upset, up in arms, whatever you wanna call it, about the Judah-ites."

"I've heard of them, sir."

"I know you have. Their top guy, who Peacekeeping thought they had flushed out and sent packin', turns up now in a new place—we don't know where, which doesn't have Carp—the potentate, any too cheery, if ya know what I mean—and this Judah guy's turnin' out more and more of this anti-Carpath—well, I guess, yeah, it's OK in that context. This guy's disseminatin' anti-Carpathia stuff everywhere. He's predictin' and says the Holy Bible prophesies that Antichrist—which is what he calls His Excellency, imagine—is gonna defile the temple and sacrifice a pig on the altar."

"You don't say."

"I *do* say, and while I wasn't there, my buddy tells me the potentate is fiery mad; I mean he's hoppin'."

"I can imagine."

"Me too. He says to the Reverend, he says somethin' along the lines of, 'Oh, yeah, well, maybe I *will* show them.' You know how he talks, never usin' contractions and like that."

"I do."

"So, and this is the genius of Nicolae Carpathia, if you'll forgive the familiar reference. He's gonna like, get this, *fulfill* this prophecy—the one in the Bible and the one by Ben Judah-ite, or, um—"

"Tsion Ben-Judah."

"Right! He's gonna sacrifice a pig on the altar of the temple in Jerusalem on purpose, knowing what the guy and the Holy Bible are sayin'. Sorta in yer face, wouldn't you say?"

"That's for sure." *In God's face, no less.*

"Well, see I don't know this yet, you follow?"

"Sure. It's on the QT from your buddy."

"Exactly. But when he, you-know-who, asks me can I get him a pig, I want to be able to tell him no problem. Can I tell him that? You're going to check with, with, ah, your people or whatever, and I'm gonna get him this pig, right?"

"I'll do my best, sir."

"I knew you would. Hot dog, you're good."

"You said that on purpose, didn't you, sir?"

"What's that?"

"Talking about a pig, and you said 'hot dog.' "

Hickman disintegrated into gales of laughter, then tried to pretend he had indeed said it on purpose. When he regained control, he said, "You know what I want, Hassid?"

"Tell me."

"I want a pig, are you ready—?"

"I'm ready."

"—big enough for His Excellency to ride."

"Sir?"

"You heard me. I want the biggest pig you've ever seen in your life. Big as a pony. Big enough to put a saddle on, not literally, but you know what I mean."

"Not sure I do, Commander."

"I'm tryin' to earn a few points here,

understand, Director? Just like you're doin' without tryin', 'cause you're just that good. But I wanna be able to suggest to His Excellency that if he's gonna take the gloves off and go toe-to-toe with his worst enemies, he oughta go 'em one better."

Take the gloves off to go toe-to-toe? Annie would have loved that mixed metaphor. "One better?"

"He ought to ride that pig into the temple!"

"Oh, my." David could not imagine Carpathia, even at his basest, lowering himself to such a spectacle.

"Oh, my is right, Hassid. You read the Bible?"

"Ever?"

"Yeah."

"Some."

"Well, isn't there a story about Jesus ridin' into Jerusalem on a donkey and people singin' and throwin' leaves and whatnot?"

"I was raised Jewish."

"So no New Testament for you. Well, anyway, there is that story, I'm pretty sure. Picture His Excellency havin' fun with that. Ridin' a pig with people paid to sing and throw stuff."

Lord, please! "I can't imagine."

"I can come up with 'em, can't I, Hassid?"

"You can, sir."

"Hey, I'd better get in there. Get on that pig for me, will ya? I'm gonna tell him it's as good as got."

"I'll let you know."

David was on his way out the door when Hickman called after him. "I forgot to tell you," he said, turning pages on his pad again. "There's a gal in Medical Services, a nurse. Here it is. She used to be a vet or something and she's shot biochips into dogs and cats."

"You don't say," David said.

"You might want to check her out, see if we can take advantage of her expertise. You know, in training people how to do this."

"I'll check her out. What's the name?"

"I don't think I have it right, Hassid. Some kind of a funny name. You'll be able to track her down."

"I'll ask for the nurse with the funny name, sir."

TWELVE

Rayford couldn't sleep. Pacing various floors in the cavernous Strong Building, he happened by Chaim's room. The door was wide open, and in the darkness he noticed the old man's silhouette. Chaim sat motionless on the bed, though Rayford knew he had to hear and see him in the corridor. Rayford poked his head in.

"You all right, Dr. Rosenzweig?"

A loud sigh through the wire-bound clenched teeth. "I don't know, my friend."

"Want to talk?"

A low chuckle. "You know my culture. Talk

is what we do. If you have time, come in. I welcome you."

Rayford pulled up a chair and sat facing Chaim in the darkness. The botanist seemed in no hurry. Finally, he said, "The young woman takes my wire out tomorrow."

"Leah, yes. You can't tell me you're worried about that."

"I can hardly contain myself waiting."

"But something else is on your mind."

Chaim fell silent again, but soon he began panting, then leaned to his pillow where he was racked with great sobs. Rayford pulled his chair closer and laid a hand on the man's shoulder. "Talk to me."

"I have lost so much!" Chaim wailed, and Rayford strained to understand him. "My family! My staff! And it is all my fault!"

"Little is our fault anymore, sir. Carpathia is in charge of everything now."

"But I was so proud! So skeptical! Tsion and Cameron and Chloe and you and everyone who cared about me warned me, tried to persuade me. But oh, no, I was too intellectual. I knew better!"

"But you came to the Lord, Chaim. We must not live in the past when all things have become new."

"But look where I was not that long ago! Tsion is joyful in spite of it all, so happy for me, so encouraging. I dare not tell him where my mind is."

"Where is it?"

"I am guilty, Captain Steele! I could do as you say, put the past behind me, if all I was dealing with was my pride and ignorance. But it led me down paths I never believed I would walk. My dearest, most trusted friends are dead because of me. Slaughtered in my house!"

Rayford resisted platitudes. "We have all lost much," he whispered. "Two wives and a son for me, many friends—too many to think about or I'd go mad."

Chaim sat up again, wiping his face with both hands. "That is my problem, Rayford. I have gone nearly mad with grief, but mostly remorse. I murdered a man! I know he is Antichrist and that he was destined to die and come back to life, but I didn't know that when I committed the act. I murdered a man who had betrayed my homeland and me. Murder! Think of it! I was a beloved statesman, yet I stooped to assassination."

"I understand rage, Chaim. I wanted to murder Carpathia myself, and I knew exactly who he was and that he would not stay dead."

"But I premeditated it, Captain, planned it many months in advance, virtually invented and manufactured the weapon myself, faked a stroke just to get myself in proximity to him without suspicion, then finished the job exactly as I had envisioned it. I am a murderer."

Rayford leaned forward and rested his elbows on his knees, head in his hands. "You know I almost saved you the work."

"I don't understand."

"You heard a gunshot before you attacked Carpathia."

"Yes."

"My gun."

"I don't believe you."

Rayford told him the story of his own anger, personality change, plotting, the purchase of the weapon, his determination to do the deed.

Chaim sat shaking his head. "I can hardly believe that the two people who dared attack Nicolae are in the same room. But in the end you could not do it. I did it with enthusiasm, and even up to the time I finally saw my need for God, I was glad I did it.

Now I suffer such regret and shame I can barely breathe."

"Can you take no solace in the fact that this was destiny, and that you cannot be guilty of murdering a man who is alive?"

"Solace? I would give all I own for a moment of peace. It isn't *whom* I did this to, Rayford. It is *that* I did it. I did not know the depth of my own wickedness."

"And yet God has saved you."

"Tell me, is one supposed to *feel* forgiven?"

"Good question. I have faced the same dilemma. I have full faith in the power of God to forgive and forget, to separate us from our sins as far as the east is from the west. But I'm human too. *I* don't forget and thus often I don't appropriate the forgiveness God extends. Because we feel guilty does not mean God does not have the power to absolve us."

"But Tsion tells me I may have a greater destiny, that I just might be the one to be used to lead my believing countrymen to safety from Antichrist. How could he say that and how could I do such a thing when I feel the way I do?"

Rayford stood. "Perhaps the fallacy is in

thinking it would have to be *you* who accomplishes this."

"I would love to be out from under the weight of it, but as Tsion says, who else? He himself cannot risk it."

"I'm saying it's something God is going to do, through you."

"But who am I? A scientist. I am not eloquent. I don't know the Word of God. I barely know God. I was not even a religious Jew until just days ago."

"Yet as a child you must have been exposed to the Torah."

"Of course."

"If Tsion is right, and not even he is sure, this could be your burning-bush experience."

"No one will ever see me as Moses."

"Are you willing to let God use you? Because if Tsion is right and you do what he thinks you should do, you *would* be a modern-day Moses."

"Ach!"

"You could be used of God to flee the evil ruler and take your people to a safe haven."

Chaim moaned and lay down again.

"Moses pled the same case you're pleading," Rayford said. "The question is whether you are willing."

"I know."

"You're right. You were depraved. We all were, until Christ saved us. God can make a miracle of your life."

Chaim mumbled.

"I'm sorry?" Rayford said.

"I said I want to be willing. I am willing to be willing."

"That's a start."

"But God is going to have to do something in me."

"He already has."

"But more. I could no more accept this assignment now than I could fly. The person who accepts this duty must have a clear conscience, confidence that comes only from God, and communication ability far beyond what I have ever possessed. I was able to hold forth in a classroom, but to speak to thousands as Tsion has done, to publicly oppose Antichrist himself, to rally the masses to do what is right? I don't see it. I just don't."

"But you are willing to trust God to work?"

"He is my only hope. I am at the end of myself."

At high noon Carpathia Time in New Babylon, David left the palace and went outside for the first time in days. He was to have his stitches removed at two that afternoon, and he looked forward to seeing Hannah Palemoon again, even in a sterile setting where they might not be able to converse freely.

The heat reminded David of the day of Nicolae's resurrection. It didn't seem right to stroll the grounds of the spectacular palace without Annie. His pain was so raw and the ache so deep that it made his scalp wound fade to insignificance. Hannah had told him that the removal of the bandage would be worse than the removal of the stitches. His uniform cap protected the wound from the sun, but David's body began to heat up in his dress uniform, and the memories of his trauma floated back.

The decimation of the world's population was reflected in the workforce at GC headquarters. What had once been its own bustling metropolis was now a shell of itself. The crowds that used to consist of enthusiastic employees were now made up of tourists and pilgrims, necks craned to catch a glimpse of someone famous.

In the distance David saw visitors crowded around one of the outdoor TV monitors that broadcast GC news twenty-four hours a day. He moseyed over and stood unnoticed at the back. The new Most High Reverend of Carpathianism, Leon Fortunato, held forth from his new office.

David could only shake his head. Leon stood before a pulpit-type lectern, but his height had seemed to change. A husky, swarthy man a tick under six feet tall, Leon wore a long burgundy-and-navy robe that flattered his physique. But when the late Peter Mathews—in a gaudy, silly-looking robe—had stood at the same podium, he had looked shorter than Leon, despite that he was several inches over six feet. Leon had to be standing on some sort of box or platform!

He reported on the worldwide competition to see which locales and regions led in the race to complete their replicas of the Carpathia statue. Of course, the United Carpathian States had an insurmountable lead, but the rest of the world competed for second place.

The report was dotted with feeds from all over the globe, showing how many communities had tried to make unique their version of the statue. Regulations stipulated that the replicas had to be at least life-size and monochromatic, but none could be as large as the original. Past that, local committees were free to exercise creativity. Most of the statues were black, but many were gold, some crystal, some fiberglass, one green, one orange, and several were twice life-size (or half the size of the original). Fortunato seemed particularly pleased with those two and announced plans to personally visit those sites.

"In the interest of full disclosure, it falls to me to report that while Israel has several replica statues in cities as disparate as Haifa and Tel Aviv, Jerusalem has not even begun theirs." Leon switched into his deep bass, solemn voice. "Speaking under the authority of the risen potentate, I say woe! Woe and beware to the enemies of the lord of this globe who would thumb their noses in the face of the most high!"

Here he switched to Uncle Leon mode, sounding like a beloved relative reading a bedtime story. "But you know, while I have been imbued with power from on high to perform all the miracles that our beloved leader performs, and whereas I have proven this power by calling down fire from heaven to destroy the disloyal, your lord,

His Excellency, is the embodiment of love and forgiveness and long-suffering. Against my counsel and better judgment, though I defer to his divine wisdom, the Supreme Potentate has asked me to announce that he knows he has devout followers in the capital of the Holy Land. Their loving lord shall not forget those loyal pilgrims, suffering under the insanity and subversion of the very leaders who have been charged with responsibility for the spiritual health of their souls.

"One week from today, the object of our adoration shall personally visit his children in Jerusalem. He will be there not only to deal forthrightly with those who oppose him—for he is, besides being a loving god, a just god—but also to bless and accept worship and praise from the citizens otherwise without voice.

"As your global pastor, let me urge the countless oppressed Carpathianists living under the thumb of misguided rebels in Jerusalem to bravely show your support to the one worthy of all honor and glory when he arrives in your home city. May it be a triumphal entry like none before it. Let me, on his behalf, personally guarantee your safety and protection against any form of retribution you might otherwise have suffered for your doing the right thing in the face of powerful opposition.

"We know that the leadership there has a thin majority of Judah-ites and Orthodox Jews who risk the vengeance of their god by continuing with their suicidal lunacy. Unless they see the error of their ways and come on bent knee to beg forgiveness of their lord, new leadership will be in place before His Excellency leaves that great city.

"And to those who swear that the temple is off-limits to the potentate himself, I say, dare not come against the army of the lord of hosts. He is a god of peace and reconciliation, but thou shalt have no other gods before him. There shall not be erected or allowed to stand any house of worship anywhere on this planet that does not recognize His Excellency as its sole object of devotion. Nicolae Carpathia, the potentate, is risen!"

The crowd around the TV shouted the customary response, and David said silently, "Jesus the Christ is risen indeed."

Fortunato reminded the world that within two days, all statues must be completed and open for worship. "And, as you know, the first one hundred cities with finished and approved units will be the first to be awarded loyalty mark application centers."

Leon had aides bring into view a flip chart he could reach from whatever he was standing on, and David noticed that as they came into view, his proximity made him look seven feet tall. Fortunato used a pointer to show the standard mark application facility. It contained a staging area, where several thousand at a time would be herded through crowd-control barriers, entertained by taped speeches from Carpathia and Fortunato. Every four minutes, a replay would show Fortunato's calling down fire from heaven on dissidents and Carpathia's actual resurrection. He paused to let the tape roll, and David had to look away. The tourists cheered the broadcast.

Fortunato returned to his demonstration drawing. The citizens would feed into a dozen or two dozen open-air booths—depending on the size of the city and the crowd—where they would be asked to decide on the design and size of their mark and whether they wanted it on their foreheads or the backs of their right hands.

"A friendly reminder," Fortunato said with a grin. "Should you procrastinate on your decision or forget due to your excitement, the standard injection will be made on your right hand, depicting the prefix that identifies your region, next to the thin scar that evidences injection of the biochip.

"We have been asked repeatedly how we are precluding counterfeit marks. While it may be impossible for any but highly skilled and trained observers to tell a fake mark from the real, biochip scanners cannot be fooled. We are so confident of the 100 percent reliability of this technology that anyone whose biochip is not authenticated by a scanner will be subject to execution without appeal. A readable, implanted biochip will be required for standard trade and commerce.

"And yes, we will have loyalty enforcement facilitators at every mark application site."

To David's surprise, this announcement was illustrated by footage of a huge, gleaming guillotine, and Fortunato actually punctuated it with a hearty laugh. "I can't imagine any citizen of the Global Community having to worry about such a device, unless he or she is still mired in the cult of the Judah-ites or Orthodox Judaism. Frankly, only the blind or those without access to television have not seen the resurrection of our god and ruler, so I can't imagine skeptics remain outside Jerusalem. Well, as you can see," and he laughed again, "they will not remain long."

Fortunato then hefted a huge stack of letters and printouts. "These, my friends, are applications from those who want to be first to show their loyalty to His Excellency by proudly having their marks applied right here in New Babylon. Any citizen from any region may have his or her mark applied here, though the code number will coincide with your home region. There is a limit to the number we can accommodate, so get your application in quickly or plan to have yours applied in your local center.

"Does the application hurt? It does not. With technology so advanced and local anesthesia so effective, you will feel only the pressure of the biochip inserter. By the time any discomfort would have passed, the anesthetic will still be working.

"Bless you, my friends, in the name of our risen lord and master, His Excellency the Potentate, Nicolae Carpathia."

Rayford returned to his bed drowsier but still unable to sleep. He spent an hour noodling assignments for the Force and finally concluded that Albie and Buck ought to go to Greece. He needed to stay for the sake of morale, and Buck needed to be able to expose the close-mindedness of the Carpathia regime.

With that settled, Rayford drifted off, planning to get Buck yet another new ID from Zeke in the morning and assign David a little more way-paving from his perch in New Babylon.

David informed the head of Food Services that Supreme Commander Hickman had need of the largest live pig available for Carpathia's Israel visit. Then he stopped in his office to check his computer before his appointment with Hannah. He found an urgent E-mail from Ming Toy.

"I did not know whom else to write to," she said. "I was distraught to hear of your loss and can only pray God's strength for you. I cannot imagine your pain.

"Mr. Hassid, have you seen my family since I left there? Last I heard, they had not seen you. I am most troubled. They have been awarded free accommodations until Chang has been processed for employment, and my father is thrilled beyond words. Mother is silent as usual, but I have heard directly from Chang, and he is desperate. He says the last thing he wants is to work for the GC, yet my father insists. Having his son serve Carpathia is the highest honor he can imagine.

"Chang has heard that all employees will receive the mark within a few weeks, but there is a rumor that new employees hired during this time may be the first to have it applied. Have you heard that? Could it be true? It makes sense in its own way. Why hire someone without knowing up front that they are loyal? And it saves their losing work time later just to stand in line for their marks.

"Father is insistent that Chang initiate his paperwork through Personnel immediately and is eager to see him among the very first to take the mark, especially if Father can witness this himself. Chang is ready to admit to my father that he is a believer in Jesus and, yes, could accurately be called a Judah-ite, but he is afraid of two things. One, that Father would report him, and two, that he would demand to know the truth about me. Trust me, Mr. Hassid; I know my father. He would sell us both out to prove his loyalty to Carpathia and the GC.

"I am urging my brother not to admit anything to Father, and yet I do not know how long he can avoid being tested to the ultimate. The only way to keep from officially applying for work there is to run away or tell my father the truth. Can you help in any way? I am sorry to trouble you with this during such a terrible time for you.

"Rest assured that I am praying for you. And while I assume you know this, Leah reports that your compatriots in the safe house are also upholding you daily.

"With utmost respect and honor, your sister in Christ, Ming Toy."

David called Personnel. "Can you give me the status on a Chang Wong?"

"Yes, sir. Impressive résumé. Mentioned

publicly, at least among the brass, by Carpathia. A no-brainer. He's going to work here as soon as we can get him processed. Only question is where. I suppose you want him; everybody else does."

"Can't say for sure. Just wondering."

"Your area makes the most sense. You wouldn't turn him down, would you?"

"Too early to tell, but I'm not a follower. Just because everybody wants him doesn't mean I should be desperate to snag him."

"True enough. But he'd be an asset."

"What's next?"

"Don't know. We expected him yesterday. It's in his court. He completes the paperwork, makes his app official, and we make an offer."

"And if he accepts?"

"He's in."

"He's not graduated high school."

"We have tutors. He could *teach* high school."

"When would he start?"

"A few days. Delay would be because of the new freeze. You saw that, right?"

"No."

"Should have it in your E-mail."

David didn't want to appear too eager. "I'll find it. Thanks."

"You want this kid if we can get him?"

David had to think fast. If he got him and then David and the others disappeared, the kid could be found out as an enemy of the state. But if their disappearance looked like an accident, there would be no suspicion of them or anyone they associated with. On the other hand, if taking the mark was prerequisite to hiring, the issue was moot. The kid would refuse, the father would turn him in, end of story. David would not be under suspicion for wanting him or spending time with him.

"Would I be able to do a preliminary with him?"

"Interview? Hmm. Not protocol, but I don't see the harm."

"Where's he staying?"

"Four-oh-five-four."

That close to Hannah. Wonder if she knows? "Thanks."

David hurried to the hospital. Hannah greeted him professionally and asked the typical questions about bleeding, discomfort, and pain. Then she asked him to follow her to a private room for removal of the stitches.

"You look OK but distracted," she said,

dousing his head with disinfectant and soaking the bandage.

"Can't imagine why," he groused.

"Sarcasm? Remember, I'm on your side."

"Did you know the Wongs are staying on your floor?"

"Who are the Wongs?"

David smacked himself in the forehead.

"Terrific," she said. "So much for sterility. Close your eyes." He obeyed and she doused him again. "So, who *are* the Wongs?"

He told her the story.

"What're you going to do?" she said.

"Bug their room."

"You can do that?"

"I can do anything."

"I'm gathering that. But how?"

"I'd tell you, but then—"

"Yeah, I know, you'd have to kill me." She looked embarrassed to have said that with his having just lost his fiancée. "I'm sorry," she whispered.

"My fault," he said. "I started it."

She lightly tugged at the bandage, making his eyes water. "Bear with me," she said, squirting more liquid.

"That stuff supposed to make it easier?"

"We tell ourselves that," she said. "Fortunately, you had a good surgeon. Oh, yeah, it was me. I cut enough hair that all we're dealing with is scalp and wound and stitches. Imagine if there was hair too."

"I don't want to think about it."

"Think about something else and I'll hurry."

"You can't just yank it?"

"Not with stitches. Those have to come out the right way. If I pull one out with the bandage, you're on the ceiling. Now try to get your mind on something else."

"Like what?"

She stopped and put her wrists on her hips, careful to keep her gloved hands from touching anything. "David, I hardly know you. How would I know what you have to think about?"

He shrugged.

"Think about freedom," she said. "About being away from here forever."

"You call that freedom? It's just another form of prison."

"I've been wondering about that," she said. "It has to be less tension, don't you think?"

"Different kind, I guess. Ow!"

"Sorry. Be brave. Tell me more."

"Well, we won't have to worry about who's watching and listening and whether my secure E-mail and phone connections have been compromised. We won't have to worry that we've already been found out and they're just letting us hang ourselves and expose others before they arrest us."

"That's what I was thinking," she said.

"But we'll never be free again. We'll be fugitives."

"So you've already ash-canned my idea."

"No, why? I assigned it to Mac and Abdullah."

"Because if it works, no one's even looking for us. We get new IDs, change our looks, and start over."

"But without the loyalty mark."

She hesitated. "Well, yes, there is that. Hold on. There we go." She held before his eyes the long bandage in a pair of surgical scissors. Besides disinfectant, it showed his blood and the imprint of his wound, two staples, and several stitches.

"Can I ask you something?" he said. "Totally off the subject."

"You mean *may I?"*

"Ah, one of those. Showing off your education."

"Sorry. Incurable."

"I guess we'll need a grammar cop at the safe house, in case Tsion and Buck are out. Anyway, why do you people think we want to see that stuff? The yucky bandage, I mean."

"Yucky?" She morphed into baby talk. "Does he hate to see that yucky stuff?"

"Doctors and nurses are forever doing what you just did. Just remove it and toss it. You think I need to see it or I won't pay?"

She shrugged.

"You all must just love this stuff," he said. "That's all I can figure. By the way, you never said anything about staples."

"You just answered your own question."

"I'm lost."

"I showed you so you know what's next. The stitches are separate, so they come out individually. It's not one of those deals where I cut or untie and then the whole thing just sort of tickles as it comes looping out. It won't hurt, but there are several. And there are two staples that have to stay in till the stitches are out, just in case, to hold everything together. When the stitches are gone, I'll know whether the scar can contain that big brain of yours. Then I have to get under each of those two staples, one at a time, with a wire cutter."

"You're joking."

"No, sir. I cut through the staple—"

"Ouch."

"Not if you don't flinch."

"You're the one who'd better not flinch."

"I'm good. I promise. Then I grip each remaining end, that would be two for each staple, and slowly curl it out."

"That's got to hurt."

She hesitated.

"I needed a real fast 'Not at all' right there."

"I admit you'll feel it more than the stitches. It's a bigger invasion, thus a busier evacuation."

"A busier evacuation? You could be in management."

"What *should* I say? The big, yucky staple displaced more tissue than the itty-bitty stitchies. If any of the scar tissue adhered to the metal, you may feel it give way."

"I don't like the sound of 'give way.' "

"What a wuss! It won't even bleed. And if I feel it's too early and it would cause trauma, we'll put it off."

"Not unless it would kill me. I mean it, Hannah. I want to be done with this."

"You don't want any reason to have to come back and talk to me."

"It's not that."

"No," she said dismissively, obviously feigning insult. "I can take it. I don't know any other believers with reasons to come around, but that's all right. Just leave me here to suffer alone."

"Get on with it."

"Shut up and I will. Now think about something else."

"Can you talk while you work?"

"Oh, sure. I told you I was good."

"Then tell me your story while you do this."

"Story's longer than the procedure, David."

"Then take your time."

"Now there! That was a sweet thing to say."

THIRTEEN

Hannah Palemoon's story actually took David's mind off what she was doing. And she did take her time, pausing between each stitch. She teased him by showing him the first, but his look stopped her.

She had been raised on a Cherokee reservation in what was now known as the United North American States. "You wouldn't believe the misconceptions about Native Americans," she said.

"Never been to the States, even when it was just the United States of America. But I read about it. They called you Indians because of Columbus's mistake."

"Exactly. He thinks he's in the West Indies, so we must be Indians. Now it's Indian this, Indian that. Indian tribes. Cowboys and Indians. Indian nation. Indian reservation. The Indian problem. American Indians—that was my favorite. And of course, anyone who hadn't visited the reservation assumed we lived in tepees."

"That's what I would have guessed," David said. "From pictures."

"The pictures are from the tourist sites. They want to see old Native American culture; we're happy to show it. Dress in the old garb, dance the old dances, sell 'em anything they want made from colorful beads. They didn't want to see our real homes."

"Not tepees, I take it."

"Just like any other depressed economy. Multifamily units, tiny houses, house trailers. And the tourists didn't want to know that my dad was a mechanic and my mom worked in the office of a plumbing company. They'd rather believe we were part of a raiding party, drank firewater, or worked in a casino."

"Your parents really didn't?"

"My mother liked to play the slots. Dad lost a paycheck one night playing blackjack. Never went back."

"And you were a vet."

"Vet's assistant, that's all. My uncle, my mother's brother, was self trained. Didn't have to be licensed or certified or any of that other stuff, like on the outside. Unless you wanted business from the outside, and he didn't. And he wasn't into weird stuff either. Tourists asked if he danced and chanted and brought dead pets back to life. He was a good reader, read everything he could find on patching up animals, because he loved them and there were so many of them."

"You didn't want to be a vet?"

"Nope. I read all the books about Clara Barton and Florence Nightingale. Did well in school, especially science, and was encouraged by a teacher to take advantage of opportunities for Native Americans at state universities. Went to Arizona State and never looked back. Cost me more because I wasn't from Arizona, but I wanted distance between me and the reservation."

"Why?"

"I wasn't ashamed or anything. I just thought I had more opportunity outside. And I did."

"Where did you hear about God?"

"Everywhere. There were Christians on the reservation. We weren't churchgoers, but we knew a lot who were. That teacher used to talk to me about Jesus. I wasn't interested. She called it 'witnessing,' and that sounded way too weird for me. Then at university. They were everywhere. You could get witnessed to walking to class."

"Never intrigued you?"

"Not enough to go to any meetings. I was afraid I would wind up in a cult or a multilevel-marketing scheme. The big thing with those kids was getting people to admit they were sinners and that they couldn't do anything about their sin. Tell you the truth, I never felt like a sinner. Not then."

"So, wrong approach for you."

"Not their fault. I *was* a sinner, of course. I was just blind to it."

"What finally made the difference?"

"When I found out who disappeared in the vanishings, I was mad. Those churchgoers I knew. Christians from university. My high school teacher."

"So you must have had an inkling."

"An inkling? I knew. People were saying God did this, and I believed them. And I hated him for it. I thought about those people and how sincere and devout they were, how they cared enough for me to tell me something that made me think they were strange. I didn't want any part of a God who would remove them and leave me here. I wanted a hero, someone to believe in, but not him. Then I saw all the news about Carpathia. The Bible talks about how so many will be deceived? I was at the top of the list. Bought the whole package. Found out he needed medical people, hopped the next plane to New York. Wasn't so sure about moving on to this beautiful, godforsaken desert, but I was still loyal then.

"I started getting squirrelly about Carpathia when he started sounding like a politician, trying to put everything in the best light. He never seemed genuinely remorseful about all the chaos and the loss. I didn't agree with him when he said all this proved that God couldn't have been behind the disappearances, because why would a loving God do that? I believed God *had* done it, and it proved he wasn't so loving after all."

Hannah finished her stitch-removal work, stripped off and discarded her rubber gloves, washed and dried her hands, and pulled on another pair of gloves. She sat on a stool next to David. "Still have the staples, but we can both use a break."

"Somebody had to lead you to God. I'm dying to know where you met another believer here."

"Didn't know there was one till I saw your mark plain as day as you lay there on the ground. I tried wiping it off, then almost danced when I realized what it was. I couldn't see mine and had never seen another, just read about it."

"Where?"

"Remember when we were told that Tsion Ben-Judah's Web site was contraband?"

"'Course."

"That was all I needed to hear. I was there. It was all Greek to me until he predicted the earthquake. First, it happened. Second, my whole reservation was swallowed up. Lost everybody. Mom, Dad, two little brothers, extended family. I'll bet we were one of the only places in the world that had no survivors. Zero."

"Wow."

"You can imagine how I felt. Grief-stricken. Alone. Angry. Amazed that the weird guy on the Net got it right."

"Can't imagine that convincing you, though. Seems you would have been madder than ever at God."

"In a way, I was. But I really began to see the light about Nicolae. You were here then, right? You heard the rumors."

David nodded.

"People said he bullied his way onto a chopper on the roof of the old headquarters building—which I have no problem with. I probably would have done the same. Self-preservation instinct and all that. But no calls for help. No orders for more rescue craft. People hanging on the struts of his chopper, screaming, pleading for their lives. He orders the pilot off the roof. Probably couldn't have saved anybody anyway, the way the thing went down. But you've got to try, don't you? Isn't *that* true leadership?

"Then he was phony again. The remorse didn't ring true. I just started doing my job and forgetting my idealism, but I couldn't tear myself away from the Ben-Judah site. Then millions and millions joined in, and so many of them became believers. I read about the mark of the sealed believer, and I was envious. I wasn't sure I wanted in yet, but I wanted to be part of some family.

"But you know what got to me about Tsion? Listen to me, calling a man like that by his first name. But that's just it. He's clearly one of the most brilliant scholars ever born. But he had a way of putting the cookies on the lower shelf for people like me. I understood what he was saying. He made it plain and clear. And he was transparent. He lost his whole family in a worse way than I did.

"He was so loving! You could sense it, feel it right through the computer. He prayed for people, ministered to them the way the best doctors do."

"And that was what finally persuaded you?"

"Actually, no. I believed he was sincere, and I came to believe he was right. But all of a sudden I went scientific on him. I was going to take this slow, not rush into anything, study it carefully. Well, he starts predicting these plagues, and here they come. Didn't take me long after that. People suffered. These were real. And he knew they were coming."

"Did you ever see yourself as a sinner?"

She stood and found the small wire cutters.

"Uh-oh," David said.

"Just relax. Listen to the nice lady's story." She gently pressed her fingers on each side of the staple and eased the cutting edge of the clippers in. With both hands she forced the handles together, and the staple broke with a snap.

David jumped.

"You still with us?" she said.

"Didn't feel a thing. Just scared me."

"Story of my life." She snapped the other while continuing. "Tsion warned us—you know this; surely you're part of the readership."

David nodded. "I've spoken to him by phone."

"You have *not!*"

He nodded.

"Don't nod with loose staples in your head. And if you lie to me again, I'll twist 'em for you."

"I'm not lying."

"I know you're not. That's what makes me *so* jealous."

"You know you're going to get to meet him someday."

"Better bring a mop and bucket. You can just squeegee me off the floor and pour me down the drain."

"Me too."

"But you know him already! You're best buds."

"Just by phone."

She mimicked him. "Just by phone. Blah, blah, blah. Yeah, we talk. He calls once in a while. 'How ya doin', Dave? Just finished my message.'"

David had to laugh and quickly realized it was the first time since . . .

"Anyway," she continued, pulling the ends of one staple neatly from his scalp. "See? Good timing, good technique. Uh-oh, do I see brain oozing there? Nope. Must be empty."

David shook his head. "The story, Hannah."

"Oh, yeah. Tsion promises us that if we start reading the Bible, it'll be like a mirror to us and we might not like what we see. Remember that?"

"*Do* I?"

The other staple came out just as easily. She made a show of presenting it to him, and he waved it away. "I didn't have a Bible and you don't exactly see them lying around here anywhere. But Tsion had that site where you could call up the whole Bible in your language. Well, not Cherokee, but you know. So I'm reading the Bible on the Net in the wee hours."

"And couldn't get enough of it?"

"Um, no. I did it wrong. I didn't read his little guide on where to start and what to look for. I just started in at the beginning and I loved all those stories in Genesis, but when I got into Exodus, and then—what's the next one?"

"Leviticus."

"Yeah. Ugh! I'm wondering, where's the mirror? I don't like what I'm seeing, all right, but it's no mirror. Finally, I go into his site where you can ask questions. Only a million people a day do that. I didn't expect him to answer personally, of course, and he didn't. Probably was on the phone with his pal Dave. But somebody pointed me to that guide place. I start with John and then Romans and then Matthew. Talk about desperate for more and seeing yourself! My besetting sin, the way Tsion described it, was pride. I was my own god. Captain of my own destiny. I got to that *Romans Road* thing, taking you down the path of being born in sin, separated from God, his gift is eternal life . . . man, I was there. Stayed up all night and didn't even feel the effects working a full shift the next day. Wanted to tell everybody, but wanted to stay alive too."

Hannah doused David's head with disinfectant and dabbed it dry with a clean towel. "I'm going to cover you with Betadyne now, friend, so you don't look like a skunk with a lateral stripe. You'll still look funny, but not from so far away. And we'd better get out of here before they send in a search party."

"Just a minute."

"Hmm?" She was dabbing at his head again.

"Just wanted to thank you. I needed to hear that. Those stories never get old."

"Thanks, David. Can you imagine how long I've wanted to tell someone that? Oh, and one more thing."

"Yeah?"

"Say hey to Tsion for me?"

"You don't either," Buck said.

"I do too!" Zeke said. "C'mere, look."

Buck followed Zeke to his room, turning to give Rayford and Chloe a do-you-believe-this? look. Sure enough, just as Zeke had claimed, hanging in his closet were four soiled, wrinkled GC uniforms. "Where in the world?"

"After that horsemen deal," Zeke said, "remember?" Buck nodded. "Dead GC all over the place. Dad cruised me around in the middle of the night, trying to stay ahead of the recovery teams. I didn't like yankin' clothes off dead bodies, but Dad and me both thought they were gifts from God. I got their IDs and everything, but you can't use the same name as goes with the uniform."

"I can't?"

Zeke sighed. "These guys turned up missin'. Unless somebody identified their naked bodies, they're listed as AWOL or unaccounted for. You show up with their name, rank, and serial number, who do you think they're gonna pin the murder on? Or the swipin' of the uni?"

"I get it."

"Yeah, huh?"

"So, what do you do, put a new name patch on? Make a new ID?"

"Yeah, only I mix and match. Well, here, first see if this one fits. It's the biggest I got."

"I can see already it's going to be short."

"But look at the cuffs in the shirt, the pants, and the jacket. They leave lots of hem in 'em so they won't have to make custom-made duds for everybody."

"You do tailoring work too, Zeke?"

"Not in front of everybody, and I don't brag on it, but yeah. I do everything. Full-service shop."

Buck found the trousers about two inches short and the waist snug. The shirt was close but needed another inch in the sleeves. Same with the jacket. The cap was way too small. Buck shook his head when Zeke rummaged around and found his sewing kit. It was all he could do to keep from bursting out laughing when the big kid popped a half dozen straight pins in his mouth and knelt to do his work.

"What do you mean, you mix and match?"

"Well," Zeke said around the pins, "your

ID is probably gonna be from a dead civilian. You've already done your own facial surgery, not on purpose, but you did. I'll dye your hair dark, use dark contacts, and shoot a picture to go with the new papers. You want to find someone you like? You've seen my files before. You pulled Greg North out of that stack. Grab a few. Pick someone about your same size and everything. The less I have to change, the better."

"Can you give me a rank above Albie's?"

"No can do," Zeke said. "See the shoulders and the collar on that jacket? That's your basic Peacekeeper. If your collar had another stripe or two and stuck straight up instead of layin' flat, you could be as high as a commander."

"And you can't do that much tailoring."

"That's big-time work. I'd hafta charge you double."

Buck smiled, but Zeke roared. "Did you almost check your wallet to see if you could handle it?"

"Almost."

"Dad says I'm a card." Zeke was suddenly sober.

"Know where your dad is yet?"

Zeke shook his head. "Didn't like what I

saw on TV, though. Something about startin' that mark thing with guys they've got behind bars already. Use 'em as test cases." He shook his head.

"Your dad won't take the mark."

"Oh, I know that. No way. Never. Which means I'll probably never see him again."

"Don't think that way, Zeke. There's always hope."

"Well, maybe, and I'm prayin'. But I'll tell ya when there's no more hope, and that's when they line these guys up for the mark. They get a choice, right?"

"That's what I understand."

"Dad won't even think about it. He's already got a mark. I've seen his and he's seen mine—that's how we know. And he won't start wonderin' if he can have both and stay alive. He'd never do a thing that looks like he's a Carpathia guy. He'll say, 'No you don't,' and they'll thump 'im right there. I don't know how they're gonna kill 'em in jails, whether they've got gill-o-teens or if they just shoot 'em. But that's how Dad's gettin' out of jail. In a box."

On the way back to his office, David felt strangely warmed and encouraged. He loved Hannah's personality and way of expressing herself. She would be a good friend. She was older than he but didn't act like it. He had begun to wonder if there was an oasis of good feeling anywhere.

David worked his magic on the computer, patching in to the bug in room 4054. He slipped on earphones and found himself in the middle of a heated argument. He heard the television and Mrs. Wong pleading, "Shh! TV! Shh! TV!"

Her husband shouted back in Chinese. David knew there were many dialects, but he didn't understand even one. It soon became clear that father and son were arguing and that the mother wanted to watch television. The only words David could make out from the males were an occasional *GC* and *Carpathia.* The son was soon in tears, the father berating him.

David recorded the conversation in the unlikely event he could download voice-activated software that would not only recognize the language and the dialect, but would also convert it to English or Hebrew, his two languages.

Suddenly he heard the father speak more harshly than ever, the son pleading and—it sounded like—collapsing in tears. The mother pleaded for quiet again, the father barked at her, and then it sounded to David as if someone picked up a phone and punched buttons. Finally, English!

"Missah Akbar, you speak Chinese? . . . Pakistani? Me no. English OK, OK? . . . Yes, Wong! Question for you. New worker get loyalty mark first, yah? . . . OK! How soon? . . . Not till then? . . . Maybe sooner, OK! Mrs. Wong and me get too? OK? Son, Chang Wong, want be first to get mark."

The boy cried out in Chinese, and it sounded as if Mr. Wong covered the phone before screaming at him. Someone left the room, David assumed Chang, and slammed a door.

"Missah Akbar, you do mark on boy, mother, father? . . . You no do? Who? . . . Moon? Walter Moon? . . . Not Moon himself? . . . Moon people, OK! Son first! Picture! Take picture son! . . . When? . . . Yes. I talk to Moon people. Bye-bye."

David heard Mr. Wong call out something more calmly, and then something from Chang, muffled. The father was angry again and had the last word. Then he whispered something in Chinese to his wife. She responded with what sounded like resignation.

David wondered if Chang had told his father why he would refuse the mark, or if he simply said no. When the apartment was silent except for the television, David saved the file and forwarded it to Ming Toy with a request. "If it's not too much trouble or too painful, it would help me to know what was said here. I'm guessing your father is pressuring Chang to get himself hired and to be among the first to take the mark. I'll try other sources inside to see how soon they're going to start administering the mark, but help me with this at your earliest convenience, if you would. I regret eavesdropping, but I'm sure you want to preclude this disaster too."

David dialed 4054. Mr. Wong answered. "Chang, please?"

"You want Chang Wong?"

"Yes, please."

"Talk to him about GC job?"

"Yes, sir."

"You Mr. Moon?"

"No. David Hassid. I met you last week."

"Yes! Mr. Hassid! Chang work for you?"

"I don't know yet. That's what I'd like to talk to him about."

"He here. You talk to him. You in computers, yes?"

"Much of my area is computers, yes."

"He best. He help you! Work for you. You talk to him. Wait . . . Chang!" He switched to Chinese, and the boy argued from the other room. Finally he came to the phone.

"Hello," the boy said, sounding as if he'd lost his best friend.

"Chang, it's David. Just listen. Your sister told me what was going on. Let me try to help. It will get your father off your back if you get interviewed by a director, right?"

"Yes."

"It'll buy us some time. You don't worry, OK?"

"I'll try not to."

"Don't say anything, but we might even find a way to get you out of here."

"Before the mark?"

"Don't say that, Chang. Just play along for now. Understand?"

"Yes, David."

"Call me Mr. Hassid, OK? We can't sound like friends, and we sure don't want to sound like fellow believers, brothers, right?"

"Right, Mr. Hassid."

"Thataboy, Chang. Let's do this right. You

call my assistant tomorrow and arrange for an appointment with me. I'll tell Tiffany to expect your call, and you tell her I asked you to call her. All right?"

"Yes, sir."

"Everything will be all right, Chang."

"I hope so."

"You can trust me."

"Yes, Mr. Hassid."

FOURTEEN

Rayford and the others were invited to listen in as Tsion grilled his former professor and mentor on the history of God's chosen people. Chaim, with the wire finally out of his mouth, slowly worked his jaw and rubbed his face, clearly relieved. He was not animated, however, and hard as it seemed Tsion tried, Chaim appeared still tormented by the same things he had discussed with Rayford a few nights before.

"Come, come, Chaim!" Tsion said. "This is exciting, dramatic, miraculous stuff. This is the greatest story ever told! I know where God has provided a place of refuge for his children, but I am not going to tell you until you are ready. You must be prepared in case God calls you to be a warrior for the Lord, to go into a battle of words and wit. Your knowledge would help carry you, but God would have to be your strength. I believe that if he confirms in your heart that you shall be his vessel, he will empower you with supernatural abilities to fight the satanic miracles of Antichrist. Can you envision the victory, my friend? How I wish I were the one going!"

"How I wish that too," Chaim said.

"No, no! If you are God's man in God's time, you must never want out of this most sacred duty and calling! The history of this country carries much discussion of a manifest destiny. Well, my brother, if ever a people had a manifest destiny, it is our people! Yours and mine! And now we include our Gentile brothers who are grafted into the branch because of their belief in Messiah and his work of grace and sacrifice and forgiveness on the cross. Jesus is Messiah! Jesus is the Christ! He is risen!"

"He is risen indeed," Chaim said, but he did not match Tsion's energy.

"Do you hear yourself?" Tsion mimicked

Chaim, mumbling, "He-is-risen-indeed. No! *He is risen, indeed!* Amen! Praise the Lord! Hallelujah! You could go to Jerusalem, a leader of men, a conqueror! You would stand up to the lying, blaspheming enemy of the Lord Most High. You would expose Antichrist to the world as the evil man indwelt by Satan and rally the devout believers to repel the mark of the beast!

"Oh, Chaim, Chaim! You are learning so much. That old brain is still good, still facile, still receptive. You are getting this—I know you are! If not you, who shall go? You seem uniquely qualified, but much as I dream it, I cannot presume to make this assignment. How I wish *I* were the one and could be there in person to see it! If it is you, I will want every detail. Should the forces of evil come against you and you should be overwhelmed by the power of the enemy, God would provide a way, a place, and you, you my friend, would lead the people to that place. And the Lord God himself would protect you and care for you and watch over you and provide for you. Do you realize, Chaim, that God has promised that it will be as in the days of old? Think of it! Weak and frail and wicked as they were, unfaithful, ignorant, impatient, and dallying with other gods, the God of the universe himself catered to the children of Israel.

"Do you understand what that means? You could lead your people, *his* people, to a place that will be almost impossible to go into or out from. If you were to be there until the Glorious Appearing of the Christ, what would you eat? What would you wear? The Bible says God himself will provide as he did in the days of old! He will send food, delicious, nourishing, fulfilling food! Manna from heaven! And do you know about your clothes?"

"No, Tsion," Chaim said wearily, a tease in his voice, "whatever you do, *do not* neglect to tell me about my clothes."

"I won't! And you will be grateful, not to mention amazed. If I amaze you, will you admit it?"

"I will admit it."

"Promise me."

"My word is my bond, my excitable young friend. Amaze me and I will say so."

"Your clothes will not wear out!" Tsion stopped with a flourish, his hands in the air.

"They won't?"

"Are you amazed?"

"Maybe. Tell me more."

"Now you want to hear it?"

"I always want to hear it, Tsion. I am just unworthy. Scared to death, unqualified, unprepared, and unworthy."

"If God calls you, you shall be none of those! You would be Moses! The Lord God of Abraham, Isaac, and Jacob would go before you, and the glory of the Lord would be your rear guard."

"I would need a rear guard? Who would be chasing me?"

"Not Pharaoh's army, I assure you. But if it were, God would make a way for you to escape. Carpathia's hordes would be pursuing you. And for all his talk of peace and disarmament, who has access to the residue of the world's weapons, surrendered willingly to the lying purveyor of peace? But if you needed the Red Sea parted yet again, God would do it! For what have we learned, my little Hebrew schoolchild?"

"Hmm?"

"Hmm? Don't *hmm?* me, Chaim! Tell the rabbi what you learned about the great stories, the miracles from the Torah."

"That they are not just stories, not just examples, myths for our encouragement."

"Excellent. But rather, what are they? What are they, my star pupil?"

"Truth."

"Truth! Yes!"

"They actually happened."

"Yes, Chaim! They happened because God is all-powerful. He says they happened—they happened. And if he says he will do it again, what?"

"He will."

"He will! Oh, the privilege, Chaim! Deal with your fears. Deal with your doubts. Give them to God. Offer yourself in all your weakness, because in our weakness we are made strong. Moses was weak. Moses was nobody. Moses had a speech impediment! Chaim! Moses, the hero of our faith, had less to offer than you do!"

"He was not a murderer."

"Yes he was! You forget! Did he not kill a man? Chaim, think! Your mind, your conscience, your heart tells you God cannot forgive you. I know the guilt is fresh. I know it is grievous. But you know, down deep, that God's grace is greater than our sin. It has to be! Otherwise we all live in vain! Is anything too hard for God? Anything too big for him? Any sin too great for him to forgive? It would be blasphemy to say so. Chaim! If you are the one who can commit a sin too great for God to forgive, you are above God. That's how we can wallow in our sin and still be guilty of pride. Who do we think we are, the only ones God cannot reach with his gift of love?

"He found you, Chaim! He pulled you from the miry clay! Humble yourself in the sight of the Lord, and he will lift you up!"

"Back to my clothes," Chaim said. "I could wear clothes from now until Jesus comes again, and they wouldn't wear out?"

Tsion sat back and waved dismissively. "Chaim, if he can save you and me, of all people, forgive us our sins, bring us back from spiritual death, this clothes thing is one of his lesser miracles. Forget the extra buttons, the patches, the thread. Go there with something you like, because you'll still be wearing it when this is all over."

David had pushed the limits of his ability to virtually set up the entire GC compound for his own remote computer monitoring. He breathed a prayer of thanks to God for allowing him to focus and work in spite of his grief. Mac and Abdullah were set to visit him in an hour to finalize the escape plan that included David and Hannah, and all four had agreed to carefully watch for believers they had been unaware of. It was already apparent that the brilliant teenager, Chang Wong, might be tagging along. David just had to figure out how to pull it off.

While waiting word from Ming Toy, David checked his archives for meetings he had recorded but never listened to. In his Carpathia file was the one with Suhail Akbar, Walter Moon, Leon Fortunato, and Jim Hickman the day he himself had chatted with Hickman. David felt a chill as he prepared to eavesdrop, and he did a quick walk-through of his area to make sure everyone was gone for the day. He could close a program and shut down with a single keystroke, but still he didn't want to be surprised by the wrong person.

Something Hannah had asked a few days before haunted him too. She had said, "How do you know there isn't someone just as technically astute as you are who is doing exactly what you're doing?"

"Such as?" he had said.

"Monitoring you, maybe."

He had brushed it off. He had developed antihacking programs, antibugging devices. He had electronic ears everywhere and believed he could hear if someone breathed a word of something like that. It was impossible, wasn't it? Surely the brass wouldn't be so free to speak if they thought he was listening in. And if they were onto him, it seemed they would have shut him down long before this.

David believed the security chips he'd inserted in his phones and E-mail programs were impenetrable, and he had tried to explain it to Hannah.

"I don't pretend to have a clue, David. Maybe you *are* the top computer genius alive, but ought you not be very careful?"

"Oh, I am."

"You are?"

"You bet."

"But you tell me of phone calls and E-mails between you and your compatriots in the States."

"Not traceable. Not hackable."

"But you trace others. You hack others."

"I'm good."

"You're living on the edge."

"There's no other way to live."

Hannah had dropped it with a shrug. He believed the only reason she raised the issue was because she cared, and she was, after all, a civilian when it came to technology. But he almost wished she hadn't planted the seed of curiosity in his mind. With every message, every transmission, every phone call, he got the niggling feeling that someone somewhere could be looking over his shoulder. Everything he knew told him it couldn't be, but there was no accounting for intuition. He ran continuous checks on his programs, searched for intruders. So far so good, but Hannah had spooked him. If nothing else, it would keep him on his toes.

David had begun the Carpathia meeting recording before he went to see Hickman, so he discovered several minutes of Carpathia alone in his office. The last time he had listened in that way he had heard Nicolae praying to Lucifer. Now, Nicolae *was* Lucifer. Did Satan pray to himself?

No, but he did talk to himself. At first David merely marveled at the fidelity of the sound. He had merely arranged a simple intercom system to both transmit and receive, based on his commands, but it worked better than he had hoped. He heard when Nicolae sighed, cleared his throat, or even hummed.

That was the strangest part. Here was a man who apparently did not sleep. Yet he seemed to exude energy, even when alone. David heard movement, walking, things being arranged. In the background he heard the workers he had encountered just outside Carpathia's office.

"Hmm," Carpathia said softly, as if thinking. "Mirrors. I need mirrors." He chuckled. "Why deprive myself of the joy others luxuriate in? They get to look at me whenever they want."

He pushed the intercom button and his assistant answered immediately. "Excellency?" Sandra said.

"Is that foreman still out there?"

"He is, Lordship. Would you like to speak with him?"

"No, just pass along a message. Better yet, step in a moment."

"My pleasure," she said, as if she meant it

with all of her being. Sandra had always seemed so cold and bored to David that he wondered how she interacted with Carpathia. She was more than twenty years his senior. David heard the squeak of a chair, as if Carpathia had sat.

Simultaneous with a soft knock, the door opened and closed. "Your Excellency," she said, to the sound of rustling.

"Sandra," Carpathia said, "you need not kneel every time you—"

"Pardon me, sir," she said, "but I beg of you not to deprive me the privilege."

"Well, of course not, if you wish, but—"

"I know you don't require it, sir, but to me it is a privilege to worship you."

He sighed without a trace of impatience, David thought.

"What a beautiful sentiment," he said at last. "I accept your devotion with deep satisfaction."

"What may I do for you, my lord?" she said. "Do me the honor of asking anything of me."

"Merely that I want several full-length mirrors in the remodeled office. I will leave it to those in charge of such matters to position them, but I believe it would add a nice touch."

"I couldn't agree more, sir. I shiver at the thought of multiple images of you in here."

"Oh, well, I thank you. Run along and deliver that message now."

"Right away, sir."

"And then you may go for the day."

"But your meeting—"

"I will welcome them. Do not feel obligated."

"As you wish, sir, but you know I would be more than happy—"

"I know."

The door opened and shut, and it sounded as if Carpathia rose once more. Just loud enough for David to hear he said, "I too shiver at the thought of multiple images of me, you homely old wench. But you do know how to make a man feel worshiped."

Now it sounded as if he was moving chairs into position. "Akbar, Fortunato, Hickman, Moon. No, Moon, Akbar, ah . . . must let Leon wonder about his proximity and access, keep him nimble. Hickman needs assurances. All right."

Back to his intercom. "Are you still out there, Sandra?"

"Yes, sir."

"Before you go, get Mr. McCullum on the phone for me, please."

David froze, then chastised himself. He didn't care that Nicolae communicated with Mac. If David couldn't trust Mac, he couldn't trust anyone.

"Captain McCullum," Carpathia said a few minutes later. "How good to speak with you. You are aware, are you not, that 10 percent of all weapons of war were ceded to the Global Community when we were known as the United Nations? . . . The rest were destroyed, and I am satisfied that our monitoring has confirmed that this was largely carried out. If any munitions remain, they are few and are likely in the hands of factions so small as to pose little threat. My question to you is, do you know where we stockpiled the armaments we received? . . . You had nothing to do with that? . . . Well, yes, of course *I* know, Captain! The question is merely probative. You are former military, you are a pilot, and you get around. I want to know if the word has leaked out where we inventory our weapons. . . . Good. That is all, Captain."

Clearly, Mac had told Nicolae he had no idea where the weapons were. As far as David knew, that was the truth. But what a massive operation that had to have been, and how was it pulled off without word getting out? And what might Carpathia be planning now?

"Gentlemen!" Carpathia said a few minutes later, welcoming the four visitors. "Please, come in."

"Allow me to be the first to kneel before you," Leon said, "and kiss your hands."

"Thank you, Reverend, but you are hardly the first."

"I meant at this meeting," Fortunato whined.

"And he won't be the last!" Hickman said, and David actually heard the smack of his lips.

"Thank you, Supreme Commander. Thank you. Chief Akbar? Thank you. Chief Moon? My thanks. Oh, Reverend, no, please. I would appreciate it if you would sit here."

"Here?" Leon said, clearly surprised.

"A problem?"

"I will sit anywhere His Excellency

wishes, of course. I would even stand, if you asked."

"I'd kneel for the whole meeting," Hickman said.

"Right here, my friend," Carpathia said, devoting much time and energy to putting people where he wanted them.

"Sir?" Leon began when they were settled. "Have you been able to sleep, get some rest?"

"You are worried about me, Reverend?"

"Of course, Excellency."

"Sleep is for mortals, my friend."

"Well spoken, sir."

"I'm sure mortal, boys, er, gents," Hickman said. "Slept like a rock last night. Out of shape, I guess. Gotta do something about this gut."

An awkward silence.

"May we begin?" Carpathia said. Hickman muttered an apology, but Nicolae was already addressing Intelligence Chief Akbar. "Suhail, I have become convinced that the location of our armaments remains confidential. Would you concur?"

"I would, sir, though I confess it baffles me."

"Baffles is right!" Hickman said. "Seems to me we had hundreds of troops involved in this thing and—oh, my bad, I'm sorry. I'll wait my turn."

David could only imagine the look Carpathia must have given Hickman. He had to have known whom he was putting in such a lofty position. Having Hickman share space with Sandra and become primarily an errand boy with a big title proved Carpathia knew exactly what he was doing.

"Peacekeeping Forces prepared to go on the offensive, Chief Moon?"

"Yes, sir. Ready to deploy, anywhere and everywhere. We can crush any resistance."

"An update, Reverend?"

"On loyalty mark, Jerusalem, religion?"

"Jerusalem, of course," Carpathia said, dripping sarcasm.

Leon was clearly hurt. "On top of it all, Excellency," he said. "Program is prepared, loyalists ready, should be a triumphal entry in every sense of the word."

"Commander Hickman," Carpathia said condescendingly, "you may put down your hand. You need not ask for the floor here."

"I can just jump in then?"

"No, you cannot just *jump in.* You have each been invited here because I need updates from your areas."

"Well, I'm ready. I have that. I—"

"And when I want your input, I shall call on you. Understood?"

"Yes, sir; sorry, sir."

"No need to apologize."

"Sorry."

"Suhail or Walter, what kind of resistance may we expect in Jerusalem?"

There was a pause, during which, David assumed, the two were looking at each other to avoid interrupting.

"Come, come, gentlemen," Carpathia said. "I have a planet to rule." He chuckled as if joking, but it wasn't funny to David.

Akbar began, slowly and articulately. David thought that in another setting, Suhail could have been an effective intelligence chief. "Frankly, Potentate, I do not believe the Judah-ites will show their faces. I am not discounting the effectiveness of their movement. Their numbers still seem large, but they are an underground cause, networked by computers. You will not likely see the mass public rally similar to the one at Kolleck Stadium when Tsion B—"

"I recall it well, Akbar. Tell me, is part of the reason they are not likely to make a fuss in Jerusalem because many of their ranks have been dissuaded by seeing a *real* resurrection—one that does not require blind faith?"

Silence, except for the clearing of a throat. David assumed it was Suhail's.

"No?"

"Surprisingly not, sir. That would certainly have persuaded me of your deity, except that I was already convinced of it."

"Me too!" Hickman said. "Sorry."

"Of course," Fortunato said, "I had personal experience that proved it. And now—well, it's not my turn, is it?"

"The truth is, Excellency," Akbar continued carefully, "our monitoring of the Judahite Web site reveals they are even more entrenched. They believe, ah, that your resurrection proves the opposite of what is so patently obvious to thinking people."

David flinched when he heard a loud bang on the table, the rolling back of a chair, and a string of expletives from Carpathia. That was something new. The Nicolae of before always kept his composure.

"Forgive me, Holiness," Akbar said. "You understand that I am merely reporting what my best analysts—"

"Yes, I know that!" Carpathia spat. "I just

do not understand what it is going to take to prove to these people who is worthy of their devotion!" He swore again, and the others seemed to feel obligated to grumble loudly about the lunacy of the skeptics. "All right!" Carpathia said finally. "You think they will just snipe at us from the comfort of their hiding places."

"Correct."

"That is unfortunate. I was so hopeful of gloating in their faces. Any confirmation that they are harboring Rosenzweig?"

David held his breath through another pause.

"I admit we're stumped," Walter Moon said. "We traced a few leads from people who thought they saw him running, taking a taxi, that kind of a thing. We know for sure that stroke was phony."

"You can say that again," Nicolae said.

"Dang straight!" Hickman offered. "Sorry."

"He deceived me," Nicolae added. "I have to give him that."

"Um, sir," Moon continued. "I, ah, am not second-guessing you, but . . ."

"Please, Walter."

"Well, you did pardon your attacker, maybe before you knew who he was."

Carpathia roared with laughter. "You do not think I knew who murdered me? I lift that limp arm of his to start the applause and a few seconds later I lurch away from the sound of a gun, he chops my feet from under me with that infernal chair, and the next thing I know I am in the lap of a madman. Well, I knew instantly what was happening, though I may never know why. But he was no frail old man. There was no stiff arm and no limp arm, no scrawny senior citizen. He rammed that blade into me, and I could hear him gutting my skull. The man was hard as a rock and strong."

"Ought to put out a worldwide all points bulletin and use all our resources to bring him in," Hickman said. "Got him on tape! Show it to the world!"

"In due time," Carpathia said, calmer now, and it sounded to David as if Nicolae had sat and joined them again. "I pardoned him, knowing that a world of loyal subjects would relish avenging me, should he ever show his face. Needless to say, we shall not prosecute a crime when that event occurs."

"Needless to say," Hickman parroted.

"And," Carpathia said, "where are we with the accomplice?"

"The nut with the gun?" Moon said. "We don't think he was Middle Eastern. Found his getup and the weapon. Matches the bullet. No prints. No leads. You're convinced they were working together?"

Carpathia sounded flabbergasted. "Convinced? I am not the law-enforcement expert here, but the timing of those two attacks was just a little too coincidental, would you not agree?"

"I would," Hickman said. "I worked that case and—"

"Proceed," Nicolae said.

"I figure they were hedgin' their bets. If one of 'em didn't get ya, the other one would. Guy with the gun could have been a diversion, but he's lucky he didn't kill anybody."

Akbar cleared his throat. "You're aware there's a connection between Ben-Judah and Rosenzweig?"

"Tell me," Nicolae said.

"Ben-Judah was once a student of Rosenzweig's."

"You don't say," Nicolae said, and it was the first time David had heard him use a contraction. "Hmm. Find Ben-Judah, and you find Rosenzweig."

"That's what I was thinkin'," Hickman said.

"I'm ready for your report, James."

"Me? Mine? You are? Oh, yes, sir. Um, everything's on track. Injector thingies, beheaders, er, um, jes' a minute. Viv, ah, Ms. Ivins gave me the correct terminology here, bear with me. Loyalty confirmation facilitators. Got those comin' or goin', depending. They're on their way here and there and wherever we need 'em. Not all of 'em, certainly. Some are being made as we speak, but we're on schedule. I found a nurse here that has experience shooting biochips into . . . into . . . well . . . dogs, I guess. But she's going to help train. And I've got a lead on your pig."

"My pig?"

"Oh! Not, I mean, if you don't need a pig, they'll just butcher it and use it here. But if you needed a pig, I'm pretty sure we've got a big one ordered."

"What would I want a pig for, James?"

"It's not that I heard . . . or knew . . . I mean . . . that you actually need a pig for anything, really. But if you ever did, just let me know, all right. You need one? For anything?"

"Who has been talking to you, Commander?"

"Um, what?"

"You heard me."

"Talking to me?"

Carpathia was suddenly shouting, cursing again. "Mr. Hickman, what is said in these meetings in my private office is sacred. Do you understand?"

"Yes, sir. I would never—"

"Sacred! The security of the Global Community depends on the confidentiality and trustworthiness of the communications in here. You've heard the old expression, 'Loose lips sink ships'?"

"Yeah, I have. I know what you mean."

"Someone told you there was a discussion in this room about my need for a pig."

"Well, I'd rather not—"

"Oh, yes, you had rather, Mr. Hickman! Violating the sacred trust of the potentate of the Global Community is a capital offense, is it not, Mr. Moon?"

"Yes, sir, it is."

"So, James, the next thing out of your mouth had better be the guilty party, or *you* will pay the ultimate price for the transgression. I'm waiting."

David could hear Hickman whimpering.

"The name, Commander. If I hear that he is your friend or that you'd rather not say or anything other than who he is, you are a dead man."

Still Hickman struggled.

"You have ten seconds, sir."

Hickman took a labored breath and coughed.

"And now five."

"He's—he's—a—"

"Mr. Moon, are you prepared to take Mr. Hickman into custody for the purpose of exec—"

"Ramon Santiago!" Hickman blurted. "But I beg of you, sir, don't—"

"Mr. Moon."

"Please! No!"

David heard Moon on his cell phone. "Moon here. Listen, take Santiago into custody. . . . Right, the one from Peace-keeping . . . right now . . . yes. Till I get there."

"You'll let me handle it personally, Walter?"

"As you wish."

"No! Please!"

"James, when it is announced tomorrow that a Peacekeeping deputy commander has been put to death, you at least will understand the gravity of the rules, won't you?"

David heard assent through Hickman's sobs. Apparently that wasn't good enough for Carpathia.

"Won't you, *Supreme* Commander?"

"Yes!"

"I thought so. And yes, I have need of a pig. A big, fat, juicy, huge-nostriled beast so overfed that it will be too lethargic to throw me, should I choose to ride it through the Via Dolorosa in the *Holy* City. Tell me, Hickman. Tell me about my pig."

"I haven't actually seen it yet," Hickman said miserably, "but—"

"But you understand my order."

"Yes." His voice was shaky.

"Big, fat, and ugly?"

"Yeah."

"I didn't hear you, James. Stinky? May I have him smelly?"

"Yeah."

"Whatever I want?"

"Yes!"

"Are you angry with me, my loyal servant?"

"Uh-huh."

"Well, thank you for your honesty. Do you understand that I want an animal that could accommodate my fist in either nostril?"

David jumped at the knock on his door. Mac and Abdullah had arrived.

FIFTEEN

Buck felt his age and was embarrassed to disembark in Kozani, Greece, with a severe case of jet lag that didn't seem to bother the older Albie. And Albie, of course, had done all the flying.

"Use it to your advantage," Albie said.

"How so?"

"It should make you cranky."

"I'm pretty even."

"Well, quit that. You're just being polite. Your natural instinct, when you'd rather be in bed, is to be testy, short, irritable. Go with it. GC Peacekeepers are macho, in charge. They have an attitude."

"So I've noticed."

"Don't ask—don't apologize. You're a busy man, on assignment, with things to do."

"Got it."

"Do you?"

"I think so."

"That didn't sound so macho."

"I've got to be that way with you too?"

"At least practice, Buck. You Americans, I swear. I had to shame your father-in-law into being the leader he was born to be. You're an international journalist and you can't playact to get things done?"

"I think I can."

"Well, show me. How did you get the big stories, get access to the best interview subjects?"

"I used the power of my position."

"Exactly."

"But I was working for *Global Weekly.*"

"More than that. You were Buck Williams, *the* Buck Williams of *Global Weekly.* It may have been your talent and your writing that made you *the* Buck Williams, but once you were him, you walked with confidence, didn't you?"

"I guess."

"I guess," Albie mocked. "Come on, Buck! You strutted!"

"You want me to strut?"

"I want you to get us a vehicle to drive to the detention center where Pastor Demeter and Mrs. Miklos and several others from their church are incarcerated."

"But wouldn't it be easier for you?"

"Why?"

"You're the superior officer. You outrank everybody we'll run into."

"Then take advantage of that. I'll be the one everybody sees but no one mentions. They will only salute. You speak with my authority. And you're wearing that beautiful uniform, tailored at *Chez Zeke*."

"I'll try."

"You're hopeless."

"I can do this."

"You're not giving me confidence."

"Watch me."

"That's what I'm afraid of. I'll be watching you get found out. Prove me wrong, Buck."

"Outta my way, old man."

"That's the spirit."

"You going to have them refuel us while we're in Ptolemaïs?"

"No, Buck, you are."

"C'mon. I don't know all that plane stuff."

"Just do it. From this point on, I am an angry, jet-lagged, ill-tempered deputy commander, and I don't want to speak."

"So it's all on me?"

"Don't ask me. I'm mute."

"Are you serious?"

But Albie wouldn't answer. The twinkle faded from his eyes and he set his jaw, scowling as they marched from the jet to the terminal, about twenty-five miles south of their destination. Buck accosted the first corporal he saw. "English?" he asked the young man.

"'Course. 'Sup?"

"I need you to hangar that aircraft and refuel it while my commanding officer and I are on assignment up the road."

"Yeah? Well, I want you to shine my boots while I'm sleeping."

"I'll pretend I didn't hear that, son."

"Yeah, good. Me too."

He started to leave and Buck swung him around with a grab of his shoulder. "Do it."

"You think I know how to jockey a plane? I'm ground forces, pal. Get some other lackey to do it."

"I'm telling you. Find someone who knows

how to do it and have it done by the time we get back, or suffer the consequences."

"You gotta be kiddin' me!"

Albie had kept his back to the conversation, and Buck was convinced he was trying not to laugh aloud.

"You got that, son?" Buck said.

"I'm outta here. I'll take my chances. You don't even know my name."

"Well, *I* do," Albie said, spinning to face the boy, suddenly ashen. "And you'll do what you're told or you'll be walking back to your hometown in civilian clothes."

"Yes, sir," the boy said, saluting. "Right away, sir."

"Don't let me down, boy," Albie called after him.

Buck gave Albie a look. "Thought you were mute."

"Somebody had to bail you out."

"He was my own rank!"

"That's why you refer to me! I've got the clout, but you've got to use it. Try again."

"What now?"

"I told you. We need a vehicle."

"Ach!"

Buck strode into the terminal, which was crawling with GC. With the crackdown on the underground churches, it would be a noisy area for a while. "Give me your papers," he told Albie.

"What for?"

"Just do it! Hand 'em over!"

"Now you're talking."

Buck stepped to the front of a line of GC Peacekeepers. "Hey!" the first in line shouted.

"Hey yourself," Buck said. "You a deputy commander or are you escorting one? Because if you're not, I'd appreciate your standing down."

"Yes, sir."

Buck raised an eyebrow at Albie, then spoke to the GC officer at a desk behind a window. "Corporal Jack Jensen on behalf of Deputy Commander Marcus Elbaz, here on assignment from the USNA. Need a vehicle for transport to Ptolemaïs."

"Yeah, you and a thousand other guys," the officer said, lazily looking over their IDs. "Seriously, you're about two hundredth in line."

"Seems to me we're near the top, sir, begging your pardon."

"How come your superior officer is USNA? He looks Middle Eastern."

"I don't do the assigning, pal. And I wouldn't recommend getting into it with him. No, better yet, it would be fun. Tell *him* he looks Middle Eastern and that you're questioning his base of operations. Go ahead. Really."

The officer pursed his lips and slid the IDs back under the window. "Something basic do ya?"

"Anything. I could push for something fancy, but we just want to get in and get out. Anyway, tell you the truth, Elbaz has been so touchy today, I don't think he deserves a nicer ride. We'll take whatever you've got."

The officer slid Buck a set of keys attached to a manila ticket. "Show this at the temporary motor pool behind the exit gate."

As they headed that way, Albie mimicked Buck. "He's been so touchy today, I don't think he deserves a nicer ride. I oughta bust you down to Boy Scout."

"You do and *you'll* be walking home in civilian clothes."

"Carpathia's up to something," Mac said, sitting next to Abdullah in David's office.

"I am going to be so glad to say good-bye to this place," Abdullah said.

David shifted in his chair. "Tell me about it."

"Well, don't you want to get out of here too?"

"I'm sorry, Smitty," David said. "I was talking to Mac."

"Oh! A thousand pardons."

"Watch him now," Mac said. "He'll be pout in a New Babylon second."

"I am not pout! Now stop teasing!"

Mac smacked Abdullah on the shoulder and the Jordanian smiled. "Anyway," Mac said, turning back to David, "Carpathia calls me a little while ago and asks me do I know where his weapons are. 'Course, I don't, but I'd sure like to. Tell you somethin', guys, people can talk all they want about the miraculous rebuilding Carpathia did all over the world. But nothin', and I mean nothin', compares to him getting all those countries to destroy 90 percent of their weapons and give him the other 10, and then him storin' 'em somewhere that nobody ever talks about."

"Loose lips sink ships," David repeated.

"You think people know but won't say?"

"Obviously."

"How does he keep a secret that big among so many people?"

"I think I just heard how," David said, and he briefed Mac and Abdullah on it.

Abdullah sat shaking his head. "Nicolae Carpathia is a bad man."

Mac looked at Abdullah and then at David. "Well, yeah! I mean, come on, Smitty. You just come to that conclusion, or have you known all along and just been keeping it from us?"

"I know you are teasing me," Abdullah said. "Just wait until I know your language good."

"You'll be dangerous; that's a fact."

David's cell phone rang. He flipped it open and held up an apologetic finger. "It's Ming," he said.

"Should we go?" Mac said.

David shook his head.

"They were fighting over what you assumed they were fighting over," she said. "My father wants Chang to take a job right away with the GC and be among the first to take the mark. Chang swears he will never take the mark."

"Did he tell your father why?"

"No, and I am coming to see that he never can unless my father himself somehow becomes a believer. I have not lost faith and I keep praying, but until that happens, Chang cannot tell him. He would expose us."

"Does your mother know?"

"No! She would eventually tell him. I'm afraid she is so intimidated that she would not be able to stand up to him in the end. David, you cannot let Chang get a job there, especially if new employees are the first to get the mark."

"It appears that prisoners are going to be first, but yes, new employees soon. As they are hired, apparently. And even the rest of us within a couple of weeks."

"What are you going to do, David? You and your friends?"

"We're talking about that now. Obviously, we run or we die."

"Can you take Chang with you?"

"Kidnap him?"

Ming was silent. Then, "Did you hear yourself, David? You want to leave him to take the mark or be beheaded for refusing so you won't run the risk of kidnapping him? Please! Kidnap him! For one thing, he will go willingly."

"I'm supposed to interview him for a job tomorrow."

"Then either find a way to eliminate him, discredit him as a potential employee, or tell him where to meet you when you escape."

"The latter is more likely. What could possibly disqualify him? He looks like a gold mine to any department, especially mine."

"Make something up. Say he has AIDS."

"And let your father kill him himself?"

"Well, how about a genetic defect?"

"Does he have one?"

"No! But work with me."

"I'm not a doctor, Ming. It would just stall things."

"That's better than nothing."

"Not if it makes me look suspicious. We're hoping to get out of here without their suspecting we are subversives."

"Great idea. Tell them you want to take Chang with you to check him out before hiring. Then, whatever happens to you happens to him. He's free and he can help you wherever you go."

"Maybe."

"It *has* to work, David. What choice is there?"

"What if they don't go for it? What if they say no, just hire him, give him the mark, and *then* take him on assignment?"

"You have to try. He's brilliant, but he's a child. He can't fend for himself. He can't even defend himself against my father."

"I'll do the best I can, Ming."

"That sounds like an excuse after everything fails."

"I'm sorry, but I can't do better than the best I can do."

"David, he's my brother! I know he's not your flesh, but can you pretend? If it was Annie, would you do your best? Or would you do whatever you had to do to save her?"

David couldn't speak.

"Oh, David! Forgive me! That was so wrong of me! Please! That was cruel."

"No. I—"

"David, please blame that on my fear and my situation."

"It's all right, M—"

"Please tell me you forgive me. I didn't mean that."

"Ming, it's all right. You're right. I understand. You put it in perspective for me. Count on me. I will do whatever I have to do to protect Chang, all right?"

"David. Do you accept my apology?"

"Of course."

"Thank you. I'll be praying for you and loving you in the Lord."

When David rang off, Mac said, "What in the world did she say, man? You looked more like me than like an Israeli there for a second."

David told him.

"Tell you what," Mac said, "and Smitty you speak for yourself on this, but if that boy's a believer and he's got the mark to prove it, he's with us. And anybody else we can find before we get out of here. Right, Smitty?"

"Right, I think. If I understand. Other believers here all go with us, yes. Of course. Right?"

"That's what we're saying."

"Mac, a question. Who else would speak for me?"

On the drive north, Buck used a secure phone to call Lukas (Laslos) Miklos. The man was distraught. "Thank you for coming, but there is nothing you can do. Surely you did not bring weapons."

"No."

"You would be so hopelessly outnumbered anyway that you would never get out alive. So why the trip? What can you do?"

"I wanted to see it firsthand, Laslos. Expose it to the world through *The Truth.*"

"Well, forgive me, Brother Williams. I love your magazine, and I read it almost as religiously as Dr. Ben-Judah's messages. But you go to all the time and trouble and expense and danger to come all the way here, and it is for a magazine article? Did you know that the guillotines have arrived?"

"What?"

"It's true. I would pass it off as a rumor myself if it weren't for the brothers and sisters who told me. The GC is carting them through town in open trucks so the people can see the consequences of thinking for themselves. We are part of the United Carpathian States, a name I have to spit when I say. Nicolae is going to make an example of us. And you are here to write an article!"

"Brother Miklos, hear me. You knew there was nothing we could do. We would make matters only worse if we tried to free your wife and pastor and fellow believers. But I thought you'd want to know we were here so we can tell you—if we get in—what the conditions are, how their spirits are, whether they have any messages for you."

Silence. Then Buck heard Laslos weeping.

"Are you all right, my friend?"

"Yes, brother. I understand. Forgive me. I am upset. It is all over the television that the guillotines will be set up first in the prisons, then at the mark sites. It is just a matter of days for us now. But it could be just hours for the prisoners. Please tell my wife I love her and am praying for her and long to see her again. And tell her that if I don't see her again in this life, I will meet her in heaven. Tell her," and he began to weep aloud, "that she was the best wife a man could have and that, that I love her with all my heart."

"I will tell her, Laslos, and I will bring you any message she may have as well."

"Thank you, my brother. I *am* grateful you have come."

"Do you know where she and the others have been taken?"

"We have an idea, but we dare not go looking or we will all be rounded up. You know our church is made up of many, many small groups that are not so small anymore. When the GC raided the main one, they took my wife and Pastor D and about seventy others, but they missed more than ninety other *groups.*"

"Wow."

"That is the good news. The worst of it is that apparently some in the original group have cracked under the strain. I can tell you without question it would not have been my wife or my pastor, but someone was tortured or scared or deceived into telling of the other groups. More raids have begun, and now they dare not meet at all. It is only a miracle I was not at the meeting with my wife, but if she becomes a martyr, I'll wish I was there to die with her."

"We came up with a question, besides a suggestion, David, and Smitty was very helpful on this, by the way," Mac said. "We tease him about the language, but that's a pretty shrewd brain in there. That's a compliment, Abdullah."

"Well, hey, cowpoke, I know that much right now!"

"I guess if I can make fun of Jordan, he can make fun of Texas. Really burned me there, didn't he? Anyway, the question is this: Do we want to play this out to the end, assumin' you're gonna have an inside track on *exactly* when employees have to take the mark? Or do we want some wiggle room?"

David thought about it. "It's more than wiggle room, Mac. It's part of the impression. If we wait till the last second and still try to make it look like we were killed, the timing alone is going to make it suspicious."

"That's what I said!" Abdullah said. "Isn't that what I said, Mac? I said that."

"That's what he said. Good point. OK, if we're going to do this sooner than the actual deadline, we have lots of options. Peacekeeping just started shipping its first loads of—what are they calling those contraptions now? Loyalty somethin's or other."

"Call 'em what they are," David said.

"OK, they shipped guillotines into Greece last night."

"Not from here," David said. "I would have known that."

"No, these were actually manufactured in Istanbul and driven down. Pretty soon they'll be flyin' 'em here and there, and you know we'll be pressed into service. You ought to pick a particularly strategic place you want to see or a shipment you want to monitor, find a reason to bring Hannah and Chang what's-his-name, and I'll have to requisition a Quasi Two."

"A Two? How will you justify that? We

want to avoid suspicion. You can fit two pilots and three passengers in something cheaper than a 15-million-Nick aircraft."

"Yeah, but let's say we want to take a huge load of guillotines and skids of biochips and injectors."

"I'm listening. Still need more ammo to justify a Two."

"Well, let's say it's somewhere that St. Nick hisself is gonna be."

"Tell him who thought of that," Abdullah said.

"I think you just did, big mouth."

"Big mouth?"

"Teasin', Smitty. Slow your camel down now."

David cocked his head. "Are you thinking what I think you're thinking?"

"Is this a game?" Abdullah said.

"We are," Mac said. "Jerusalem."

David sat considering the possibilities. "I pass the word up the line that we want to be there, bring the injection expert and my best new computer prospect. We want to carry the maximum cargo load in an impressive craft that will look good for the potentate, play to his ego."

"You think he's egotistical?" Mac said, as seriously as if he meant it.

David smiled.

"Is he joking again?" Abdullah said. "Not enough cloth in Jordan to make a turban for Nicolae's head."

Mac threw his head back and laughed.

David was still deep in thought. "And the Quasi Two can be flown remotely."

"Just about any plane can nowadays, but I've got lots of experience with these."

"So we land somewhere out of sight on our way there. Then, from the safety of the ground, you fly that very expensive jet, with all that precious cargo—except us—in it, nose down right into the middle of one of the deepest bodies of water we can find."

"With people watching."

"Come again?"

"Let 'em see it! You wanted us to think about a logical explanation for the accident. Well, forgive the painful subject, but we recently lost our cargo chief. She would have prohibited that much weight on that particular plane, but me bein' a veteran, I thought it would handle it. Flyin' it remote and also broadcasting from it remote, I start hollerin' about a weight shift, cargo rolling, hard to control, Mayday, good-bye cruel world."

"You guys are brilliant."

"Thank you."

"Both of us," Abdullah said. "Right?"

"Of course," David said.

"Just thought of one more good one," Abdullah said.

"Hold on now, Smitty," Mac said. "Is this new to me?"

"Slow down your pony. You'll like it. You want to do this in front of people, do it in Tel Aviv. Carpathia is flying through there. Do air show for him and crowds. Crash into Mediterranean, so deep they know we're dead and plane is too deep to bother with search."

"And where are we supposed to be during all this?" Mac said. "It's going to be awfully hard to hide in Tel Aviv with Carpathia and all his crowds."

"We don't take off from Tel Aviv. We come straight from here to show, only they don't know we stopped in Jordan. I know that place. We can land where no one sees. Send plane to Tel Aviv, do show, crash."

"From how far away do you think I can remotely fly that plane, Smitty?"

"Sort of not remote. Take off remote, but flight plan, tricks, everything programmed into computer."

Mac looked from Abdullah to David. "He may just have something there."

"Really?" David said. "You can program the thing that specifically?"

"It would take some time."

"Get on it."

"Surprise, surprise," Abdullah said. "Camel jockey come up with one."

David's cell phone rang. "Readout says *urgent* from Hannah."

"Take it," Mac said.

"Hey, what's up?" David said.

"You're 100 percent certain this connection is secure?"

"Absolutely. You all right?"

"I'm in a utility closet. Did you know Carpathia had a Peacekeeper executed today?"

"Actually, I did. Santiago?"

"Thanks for telling me. I just had to go get the body from Security lockup."

"There wasn't time to tell you, Hannah. Anyway, who knew you'd get assigned?"

"It was awful. I deal with death all the time, but he was shot between the eyes at point-blank range. And they aren't even pretending it's anything but what it was. He was executed by Carpathia himself! You know what for? Well, of course you do. You know everything."

"I heard he talked too much."

"Doesn't sound very technical to me, David, but that's what I heard too. Apparently he told someone something that Carpathia said in a private meeting."

"I'm sorry you got in the middle of it, Hannah."

"Yeah, well, I think I know who ratted him out."

"You do?"

"Do you?" she said.

"Actually, I do."

"David, how can you live with this stuff?"

"Don't think it's easy."

"So, who told? Who got Santiago executed?"

"You said you knew, Hannah."

"You'll confirm it if I'm right?"

"Sure."

"Hickman."

"How'd you know?"

"I'm right, David?"

"You're right."

"He was just delivered to the morgue. Someone found him in his office with a self-inflicted gunshot wound to the temple."

SIXTEEN

Buck and Albie joined and separated from and joined again a caravan of GC vehicles picking its way through what was left of Ptolemaïs. "Would you look at that," Albie said, nodding toward open trucks carrying guillotines. "They're ugly, but there's really not much to 'em, is there?"

Buck shook his head. "That's one of my sidebar stories, how easily they can be assembled. They're simple machines with basic, pattern-cut parts. Each is basically wood, screws, blade, spring, and rope. That's why it was so easy for the GC to send out the specs and let anybody who wanted work and had the materials to have at it. You've got huge manufacturing plants reopening to mass-produce these, competing with amateur craftsmen in their backyards."

"All for something the GC says will serve as a—what did they call it, officially?"

"Visual deterrent. They put just one at each mark application site, and everyone is supposed to fall in line."

Albie stopped where a GC Peacekeeper was directing traffic. He signaled the young woman over. "I'm working here," she said testily until she recognized the uniform. She saluted. "At your service, Commander."

"We've been assigned the main detention facility, but I left the manifest in my bag. Are we close?"

"The main facility, sir?"

"I think that's what it said."

"Well, they're all together about three clicks west. Take a left at your next intersection, and follow the unpaved road around a curve until it joins the rebuilt highway again. The center will be on your right, just inside the city. Can't miss it. Massive, surrounded by barbed wire and more of us. Better hurry, though, if you want to see the fun. They're going to do some chopping tonight if the rebels don't soil themselves and change their minds."

"Yeah?"

"Word I get is they're lining them up and sorting them out now. The ones who go back to their cells with their heads attached will have a new tattoo tomorrow."

David was exhausted. It was nearly 2300 hours Carpathia Time as he trudged from his office toward his quarters. He was stunned to hear energetic steps behind him and turned to see Viv Ivins, looking as fresh and gung ho as she did every morning. She carried a leather portfolio and smiled brightly at David.

"Evening, Director Hassid," she called out as she drew alongside.

"Ma'am."

"Great days, hmm?"

He didn't know how long he could maintain the charade. "Interesting days, anyway," he said.

She stopped. "I love when things fall into place."

He thought that an unfortunate choice of words, given her personal coordination of guillotine production and distribution.

"Things humming along, are they?" he said.

"I've persuaded top brass not to display loyalty enforcement facilitators here at the palace."

"Oh?"

"Not the best image."

"They're showing up all over the world."

"And that's fine. I can live with that. In fact, I'm all for it. Outside the capital city and the headquarters in particular, you will have certain elements who need the visual aid, a reminder of the seriousness of this test of loyalty. One would have to be pathologically committed to one's cause to really decide against the mark. Seeing the consequence standing right before you as you make your decision will persuade those who merely want a little attention for stalling with their choice."

"But not here."

"Not necessary. If a person was not loyal to the risen potentate, why would he or she want to work here? What I want to see produced here are pictures, still and moving, of happy, willing, joyful loyalists. The citizenry of the Global Community should see rapture on the faces of those it depends upon to administer the new world order. No enforcement is needed here. We are the examples to the world of the joy of commitment, the sense of fulfillment when one takes his stand. Follow?"

"Sure. And I have to say, I like the idea of those ugly contraptions not dotting the landscape here."

"I couldn't agree more. We start with new hires tomorrow, and there is much enthusiasm among them over being among the first to receive the potentate's mark. All are opting for his image on their foreheads. I plan to go for the simple understatement, but I have to say, Mr. Hassid, it's fun to see these kids today with their eagerness to stand out. You're interviewing a prospect tomorrow."

"Right."

"The Asian prodigy."

"That's him."

"What a family! His father is pleading to have his son be the first to receive the mark. It's too late for that, as we're beginning with political prisoners, but he very well could be the first GC employee."

David blanched and tried to cover. "But he's not been hired yet."

"It's a foregone conclusion though, right?"

"Well, I need to talk with him at length, determine his suitability to take his last year of high school here, be away from his parents for the first time, see where he fits best. . . ."

"But the odds of him not being hired somewhere here are minuscule. We could process him first and he would, in essence, be preapproved to work in any department. Sort of like a preapproved mortgage. First you qualify, then you can make an offer on anything in your price range."

"I wouldn't do that," David blurted.

"Why not?"

"It just doesn't seem as buttoned-down as we like to be. Let's let the process run its course—do it right."

"Oh, Mr. Hassid, honestly. What would be the harm?"

He shrugged. "I was told the boy is scared to death of needles and is fighting the whole idea."

"Even to the point where he would pass up a golden opportunity here? He's going to have to take the mark in the United Asian States anyway, or he'll lose more than a job."

"Maybe he'll get used to the idea by then."

"Oh, pish-posh, Director Hassid. If he's so brilliant, it's time for him to grow up. He may fight it, but it'll be over in seconds and he'll see he made a big to-do about nothing."

"Well, my meeting with him is at 0900 hours. It can wait till after that, can't it? I'd hate to try to interview him after he's been through a trauma."

"A trauma? I just told you—"

"But he'll still be upset."

"I can't imagine them administering marks before 0900 anyway."

In his room a few minutes later, David used his subnotebook to double-check his secretary's schedule. She had not informed him of a time for his appointment with Chang, and a quick look at her calendar showed why. The meeting had been confirmed at the end of the day for 1400 hours, two o'clock. It was something she would tell him in the morning.

David changed it on her calendar to 0900, then hacked into Personnel's computer and did the same. He phoned 4054 and left a voice message: "Chang, our interview tomorrow has been changed to 9 A.M. Please do not go to Personnel or anywhere else until we've met. See you then."

While he was finishing his message, his phone told him he had a call waiting. He punched in to find Ming, distraught. "It's started here," she said. "Has it started there?"

"Slow down, Ming. What's started?"

"Application of the mark! The equipment arrived at Buffer this morning, and they're already using it tonight."

"Prisoners are getting the chip?"

"Yes! I can't imagine it will be much longer for us staff. I need to bolt soon, but I wanted to check."

"Any believers there? Anyone refusing the mark?"

"Not a one. They're lining up for this thing as if they've been loyal scouts forever. I think they're hoping they'll get good behavior points. Truth is, they'll still be rotting here, but with a mark on head or hand."

David told her of his conversation with Viv and what he had done about it. "Oh, no, no," she said. "At nine you must make Chang disappear. Get him out of there."

"We're not prepared to leave yet, Ming."

"What are you going to do?"

"I'll have to make up something, I guess. Some reason why he is just not ready.

Maybe I'll say I found evidence of immaturity, that I just think he's too young to fit in."

"You're a director, David. Make it convincing. This has to work."

"I have all night to think about it."

"And I have all night to pray about it."

"I'll take all I can get, Ming. Listen, let me do something for you. I can get you reassigned to USNA."

"You could?"

"Of course. I just do it through the computer and no one questions it. They see it's approved by someone higher than their level, and they don't rock the boat. Where do you want to go?"

"There are prisons all over the States," she said. "But I'm never actually going to get to one, right?"

"Right. We get you assigned, get you on a plane, but then lose you somehow. You run off and we can't find you. But then you're on your own. You need to get to the safe house in Chicago."

"Would they have me?"

"Ming! Leah has told everyone about you. They can't wait to welcome you. They knew you and your brother would eventually have to wind up there. We can use you both. Now where shall I assign you in the States? Somewhere close enough to Chicago so you can get to the safe house but not so suspiciously close that people start putting two and two together."

"I don't know the States," she said. "There is a huge facility in Baltimore that always needs personnel."

"That's a long way from Chicago. Wait! Can you get to Greece?"

"When?"

"As soon as possible, even tonight."

"I guess that's up to you. Make my transfer highest priority, and if you want GC here to get me to Greece, they'll have to do it. But David, Greece is a hot spot right now, crawling with GC and making an example of political prisoners. I don't want to work or hide there."

David told her how she would get to the States from Greece, and it would appear GC was escorting her.

"There is a God," she said. "Where do I meet these men?"

"Get to the airport at Kozani. They'll find you."

"Can you get Chang there too? Please, David, do it! Get him out of my parents' quarters, get him assigned somewhere, and have one of your pilots get him to Greece. We can go to the safe house together."

"Ming, please. It has to make sense. I pull a stunt like that, your parents lose track of Chang, and it all comes back to me—not to mention you! You *both* are sent somewhere and then wind up lost? Think, Ming. I know you're desperate and that you care, but let me work on the logistics. The last thing I want is for the GC spotlight to turn on us."

"I know, David. I understand. I'm thinking with my heart."

"Nothing wrong with that," he said. "Until we quit thinking at all and make things worse."

"We in trouble?" a Greece-based GC Peacekeeping chief at the detention center asked Buck when he saw he was accompanied by a deputy commander. "We do everything by the book."

"This looks like a madhouse, frankly," Buck said, surveying the complex of five rather plain, industrial buildings that had probably once been factories. The windows were covered with bars, and the perimeter was a tangle of fence and razor wire. But the place was crowded with GC in lines, peering at printouts in the night, using flashlights to see where various prisoners were located.

"We do all we can with what we have to work with," the chief said, nervously eyeing Albie.

Buck continued to do the talking. "How many prisoners at this facility?"

"About nine hundred."

"You've got that many GC here."

"Well, not quite, sir."

"What are they all doing? Are they assigned?"

"Most are running the mark center in the middle building."

"What is in the other buildings?"

"Teenagers through early twenties in the first building, males in the west wing, females in the east."

"Individual cells?"

"Hardly. Prisoners are incarcerated in large, common areas that used to be production lines."

"And in the other buildings?"

"Women in the next. None in the center. Men in the last two."

"What are the majority of these people charged with?"

"Mostly felonies, some petty theft, larceny."

"Any violent criminals?"

The chief nodded back over his shoulder. "Murderers, armed robbers, and the like, right there."

"Political prisoners?"

"Mostly in the second building, but religious dissidents, at least the men, are right here too." He motioned to the last building again.

"You've got dissidents in with violent criminals?" Buck said, leaning forward as if to get a better look at the man's nameplate.

"Where they're placed is not my call, sir. I'm coordinating the loyalty mark application. And I need to be in that center building in about five minutes. You want to help—I've got a crew of six moving from building to building, starting with the west, doing preliminary sorting."

"Meaning?"

"Determining whether any plan to refuse the mark."

"And if so?"

"They are to identify themselves immediately. We're not going to waste time letting people wait until they're in line to decide whether they want to live or die."

"What if some change their minds in line?"

"Decide at the last minute they don't want the mark after all? I don't foresee that!"

"But what if they do?"

"We deal with that quickly. But for the most part, we want to know in advance so we don't hold things up. Now, gentlemen, I have orders. Will you help with the culling or not?"

"Will this be going on simultaneously in all the buildings?" Buck asked, not wanting to miss the pastor or Mrs. Miklos.

"No. We're starting in the west building. Prisoners will be escorted to the center building for processing, then back before those in the next building go. And so forth."

"We'll help," Buck said.

The chief shouted, "Athenas!" and a stocky, middle-aged Peacekeeper with a one-inch, black crew cut stepped up, three men and two women in uniform behind him. "Ready, Alex?"

"Ready, sir," Alex said, with a high-pitched voice that didn't match his physique.

"Take Jensen and Elbaz here with you."

"I have sufficient staff, sir."

The chief lowered his head and stared at

Athenas. "They're here from USNA, and if you didn't notice, A. A., Mr. Elbaz is a dep-u-ty com-man-der?"

"Yes, sir. Would Mr. Elbaz care to lead?"

Albie stuck out his lower lip and shook his head.

It was two in the afternoon in Chicago, and the remaining Trib Force members crowded around the television. The local GC news reported that mark applications had begun at local jails and prisons.

Zeke sat rocking before the TV, his hands over his mouth. Rayford asked if Chaim's Jerusalem disguise was ready. Zeke kept his eyes on the screen and took his hands from his mouth only long enough to say, "All but the robe. Done by tonight."

Tsion had come up with the idea of letting Zeke change Chaim's appearance exactly as he had been planning, but also outfitting him in sandals and a thick, brown, hooded robe that extended far enough in front of his face to hide his features. The whole garment would go over his head and the hem would settle an inch off the ground, the waist cinched with a braided rope. Everyone agreed it sounded humble and nondescript, and yet ominous enough once Chaim was seen by crowds as in charge and with something to say.

Chaim was slowly accepting the idea, provided he could playact from the shadows of his garb. "I still say Tsion ought to go."

"Let me promise you, my friend," Tsion said. "Allow God to use you mightily to get his people to safety, and I will come and address them in person sometime."

The TV anchorman announced that while the area GC had not expected to need the loyalty enforcement facilitators, one prisoner had reportedly refused to take the mark and had been executed. "This occurred at what was formerly known as the DuPage County Jail, and execution of the dissident was carried out less than ninety minutes ago. The rebel, serving an indeterminate sentence for black market trafficking of fuel oil, has been identified as fifty-four-year-old Gustav Zuckermandel, formerly of Des Plaines."

Zeke buried his face in his hands and toppled onto his side, where he lay crying quietly. One by one the rest of the Force approached to merely lay a hand on him and cry with him. Tsion, Chaim, Rayford, Leah, and Chloe surrounded him and Tsion prayed.

"Our Father, once again we face the wrenching loss of a loved one. Shower our young brother with hope eternal and remind us all that we will one day see again this brave martyr."

When Tsion finished, Zeke drew a sleeve across his wet face, moved to his hands and knees, and then awkwardly rose.

"You all right, son?" Rayford asked.

"Got work to do is all," Zeke said, averting his eyes. And he shuffled back toward his room.

Buck had a bad taste in his mouth. He had been in these situations before, had seen enough depravity and mayhem to last several lifetimes. But he wished he and Albie had brought high-powered automatic weapons so they could at least attempt a rescue. How, in his flesh, he wanted to spray deadly projectiles into the swarming GC. How he would love to have stormed the detention barracks, looking for people with the mark of Christ and ferrying them to safety.

But here was an impossible situation.

Prophecy was once again coming to life before his eyes, and he would not be able to turn away. At the west building, the eight members of the culling team were checked in past the outer fence, and then again at the main entrance.

Buck was assaulted by the stench as soon as they had cleared the main corridor. Inside a huge cage milled more than a hundred male teenagers, some looking tough, others petrified. The cage was surrounded with four to five guards on a side, weapons in hand, smoking, reading magazines, and looking bored.

The teenagers jumped and cheered and applauded when the team entered. "Freedom!" one shouted while the rest laughed. "They've come to free us!" And others jeered and mocked.

Athenas stepped away from the others and put up both hands for quiet. Buck sidled to a guard, who dropped his magazine and straightened up. "Sir?" he said.

"What's the smell, soldier?"

"The cans, sir. In the corners, see?"

Buck looked to the four corners of the cage where 55-gallon drums stood. Each had a makeshift wooden set of steps next to it and was covered by an ill-fitting toilet seat. "This building has no facilities?"

"Only for us," the guard said. "Just down that hall."

Buck shook his head. "They can't be led there periodically?"

"Not enough of us to risk that."

Alex Athenas had finally commanded the prisoners' attention. "You are privileged to be among the first to display your loyalty and devotion to His Excellency, the risen potentate of the Global Community, Nicolae Carpathia!"

To Buck's amazement, this was met with enthusiastic cheering and applause that went on for almost a minute. Some teens broke into chants and songs, lauding Carpathia.

Athenas finally quieted them again. "In a few moments you will be led to the central building, where you will tell the staff whether you want your loyalty mark on your forehead or your right hand. The area you choose will then be disinfected with an alcohol solution. When it is your turn, you will enter a cubicle, where you will sit and be injected with a biochip, while simultaneously tattooed with the prefix 216, which identifies you as a citizen of the United Carpathian States. The application takes just seconds. The disinfectant also contains a local anesthetic, and you should experience no discomfort.

"Any acts of disorderly conduct will be met with immediate justice. For you illiterates, that means you will be dead before you hit the floor."

This was met with more hooting and hollering, but Buck found himself staring at a boy in the middle of the crowd. He had black, curly hair, was thin and pasty, and wore tilting glasses that appeared to have one lens missing. The boy looked barely old enough to be in this crowd, but what caught Buck's eye was the shadow on his forehead. Or was it a smudge? Or was it the seal of God?

"Excuse me, officer!" Buck said, striding past Athenas and peering into the cage. The hooting stopped and the prisoners stared. "You, there! Yes, you! Step forward!"

The young man made his way through the crowd to the front of the cage, where he stood quaking. "Someone open this door!" Buck barked. No one moved. He whirled to look at the guard he had spoken to, who shuffled nervously and looked at Athenas.

"The rest of you back off," Athenas said, and he nodded to the guard, who unlocked the cage.

Buck marched in and grabbed the boy by the arm, his ratty, gray sweater bunching under Buck's fingers. He dragged him out of the cage, past Athenas and the other guards, scolding him the whole way. "You mock Global Community Peacekeepers, young man? You'll learn respect."

"No, sir, please—I, I—"

"Shut up and keep moving!"

Buck dragged him past the guards at the entrance, who called after him, "Wait! Who is that! We have to process him out!"

"Later!" Buck said.

"Where are we going?" the boy pleaded with a Greek accent.

"Home," Buck whispered.

"But my parents are here."

"Give me their names," Buck said, and he wrote them down. "I can't guarantee they'll get out. But you're not going to die tonight."

"You're a believer?"

Buck nodded and shushed him.

They blew past the guards at the outer

gate, and Buck marched him to the GC jeep across the road. Past the lights and into the shadows, few heads had even turned to watch. "Front passenger side," Buck said. "Any other believers in the cage?"

The boy shook his head. "Never saw anyone."

"Give me the name of one of the guys in the cage, just one."

"Who?"

"Anyone. Just give me a name."

"Ah, Paulo Ganter."

"Got it. Now listen. You are to sit here, right here in this jeep, until I get back. What you must not do—are you listening?—is make sure that no one is watching. Because if you discover that, you might be tempted to make a run for it and not stop until you are somewhere safe. Then I would get back out here later and wonder whatever happened to my prisoner. Understand?"

"I think so. You don't want me to do this?"

"Of course not. I don't know what I'd do about an escapee. Do you?"

The boy managed a weak smile.

"You know what?" Buck said. "I don't think anybody's watching now." Feeling like Anis, the mysterious border guard who had discovered Tsion under the seat of the bus so long ago, Buck put one hand on the boy's shoulder and another on his head. And he said, "And now may the Lord bless you. May the Lord make his face to shine upon you and give you peace. Godspeed, son."

Buck trotted back to the gate, and when he glanced over his shoulder, the boy was gone.

The gate guards let Buck through and the ones at the building asked, "Who was that?"

"Ganter, Paulo," he said. "Transferred custody to the United North American States." They were flipping through their printouts as he hurried back in.

Alex Athenas was finishing. "Are there any here who will be choosing to reject the loyalty mark?"

The group laughed and waved derisively at him.

"None then? No one? Anyone?"

The prisoners looked at each other and quieted. Buck waited and watched to see if the boy had been wrong and there were any other believers who might take a stand.

"What if we say no?" a tough called out, smirking.

"You know the consequences," Alex said. The boy drew a finger across his neck. "That's right," Alex added. "Any questions?"

"No rebels here!" someone shouted. "All loyal, upstanding citizens!"

"That's what we like to hear. No questions?"

"Do we get to choose what image we want?"

"No. Because of your circumstances, you are allowed only the basic chip and number tattoo."

The prisoners groused loudly, and Athenas signaled to his team and the other armed guards to get into position. "This will be done in an orderly fashion," he said. "Or you will wish you had opted to reject the mark."

SEVENTEEN

Rayford stopped to check in on Zeke, whom he found busy on Chaim's robe. Zeke said, "Got enough material. Thinking about makin' him two."

"You heard what Tsion said about clothes in the safe haven?"

Zeke nodded. "He might want variety though. And I didn't hear Tsion say whether the clothes get dirty."

Rayford shrugged. "I admired your dad, Zeke. You know that?"

Zeke nodded, still working.

"He was courageous, right to the end."

"Didn't surprise me," Zeke said. "I told you he'd do that, didn't I?"

"You had him pegged. I pray we'll all show that kind of courage."

Zeke looked up and shook his head, his eyes distant. "I wish he hadn't got caught. Bad timing. He coulda done a lot more for the believers. Like I'm gonna do."

"I admire you too, Zeke. We all do."

Zeke nodded again.

"Don't forget to mourn and grieve too, you know. There's nothing wrong with that."

"I can't help it. I miss him already."

"I'm just saying, don't pretend—you don't have to look strong to us. We've all suffered terrible losses, and even if the Lord helps us through it, we don't have to like it. The Bible doesn't say we're not to mourn. It just says we're not to mourn the way people do who have no hope. Mourn with all your might, Zeke, because we *do* have hope. We *know* we're going to see our loved ones again."

Zeke suddenly stood and thrust out his hand. Rayford shook it. "I don't s'pose I dare go try to get his body."

Rayford shook his head. "The first thing

they're going to want is to know your connection. And you know the second thing."

"Whether I want the mark."

"We're crippled with the loss of your dad, Zeke. I don't know what we'd do if we lost you too."

"I just hate to think what they're gonna do with him. I try not to think about . . . you know . . . his head being . . . you know . . ."

"I know. But no matter what they do with your dad's body, God knows. He has his eye on your father. His soul is in heaven now, and his body will eventually be there too, new and improved. If God can resurrect a cremated body—you know what that means?"

"Burned up, yeah."

"Then he can resurrect anybody. Remember, he created us from the dust of the earth."

"Thanks, Captain Steele. Bad as this is, there's no other place I'd rather have been when I heard about it. I sure love all you guys."

"And we love you, Zeke."

Rayford walked out and shut the door, noticing Tsion just out of sight of the doorway, leaning against the wall, arms folded.

"Excuse me," Dr. Ben-Judah said. "I didn't intend to listen in. I didn't know you were there. You must have had the same idea I did."

"It's all right."

"I'm glad I heard that, Rayford. God has restored you to leadership. You did just what I know the Lord would have wanted you to do, and you did it well."

"Thanks, Tsion. God's been more patient with me than I deserve."

"Isn't that true with all of us?"

They walked back toward the commons. "I spoke with Chloe a few moments ago," Tsion said. "I hope I wasn't out of line."

"You can't be out of line, Doc. You know that. What was it about?"

"I was just checking to see how she was doing with the assignment you gave her. I have a vested interest, you know."

"In the call for planes and pilots? I should say you do! So, save me a conversation. How's it going?"

"She was amused and eager to tell me, actually. She put out the request for brave Commodity Co-op members willing to lend their planes and cars and fuel and time to the cause of Messiah in Jerusalem—and she told them it would be soon. She reports that the response has been overwhelming. The element of danger must make these men and women rally. She says they are more willing to throw caution to the wind for this scheme than they are to make the routine flights that keep the co-op running."

Around the corner Kenny Bruce came chugging, chased by Leah. He appeared lost in the fantasy that he *had* to elude her, though he loved her hugs and tickles. "Grandpa!" he squealed, reaching for Rayford. But at the last instant he changed course, leaping into the rabbi's arms. "Unca Zone!"

Leah laughed and grabbed for him. "That old man can't save you!" she said, and he buried his head in Tsion's chest.

"Old man?" Tsion said. "Miss Leah, you have wounded me!"

Tsion carried Kenny back to his mother, and Leah lingered. "Rayford, I feel useful here, helping Chloe—who's incredible, by the way. That girl could run any size corporation. And I love helping with that precious child."

"But—?"

"You know what's coming."

He nodded. "I'm still finalizing assignments," he said. "But yours includes getting out of here awhile."

"Oh, thank you, Ray. I don't want to be selfish, and I know Chloe is as antsy as I am."

"She has responsibilities here. More than you do."

"It doesn't seem fair to her."

"But she takes her role seriously, and I think she's resigned to it."

"Well," Leah said, "I can't speak for her, but I would feel trapped."

"Trapped by motherhood?"

Leah smiled. "Spoken like a man. As someone who has been there, let me tell you, at times you need a break. It doesn't have to be long, and you can't wait to get back. But, well—it's not my business. But if you find a place for her outside, even a short assignment, I'll be happy to spell her."

"You can do what she does? Both the co-op and looking after the baby?"

"Sure. It's only the men around here who are incapable of that." Rayford shot her a double take. "I'm kidding, Ray. But tell me, am I going to get to go to Israel?"

"You *want* to be there?"

"I was stuck in Belgium last time. All the good stuff happens in Jerusalem."

"The dangerous stuff."

"And your point?"

He cocked his head. "Oh, yeah. You live for that stuff."

"I live to serve, Ray. I'm not bragging. It's what I do. It was, even before I became a believer. I want to be valuable to the cause. I'm not even suspicious. No one's out trying to hunt me down. And with that wacky dental appliance in and if I let Zeke touch up the hair, I'm invisible."

"It would take more than that to make you Middle Eastern."

"Maybe this David character can make me GC then. Give me a reason to be over there."

Rayford raised his eyebrows. "Maybe," he said. "You never know."

Buck and Albie stood with the culling squad in the female teens' area. Buck found it hard to believe the conditions were the same as for the men. There were two women guards, but the rest were men. The girls were not as noisy and raucous as the boys, but the makeup of the group was similar. There were tough girls and apparent victims, but all were curious.

Buck scoured the group, and a tall brunet stared back at him. He was convinced they had seen each other's mark at the same time. Her eyes grew wide, and he tried to communicate with his that she must not give him away. As Alex Athenas ran through his explanation, Buck casually moved close to Albie.

"I'd better not push my luck. Think you can get one out of here?"

"Maybe," Albie said. "You're not thinking of trying this in every building, are you?"

"I hate doing nothing."

"Me too, but we're going to get ourselves killed. And what about when there's a bunch of 'em?"

"I can worry about them only one at a time."

Albie sighed. "Where is she?" Buck pointed her out. "Watch and learn, buddy boy," Albie said.

Albie rushed the cage, shouting. Alex fell silent and watched with everyone else as Albie prowled up and back before the wire mesh, eyes on his prey. "You! You from the North American States?"

The girl froze, her eyes darting at Buck, who nodded slightly, and back at Albie. “No,” she said, her voice a constricted squeak. “I’m—”

“Don’t lie to me, dirt ball! I’d know you anywhere.” Albie whirled in a rage that almost convinced Buck. “Alex, get somebody to open this cage.” He turned back, pointing at the girl. “Step to the door! Now! Hands behind your head.”

She advanced, stiff legged and shuddering, as the gate was unlocked.

Albie grabbed her and wrenched her out. “Cuffs,” he announced, and a guard tossed him a pair. “Key too,” he said. “I’ll bring ’em back.” He pushed her up against the cage and drew her hands down to hook her up. He slipped the key in his pocket and guided her out.

“Have fun,” a guard whispered as they passed.

Albie turned on him, grabbed his jacket, and shoved him against the wall. “Say again, soldier?”

“Sorry, sir. That was uncalled for.”

Albie gave him another shove and turned back to the girl, hustling her out. He returned a few minutes later and returned cuffs and key to the lender.

Buck was shocked when a girl with a pronounced Greek accent responded in the affirmative to Officer Athenas's main question. The other girls whirled to see who it was, and Buck leaned in to see if he could detect a mark on her forehead. There was none.

"You're refusing the loyalty mark of the Global Community?" Alex said.

"I'd certainly like to think about it," she said. "It seems a drastic move, not something to enter into lightly."

"You understand the consequences?"

"I'd just like to think it over."

"Fair enough. Anyone else?" No one. "Young lady, because you are the only one in this facility, rather than being sent straight to the confirmation facilitator, you may mull this over while in line. Your male counterparts are almost finished with the procedure, and where you wind up in line will determine how much time you have to decide. When you get to the place in the queue where you are asked where you would like the mark affixed, that will be your final chance to elect not to have it at all."

"And then?"

"You will be directed to the confirmation facili—"

"You know what that is, girl?" a teen called out.

"You're dead!"

"Guillotine! Head chopped off."

The girls quieted and Athenas looked at her. "Still want to think it over?"

"What, are they serious? You're going to chop my head off for wanting to think this through?"

"Not for thinking, miss. For deciding against. If you decide for, you just choose where."

"So I don't really have a choice."

"Where you been?" one of the girls said, and others joined in.

"Of course you have a choice," Alex said. "I believe I've made it clear. Accept the mark or accept the alternative."

"The mark or death, you're saying?"

"Still want to think it over?"

She shook her head.

One of the girls said, "You sure made that harder than it needed to be."

"Well, I didn't know there was really no choice."

Before proceeding to the adult women's lockup, Buck and Albie followed the young women to the lines in the middle building. It had already become a model of efficiency. The prisoners moved along steadily. They were ready with their forehead or hand choices, and the disinfectant/anesthesia was applied quickly. The injectors sounded like electric staplers, and while some recipients flinched, no one seemed to feel pain.

Almost all the teen males took their marks on their foreheads, and one of the last, as he got back in line, raised both arms and shouted, "Long live Carpathia!" That soon became the custom, as it did with the young women choosing to receive the mark on their hands.

Buck stood staring, wishing he could preach. They had made their choices, yes, but did they *really* know what they were choosing? It wasn't between loyalty and death; it was between heaven or hell, eternal life or eternal damnation.

His heart raced as the line of young women neared its end, and they were herded back. In the next building he expected to see Mrs. Miklos. How many of her friends would be there with her?

The women's facility was surreal, in that there was no cage. The guards, again, were mostly men, and they apparently didn't expect trouble. The women sat, mostly passive, chatting quietly, but their curious eyes also took in the Athenas squad.

Buck strolled around the outside of the group of women, looking for Laslos's wife. Finally he noticed a group of about twenty women in a back corner, on their knees. In the middle of the group, praying, was Mrs. Miklos.

"Shut up and listen up!" a guard bellowed, and most of the women came to attention. "This here's Officer Athenas, and he's got announcements and instructions."

Alex began, but the women in the back—who Buck assumed were Mrs. Miklos's believing friends—paid no attention and continued praying. Some gazed toward heaven, and Buck saw the marks on their foreheads. Others peered up and around the crowd at Alex, and Buck noticed that some of them had no mark. Laslos's wife had apparently been trying to recruit new believers.

Athenas grew impatient with those kneeling in the back. "Ladies, please!" he said, but they ignored him. He nodded to one of his female assistants, who handed her high-powered rifle and side arm to a compatriot, pulled out her baton, and moved directly into the tough-looking women in the front, heading toward the rear. A young, thick, healthy woman, she stared down the menacing ones, clearly knowing that her comrades had her back.

"As I was saying," Alex took up again, but he stopped when the attention of the women diverted to where his guard was headed.

"Ladies!" the guard bellowed. "You will cease and desist, face the front, and give Officer Athenas your full attention."

Many did just that. Some stood and moved away from the group. Others remained kneeling but looked up. Still others kept their heads bowed and eyes closed, lips moving in prayer. Mrs. Miklos, kneeling with her back to the guard, kept her hands folded, head bowed, eyes closed, praying softly.

The guard poked her with the baton, and she nearly lost her balance. When Mrs. Miklos turned to look up at her, the guard bent close and shouted, "Do you understand me, ma'am?"

Mrs. Miklos smiled shyly, reset herself, and returned to prayer. The guard, clearly incensed, put both hands around the end of the stick, set herself, pulled the baton back, and stepped into her swing.

Buck was barely able to hold his voice, and Albie had to grab and hold him back as the hardwood baton cracked loudly off the back of Mrs. Miklos's head.

Blood splattered several of the women as Laslos's wife pitched forward, arms and legs twitching. Several women screamed. Many of the kneelers, even those with marks on their foreheads, stood and rushed to join the main group. One woman dropped to her knees to check on her injured friend, and the guard caught her just below her nose with a second vicious swing.

Buck heard teeth shatter, and she cried out as the back of her head hit the floor and her hands came up to cover her face.

The guard marched back to the front, the sea of women parting for her. Miraculously, Mrs. Miklos drew herself up to her hands and knees and slowly, majestically returned to her kneeling position, hands folded before her.

With her back to the rest, the gaping wound, emitting great back issues of blood that ran down her hair and onto her sweater, was exposed to everyone. Most averted their eyes, but Buck stared at the white of her skull at the top of the laceration. Her skull had shattered and surely bone had been driven into her brain. And yet there she knelt, silently continuing to pray.

The other woman, rolling onto her stomach, also slowly drew herself up, spitting teeth, blood gushing down her chin, and returned to prayer. Buck felt a tingle at the base of his spine, imagining the blinding pain.

The guard retrieved her weapons with a look of satisfaction and exhilaration. The crowd behaved with a who-wants-to-be-next? attitude, and Alex said, "We'll see who's strong enough to stand in the enforcement facilitator line."

Buck, his pulse racing and his breath coming in gasps, stood stock-still as Alex finally reached the pivotal question. "Just so we'll know," he said, "how many will be rejecting the mark of loyalty and choosing the alternative?"

Mrs. Miklos stood and turned to face him. Her face was drained of color, eyelids fluttering. Her chest heaved with the effort of merely breathing. Blood pooled behind her from the ugly wound. She shook like a victim of advanced Parkinson's, and yet she raised both hands, a beatific smile softening her macabre face.

"You choose execution by guillotine rather than the mark of loyalty," Alex clarified.

The woman next to Laslos's wife, her face swelling, her nose red, upper teeth gone, stood and raised both hands, smiling a cadaverous grin.

"Two of you then?"

But there were more, and now the rest of the women stood just to see who was making the choice. From the original group of the kneeling devout stood a half dozen, smiling, hands lifted. "You all want to die tonight?" Alex shouted, as if it was the most ridiculous thing he had ever heard. "I'm counting eight. You eight will—now nine—will go to the extreme right when you—all right, now ten—when you are led to the processing center. OK, you can lower your hands now. Two more. OK, twelve of you. No need to keep your hands up!"

A couple of women in front looked at each other and started toward the back, marks of the believer appearing on their foreheads as they lifted their hands.

"All right," Alex said. "Those taking the mark stay left as we enter the center. Suicides stay to the right." And as he said it, three more lined up behind the bleeding women.

Buck fought tears. He could give in to emotion and wind up a martyr this very night, and in the heat of the moment, that didn't sound so bad. But he had a wife and a child and compatriots who counted on him. He stood blinking, panting, fighting to maintain control. These women were heroes of the faith. They would join the great blood-washed who literally made their bodies living sacrifices, soon to be martyred and appear under the very altar of God in heaven in snow-white robes of righteousness. He couldn't help but envy them!

As the women were led out, Alex shouted over the din, "You can change your mind! If you have chosen this ridiculous option and wish you hadn't, simply step out of one line and into the other!"

But as the courageous filed past Buck, he saw the mark on each forehead and knew there would be no one turning back—no, not one. He fell into step with the female guard leading the doomed to the guillotine line. This proved no end of fascination to the others, who stared as they themselves stood in the loyalty lines, deciding where they would bear the mark of Nicolae.

When the guard moved past the head of the line to talk to the two men who would work the death machine, Buck stepped close to Mrs. Miklos and tried to appear as if he were interrogating her. "Laslos wanted me to tell you he loves you with all of his heart and will see you in heaven."

She turned toward him with a start, blood still oozing down her back. She stared at the uniform and then at Buck's forehead. Then at his face. "I know you," she said.

He nodded.

"I don't believe you have met Mrs. Demeter," she said.

Buck was startled. The pastor's wife had taken the blow to the face. "I'd shake your hand," she whispered through her ruined mouth. "But then you'd be in line with us."

Mrs. Miklos bent close to Buck. "Tell Laslos thank you for leading me to Jesus. I see him. I see him. I see my Savior and can't wait to be with him!"

With that her knees buckled and Buck caught her. The guard reappeared and grabbed her. "No you don't, lady!" she said. "You chose this, and you're going to take it standing up." It was all Buck could do not to punch the woman in the face. She turned to him and said, "What are we going to do with all these bodies? We weren't prepared for anything like this."

Buck headed to the back, where the guards were lined along the wall. This was the first they would see of any executions, and it was clear they weren't about to miss it. Albie joined him, clearly overcome.

"That was Pastor D's wife with Mrs. Miklos."

Albie shook his head. "They're champions, Buck. I don't know if I can watch this."

"Let's get out of here."

"Maybe we should be here with them."

"We shall start with enforcement," Alex Athenas announced. "Any who wish to switch lines may do so at any time. Ladies, once you have been secured in position in the apparatus, no change of mind will be honored. Inform someone before that or suffer the consequences."

Buck stood paralyzed as Mrs. Miklos was led to the ugly machine. "Has that been tested?" Athenas shouted. "I want no malfunctions."

"Affirmative!" answered the assistant, who would trade roles with the executioner with each victim.

"Carry on!"

From thirty feet away Buck read the lips of the executioner. "Last chance, ma'am."

Laslos's wife knelt and the assistant positioned her.

"Turn her around!" someone yelled. "We want to see it happen!"

Albie turned on the man. "Shut up! This is not for your amusement!"

The room fell tomb silent. In the stillness Buck heard Mrs. Miklos's delicate voice. "My Jesus, I love thee, I know thou art mine."

A sob attacked his throat. Seemingly all in one motion, the assistant fastened the clamp and stood quickly with both hands raised to indicate he was clear of the blade path while the other yanked the short cord. The heavy blade raced to the bottom of the shaft. Buck pushed past the others and out into the night air, disgusted at the cheer that met the sickening thud.

He was glad for the vomit that gushed from him, allowing him to sob openly. Tears cascaded as he thought of the cold workmanlike crews that would remove heads and bodies and make room for the next and the next and the next.

As he stood in the cool grass, convulsing now in dry heaves, he covered his ears in a vain attempt to muffle the thuds and cheers, thuds and cheers. Albie emerged and rested a hand on his back. His voice was thick as he bent and gently pulled Buck's hands away from his ears.

"When I get to heaven," he whispered, "after Jesus, those women are the first people I want to see."

EIGHTEEN

Chaim took to pacing around in the Strong Building, repeating lines over and over. He usually carried a Bible, Rayford noticed, but sometimes a commentary or his own notes.

He didn't sound eloquent or forceful or confident to Rayford. It was as if all he was trying to accomplish was getting the basics down and having some idea what he was talking about. He also looked miserable, and Rayford wanted to counsel him again on where he stood with God, but he didn't feel qualified to make Chaim feel better about himself. Chaim apparently didn't see

Tsion as a personal mentor but only as a teacher and tireless motivator.

It struck Rayford that they all had had to endure the same doubts and fears when first they became believers. They had missed the truth, then feared they had come to God only as a last-ditch effort to avoid hell. Was it valid? The Bible said they were new creatures, that old things had passed away and all had become new. Rayford had worked hard to accept for himself the truth that God now saw him, in essence, *through* his sinless Son, the Christ.

But it had been almost impossible. He was new inside, yes. From a spiritual standpoint he knew it was true. But in many ways he struggled with his same old self. And while God's truth about him should have carried more weight than his finite emotions, they were loudly at the forefront of his conscience every day. Who was he to tell Chaim Rosenzweig to just have faith and trust that God knew him and understood him better than Chaim himself ever could?

But if there was someone who seemed healthier more quickly than most, it was Hattie. The irony of that was not lost on Rayford. Fewer than twenty-four hours before she became a believer, she was suicidal. Months before, she had admitted to any Trib Force member who had the endurance to debate her that she understood and believed the whole truth about the salvation gospel of Christ. She simply had decided, on her own, to willfully reject it because, even if God didn't seem to care that she didn't deserve it, she did care. She was saying, in effect, that God could offer her the forgiveness of her sins without qualification, but she didn't have to accept it.

But once she finally received the gift, her mere persistence was wearing. In many ways she was the same forthright woman she had been before, nearly as obnoxious as a new believer as she had been as a holdout. But of course, everyone was happy she was finally on the team.

Chaim, if Rayford could judge by facial expressions, was at least bemused by her. He was the next newest believer, so perhaps he identified with her. Yet Chaim was not responding as she was at all. Was it healthy envy that made him seem intrigued with her patter? Did he wonder why he hadn't been bestowed with such abandonment with his commitment to the truth?

Rayford didn't want to get ahead of himself, didn't want to take too literally Tsion's compliments about his return to effective leadership. But sometimes the surprise move, the one against the groove, was effective. Should he—dare he—conspire with Hattie to get her to see if she could jostle Dr. Rosenzweig off of square one? Tsion had become convinced that Chaim was God's man for this time, and Rayford had learned to trust the rabbi's intuition. But Chaim was going to have to progress a long way in a short time if he was to become the vessel Tsion envisioned.

Hattie had fed and was changing Kenny when Rayford approached her. What a bonus for Kenny that he had so many parent figures! The men doted on him, and even Zeke, though slightly intimidated, was extremely gentle and loving toward him. The women seemed intuitively to know when to spell each other, mothering him, but of course, most of the responsibility fell to Chloe.

"Have a minute?" Rayford asked Hattie as she lay the freshly powdered and dressed boy over her shoulder and sat rocking him.

"If this guy is drowsy, I've got all the time

in the world, which—according to our favorite rabbi—is slightly less than three and a half years."

Hattie isn't as funny as she sees herself, *Rayford thought*, but there is something to be said for consistancy.

"Could I get you to do me a favor?" Rayford said.

"Anything."

"Don't be too quick to say that, Hattie."

"I mean it. Anything. If it helps you, I'll do it."

"Well, if you succeed, it helps the cause."

"Say no more. I'm there."

"It has to do with Chaim."

"Isn't he the best?"

"He's great, Hattie. But he needs something Tsion and I don't seem to be able to give him."

"Rayford! He's twice my age!"

So as not to draw suspicion, Buck suggested he and Albie get a head start on the next group by heading directly to the building immediately east of the processing center. This housed the lesser criminals, according to the organizing officer. Yet he had also said that the religious dissidents were in with the worst felons in the easternmost facility.

The two approached the guards at Building 4. "Ready for us?" one said with a Cockney lilt.

"Soon," Buck said. "You're next."

"Heard whooping and hollering. Somebody choose the blade?"

Buck nodded but tried to make it clear he didn't want to talk about it.

"More'n one?" the man added.

Buck nodded again. "Wasn't pretty."

"Yeah? Wish I'd seen it. Never saw somebody buy it before. You watched, eh?"

"Told you it wasn't pretty. How would I know otherwise?"

"Sor-*ry!* I'm just askin'. How many you see then?"

"Just the one."

"But there were more? How about you, Commander? You stay for the whole show?"

"Leave it alone, Corporal," Albie snapped. "Several women chose it and showed more bravery than any man I ever saw."

"That right, is it? But they wasn't loyal to the potentate now then, was they?"

"They stood by their convictions," Albie said.

"Convictions and sentences, sounds like to me, mate."

"Would you choose to die if you felt that deeply?"

"I *do* feel that deeply, gents. Only I'm on the other side of it now, ain't I? I choose what makes sense. Man rises from the dead—he's got my vote."

The armed guards led the somber survivors back to the women's building while Athenas's crew caught up to Buck and Albie. Buck noticed that Alex's people seemed as subdued as the women prisoners. But their guards seemed energized.

"Let's get this done," Athenas said, leading the way in.

These were clearly white-collar criminals or small-timers. No bravado, no threats, little noise at all. They listened, no one opted for the guillotine, and they filed out quietly to be processed. Buck was repulsed at the smell of blood that hung in the center. Word quietly spread throughout the men that several women had been beheaded in that very room, and the men grew even quieter. The workers assigned to the guillotine seemed relieved to have a break.

Buck watched the process, despairing at the masses who ignorantly sealed their fate. The workers had grown smooth with experience, and the operation went faster and faster. Line up, decide, swab, sit, inject, back in line, file out. Ironically, real life bloomed at the point of bloody death. Men receiving what looked like an innocuous mark they thought kept them alive sealed their real death sentences. From death, life. From life, death.

Buck was eager to meet Pastor Demeter, about whom Rayford had said so much. Yet he dreaded the confrontation with the worst of the worst criminals in Building 5, knowing that many believing men would choose the right but ugly fate.

His phone vibrated. The readout said, "Top priority. Rendezvous at Kozani no earlier than 0100 hours with GC penal officer reassigned from Buffer to USNA. Urgent. Her papers will specify destination. Late twenties, dark hair, Ming Toy. Sealed."

"We'll have company tonight," Buck told Albie. "It will be refreshing to have a sister aboard who won't remind me of this place every time I look at her."

"I understand," Albie said. "I could have

lived a lifetime without having seen this and not felt I missed a thing."

It was late afternoon at the safe house, and everyone was busy except Rayford. Zeke was sewing. Tsion writing. Chloe working on the computer. Leah copying. Chaim cramming. Kenny sleeping. And Hattie, with a wink to Rayford, approaching Chaim.

The old man looked up at her from a couch, seemingly intrigued. Rayford sat nearby, ostensibly buried in a book. "Ready for an interruption?" she said. "Because I can't be dissuaded." She sat on the floor near his feet.

"As I don't appear to have a choice, Miss Durham, I could use a diversion. Something on your mind?"

"You're new at this too," she said, "but I've noticed you're not all over the place talking about it."

"I'm on assignment. Heavy study load. You remember from college?"

"Didn't finish. Wanted to see the world. But, hey, you won't let the studying get in the way of the thrill, will you? This has to be more than a class or that would take the fun out of it."

"Fun I don't associate with this. I came to the faith, you and I both did, at the worst possible time in history to enjoy it. It's about survival now. Joy comes later. Or if we had come to the faith before the Rapture, I could see where I might have enjoyed it more."

She scowled. "I don't mean fun fun, like ha-ha fun. But we can let it reach us, can't we? Inside? Get to us?"

He let his head bob from side to side. "I suppose."

"Do you? Your eyes and your body language tell me you're still not with the picture."

"Oh, make no mistake. I'm in. I believe. I have the faith."

"But you don't have the joy."

"I told you about the joy."

"I can't debate a brain like you, but I'm not giving up on this. I don't care if you are ten times more educated—I want you to understand this."

"I'll try," he said. "What do you want me to agree with?"

"Just that we have so much to be thankful for."

"Oh, I agree with that."

"But it has to thrill you!"

"In its own way, it does. Or I should say, in my own way."

Hattie slumped and sighed. "This is beyond me. I can't convince you. But I'm so thrilled that you are my brother, and I am on fire about what God is calling you to do."

"Now see, Miss Durham, that is where I suppose we differ or disagree. I have come to see that Tsion is right, that I am in a unique position to be involved in something strategic. I have resigned myself to the fact that it is inevitable and that I must do it. But I do not warm to it, long for it, look forward to it."

"I do!"

"Listen to me now, Miss Durham."

"Sorry."

"I accept this mantle with great gravity and heaviness of heart. I am working not to be a coward or even reluctant or resistant. This is not something one should eagerly embrace as some sort of honor or achievement. Do you understand?"

She nodded. "You're right; I'm sure you are. But does it also humble you that God would choose you for something like this?"

"Oh, I'm humbled all right. But there are times when I can identify with the Lord Messiah himself when he prayed and asked that if possible, his Father would let this cup pass from him."

Hattie nodded. "But he also added, 'Not my will, but yours be done.' "

"He did indeed," Chaim said. "Pray for me that I will approach that same level of brokenness and willingness."

"Well," she said, standing, "I just want to tell you that I know God is going to do great things through you. I will be praying for you every step of the way."

Chaim seemed unable to speak. Finally his eyes filled and he rasped, "Thank you very much, my young sister. That means more to me than I can say."

As Buck trudged into the last building, he found himself next to Alex Athenas, going over his notes. "Ugly work," Buck said.

Alex grunted. "Uglier than I thought. Who'd have guessed those women would be so resolute? We're going to run into some of their husbands now. We'll find out who's tougher."

"I find it hard to believe you've got religious dissidents in with hardened criminals."

"That's not my call. I've got one job here."

"I wouldn't want it."

"I didn't ask for it."

"Don't you agree the mix in this building is strange?"

The others passed as Alex stopped and looked Buck full in the face, making him uncomfortable. "Let me ask you something, Jensen. Have you ever talked to Nicolae Carpathia?"

Buck froze. Why would he guess that? "It's been a long time," Buck said.

"Well, I have. And he sees the dissidents as every bit as dangerous as the criminals. Well, they're both criminals."

"Murderers and people of faith?"

"People of the wrong faith, the divisive faith, the intolerant faith."

Buck stepped closer. "Alex, listen to yourself. You just sent more than a dozen women to their deaths because they don't share Nicolae Carpathia's faith. And you call *them* intolerant?"

Alex stared back. "I've got a mind to turn you in. You make me wonder about your loyalty."

"Maybe I'm wondering about it too. Whatever happened to freedom?"

"We've still got freedom, Jack," Alex spat.

"These people can decide for themselves whether they want to live or die."

Buck followed him in. This was by far the largest holding room, men of all ages milling about, talking. Buck noticed at least two dozen men with the mark of God on their foreheads, and they all seemed to be earnestly pleading with small groups of others. Strangely, the others seemed to be listening.

Buck caught Albie's eye. "See all of them?" he mouthed. Albie nodded sadly. It was great to see so many believers, but that meant more carnage was not far off. Buck wondered how he would identify Pastor Demeter without calling him out.

He asked a guard, "Who's the leader of the dissidents?"

"The local Judah-ites?"

Buck shrugged. "That what they call them here?"

The guard nodded and pointed to where a tall, dark-haired man was surrounded by at least a dozen others. He was speaking earnestly and quickly, gesturing. Rayford had said the man had the gift of evangelism, and he must have been exercising it with desperation. Buck moved to where he could hear.

"'But God demonstrates His own love toward us, in that while we were still sinners, Christ died for us.' That's you and me, gentlemen. I'm pleading with you not to take this mark. Receive Christ, get your sins forgiven, stake your claim with the God of the universe."

"It could cost us our lives," one said.

"It *will* cost you your life, friend. You think I don't know this is a hard thing? Ask yourself, do I want to be with God in heaven this very night, or do I want to pledge my loyalty to Satan and never be able to change my mind? Tonight you'll be dead for an instant and then in the presence of God. Or you can live another few years and spend eternity in hell. The choice is yours."

"I want God," a man said.

"You know the consequences?"

"Yes, hurry."

"Pray with me." They knelt.

"On your feet, everyone!" Alex called out.

"God, I know I'm a sinner," Pastor D began, and the man repeated it.

"I said on your feet!"

"Forgive my sins and come into my life and save me."

"Don't make me send a guard in there to break your heads!"

"Thank you for sending your Son to die on the cross for me."

"All right, get in there!"

"I accept your gift and receive you right now."

"Don't say I didn't warn you!"

Buck noticed that other men were repeating the prayer too, though their eyes were open and they faced the front, standing.

"Amen."

Just as the guard got to Pastor D, he stood and pulled the other man up.

"You two listen up now!"

As the guard left, Buck heard a man whisper, "Pray that again."

Pastor D started in again, quietly, still appearing to be paying attention as Alex finished his information. All throughout the cage, other men were praying and leading others to do the same. The murmuring floated toward the guards, but it was hard to pin on one person.

"I need to know if any of you will be rejecting the mark of loyalty so we can get you in the right line now!"

"Put me in the other line!" Pastor D called out.

"You're rejecting?"

"Yes, sir!"

"You understand the consequences?"

"Yes. I reject the authority of the ruler of this world and wish to—"

"I didn't ask for your philosophy, sir. Just get in the line to my right as—"

"I wish to pledge my allegiance to the true and living God and his Son, Jesus Christ!"

"I said be quiet!"

"He is the one who offers the free gift of salvation to anyone who believes!"

"Silence that man!"

"What are you going to do, kill me twice? Oh, that I could die twice for my God!"

"Anyone else?"

"Me!"

"Me too!"

"Count me in!"

"Sign me up!"

And one after the other, as the men chose their own deaths, they began to holler their reasons.

"I just became a believer tonight, right here! Do it, men! It's true! God loves you!"

"Silence!"

"I was arrested because I was worshiping God with fellow believers! God will never leave you or forsake you!"

"Guards!"

The guards followed Alex's men into the cage, throwing men to the ground, stomping their heads and faces.

"Do not resist!" Pastor D shouted. "We'll be out of our misery soon! May the very men who beat us listen to our report before it's too late!"

He was smacked atop the head with a baton and crumbled to the floor. A criminal who Buck noticed did not have the seal of God on his forehead grabbed the guard around the neck from behind and threw him down as others climbed atop.

"Don't resist, brothers!" a believer yelled. "Just speak the truth!"

But the unbelievers were rioting. "I'm taking Carpathia's mark!" one screamed. "But stop hurting these men! I'm a coward, but they are brave! Agree with them or not, they have more courage than any of us!"

A guard jumped him and wrapped his arms around the man's head, a hand on his chin. He yanked until the neck snapped and the man fell dead.

Alex, who remained outside the cage guarding his men's weapons, grabbed one and fired into the air, squelching the bravado of most unbelievers. "I will authorize my people to shoot to kill!" he said. "Now get to my left if you are accepting the mark of loyalty to the Global Community and our risen potentate. And get to the right if—"

"There is one God and one Mediator between God and men, the Man Christ Jesus!"

"Silence that man!"

The believers helped Pastor D up, but he could not stand alone. They carried him to the front of the line to Alex's right, and dozens of others fell in behind. Suddenly they began singing, "What can wash away my sin? Nothing but the blood of Jesus! What can make me whole again? Nothing but the blood of Jesus!"

"Herd them out! Shut them up! Guillotine line first! Move! Move!"

"O precious is the flow, that makes me white as snow! No other fount I know! Nothing but the blood of Jesus!"

As the line passed Buck, he grabbed Pastor D by the shirt and pulled him up, as if forcing him to walk. He whispered desperately in his ear, "Jesus is risen!"

Demetrius Demeter, he of the gift of evangelism, eyes rolling back, tongue thick, legs failing, mumbled, "Christ is risen indeed!"

Buck watched the staggering band, each with the seal of God on his forehead, march to the death room, singing of the blood of Jesus and accepting the blows. He could not follow them in, knew he could not endure witnessing the deaths of these saints, old and new. Eyes filling, he found Albie in the crowd and motioned with a nod that he should follow. They strode quickly to the jeep, but not soon enough to avoid hearing the first slide and thud and the cheering of the bloodthirsty crowd.

Buck fired up the engine to drown out the sounds and squealed off into the night. He and Albie shared not a word as they raced south twenty-five miles to the airport at Kozani. Buck skidded to a stop by the motor pool and they leapt out, hurrying through the gate.

"Key in it?" someone called, and Buck nodded, not trusting himself to speak.

As he and Albie marched across the tarmac toward the runway and the hangar where their refueled jet awaited, Buck saw a tiny Asian woman sitting next to a huge suitcase and a smaller bag on a bench under a light pole. Something about the way the light illuminated her red, GC prison-system uniform made her look angelic.

She appeared tentative when she saw them and stood, pulling her orders from her pocket. She was a sliver of reality, a link to life, to safety, a cup of cold water in a desert of despair.

"Tell me you're Ming Toy," Buck said brusquely, barely trusting his voice.

"I am. Mr. Williams?"

Buck nodded.

"And Mr. Albie?"

"Jensen and Elbaz until we board, ma'am, please," Albie said, and Buck could tell he was just as ragged emotionally.

"Let me see your papers," Buck said, picking up her suitcase while Albie grabbed the other bag.

"Let me carry something, gentlemen. You have no idea how I appreciate this."

"Until we get on that plane, Ms. Toy," Albie said, "we're just following orders and ferrying an employee from one assignment to another."

"I understand."

"Once we're on board, we can make nice."

Buck tossed her suitcase behind the backseat, then helped her aboard and pointed to a seat. As she buckled in, Albie slipped behind the controls. Buck sat next to him but did not strap himself in. He turned so his knees were between his chair and Albie's and grabbed a clipboard.

He faced the silent woman behind him. "Ms. Toy," he said, and he began to sob. "We have to do a preflight checklist and get clearance for takeoff." She squinted at him in much the same way he assumed she must deal with the prisoners at Buffer. She had to be wondering what in the world was wrong with this man. "But once we are airborne," he said between great gasps, "we are going to tell you what a miracle you are and why we so badly needed you to be on this plane tonight." He caught his breath and added, "And we're going to tell you a story you won't believe."

NINETEEN

David awoke every few hours, peeking at his clock. Finally, at 0600, he rolled out of bed, ran a hard five miles, ate, showered, and dressed. He was in his office by 0730.

"You change this appointment?" his assistant asked.

"Yeah, sorry, Tiff. A conflict?"

"No, just curious."

David called 4054, just to make sure Chang was still there and planning to come at 0900. When David identified himself, Mrs. Wong said, "Missah Wong not here right now. I have him call you back, OK?"

"Is Chang there?"

"No. Chang with father."

"Do you know where they are?"

"See Missah Moon."

"They are with Mr. Moon now?"

"I have him call you back."

"Ma'am, Mrs. Wong, are your husband and your son with Mr. Moon now?"

"I no understand. Call Missah Moon."

David called Moon's office and was told Walter was in Personnel. Personnel told him the executives were in a meeting. "Can you tell me if they have begun applying marks to new hires?"

"Not that I know of, but that *is* supposed to be today, and that *is* what the meeting is about."

"Can you tell me if one of my candidates is there, Chang Wong?"

"I believe I did see him and his father in here this morning with Mr. Moon."

"Where are they now?"

"I have no idea. Would you like their room number? They're staying here at—"

"No, thanks. I really need to talk to Moon."

"I told you, sir, he is in a meeting with Personnel execs."

"It's an emergency."

"So you say."

"Ma'am, I am a director. Would you please interrupt the meeting and tell Mr. Moon I need to speak with him immediately."

"No."

"Excuse me?"

"I have been in trouble for just that kind of thing before. If it's that important, you may feel free to interrupt the meeting yourself."

David slammed the phone down and jogged to Personnel. He found the conference room empty, then found the receptionist. She held him off with a raised hand as she handled another call.

"Ask them to hold a second," he said. "This is important."

"Just a moment, please."

"*Thank* you! Now, I—"

"I didn't put this call on hold to help you. I put them on hold to ask you to wait your turn."

"But I—"

She held up a hand again and returned to her call. Another phone rang while she was finishing, and she went directly to it. David leaned across her desk and depressed the cradle button.

"Director Hassid! I'll report you for this!"

"You'd better get me fired before I get you fired," he said. "Now where is this meeting?"

"I don't know."

"It's not here; where is it?"

"Off-site, obviously."

"Where?"

"I honestly don't know, but my guess would be the basement of Building D."

"That's a quarter mile from here! Why didn't you tell me it was there when you told me to interrupt it myself?"

"I didn't know you'd actually do it."

Her phone rang again.

"Don't answer that."

"It's my job."

"Answer it and it'll be your job. Why would the meeting be in D?"

"I don't know that it is. I said it was a guess."

"Why *might* it be there?"

"Because that's where they're setting up the loyalty mark application center." And she answered her phone.

David slammed both palms on her desk, making her jump and then apologize to the caller. As he pushed through the door, she called after him in a singsong tone. "Oh, Director Hassid! You might want to take this call. It's your assistant."

He rushed back, only to get a condescending look. "Like I'm going to let you use my phone." She pointed to a phone on a table in the waiting area.

"This is David."

"Hey. Just got a call from Walter Moon."

"Where is he?"

"I'm sorry. He didn't say and I didn't think to ask. Want me to find him?"

"What did he want?"

"He said he would be delivering your 0900 appointment personally, that he and the candidate's father were most excited about your interest, you know the drill."

"What was he doing with Moon this morning?"

"No idea, sir, but I'll find out if you want."

"Find Moon and call me back on my cell."

David hurried to Building D and found the basement cordoned off. He had to use every line in the book to talk his way past Security. When he was finally able to peek through the double doors that led into a huge meeting room, he got his first glimpse of the setup for applying the mark. Crowd-control barricades were arranged to funnel people to processing points and finally to the cubicles where the last of the injection guns were being plugged in and tested.

"What's all this for?" David asked a woman arranging chairs.

"Oh, come on, you know."

"But why so big? I thought they were just doing new employees first."

She shrugged. "The rest of us will be next. Might as well have everything in place and tested, huh? I can't wait. This is the dream of a lifetime."

"Have you seen Security Chief Moon this morning?"

"Actually he *was* here a while ago."

"With anyone?"

"Couldn't tell you who. Some guys from Personnel, I know."

"Anyone else?"

She nodded. "I didn't pay attention, though."

"Any idea where he is now?"

She shook her head. "I suppose you've heard the rumors, though."

"Tell me."

She smiled. "You poor managers miss the gossip, don't you?"

"We often do."

"I figure you start most of it, or at least your decisions do."

"Granted. What's the word this morning?"

"That Moon's in line for Supreme Commander."

"You don't say."

"I like him. I think he'd be good at it."

David's cell phone vibrated and he excused himself. "Moon's people now say he's in with Carpathia," Tiffany said.

"Alone?"

"David, I'm sorry. I didn't ask. I'll find out whatever you want, but I have to know in advance what I'm looking for."

"My fault. Did they happen to say whether Walter is still bringing Chang at 0900?"

"Yea! I know one! Yes."

"Really?"

"Honest."

"Is Chang with him and Carpathia now?"

"Sorry. No idea."

"I'm on my way back."

David used his cell phone as he walked and tried the Chang apartment again. This time Mr. Wong answered. Encouraged, David asked for Chang. "He not available right now. He see you at nine, yes?"

"That's right. Is he OK?"

"Better than OK! Very excited! Missah Moon come get us to bring to see you."

"You're coming too?"

"If OK. May I?"

David sighed. "Why not?"

"No?"

"Yeah, sure."

Back in his office, with fifteen minutes to spare, he patched in to Carpathia's office. The first thing he heard was Nicolae's voice. "Hickman was a buffoon! I'm better off without him. I don't know what Leon was thinking."

"Probably that he was going to have your job and Jim would be easy to manage."

Carpathia laughed. "You're a good judge of character, Walter. It came down to you and Suhail. He has an impressive résumé, but he's so new to his current position."

"And can you trust a Pakistani? I don't understand those types."

"Who can you trust these days, Walter? Now listen, I don't know how you stand on pomp and circumstance, but I don't want to make a big deal of this. You'll have an appropriate office you won't have to share with anyone, but I just want to announce your appointment and not get into a lot of ceremony."

"Perfect," Walter said. "I don't want to take any attention from you, sir."

David thought Walter sounded disingenuous and almost palpably disappointed. He was right, though, in pandering to Carpathia's ego. No one was going to steal that thunder anyway.

"Walter," Carpathia said, "how are we coming with the GCMM?"

Moon sounded surprised. "Sir, the Morale Monitors have been in place for a long time. I get input from them every day, and I know Suhail counts on their intelligence briefings."

It was clear Carpathia was impatient. "Mr. Moon, surely you caught my drift recently when I spoke of mobilizing a great enforcement throng from every tribe and nation who would—"

"Of course, Potentate. I am working with Chief Akbar now to—"

"I don't believe it! You missed it! Walter, I am determined to surround myself with people who understand me intuitively!"

"I'm sorry, Excellency. I—"

"For all of Leon's foibles and idiosyncrasies, he is a man who stays with me, anticipating my needs and desires and strategies. Do you kn—"

"That's the kind of subordinate I want to b—"

"Don't interrupt me, please!"

"I apologize."

"Do you know where Leon is now?"

"I heard he had flown to the United European Sta—"

"He is in Vatican City, Walter! He has called together the ten regional potentates and has asked each to bring his most trusted and loyal spiritual leader to join them in that former great bastion of Christianity."

"I don't underst—"

"Of course you don't! Think, man! At this very moment I imagine Reverend Fortunato is kneeling in the Sistine Chapel, the subpotentates and the spiritual leader from each region who will represent Carpathianism throughout the globe laying hands on him and committing him to the great task before him."

"I should like to have been there, Excellency."

"You're my chief of security and you didn't even know this! I'm going to make you Supreme Commander, but you have to get in step!"

"I'll do my best."

"Leon called me at dawn, telling me with great relish that he had ordered destroyed every Vatican relic, every icon, every piece of artwork that paid homage to the impotent God of the Bible. There were those among the potentates and even among the Carpathianists who suggested that these so-called priceless treasures at least be moved here to the palace to preserve their worth and to remind us of history. History! I don't know when I've been prouder of Leon. Before he returns, the Vatican will be left no vestiges of any sort of tribute to any god but the one my people can see and touch and hear."

"Amen, Your Holiness. You are risen indeed."

"Of course, and the whole world was watching! Now when I spoke the other day of a host of enforcers, I wanted you to gather that I meant the very core of my most loyal troops, the GCMM. They are already armed. I want them supported! I want them fully equipped! I want you to marry them with our munitions so their monitoring will have teeth. They should be respected and revered to the point of fear."

"You want the citizenry afraid, sir?"

"Walter! No man need fear me who loves and worships me. You know that."

"I do, sir."

"If any man, woman, young person, or child has reason to feel guilty when encountering a member of the Global Community Morale Monitoring Force, then yes, I want them shaking in their boots!"

"I understand, Excellency."

"Do you, Walter? I really need to know."

"I absolutely do, sir."

"I don't care whom you replace yourself with as chief of security. All I want you to know is that I hold you personally responsible for carrying out this wish."

"Of giving more muscle to the GCMM."

"The understatement of the century."

"Any budget for this?"

"Walter, you report directly to me. I control the globe politically, militarily, spiritually, and economically. I have a bottomless sea of resources. Spare not one Nick in your effort to make the GCMM the most powerful enforcement juggernaut the world has ever seen."

"Yes, sir!"

"Have fun with it! Enjoy it! But don't dawdle. I want a full contingent, at least one hundred thousand fully equipped troops, in Israel when I return there in triumph."

"Sir, that is but days away."

"Do we not have the personnel?"

"We do."

"Do we not have the armaments?"

"We do. Are you lifting the embargo against showing military-style strength in the form of tanks, fighters, bombers, and other such?"

"You're catching on, Walter. I want to crush resistance in Israel before it even arises. From whom should I expect opposition?"

"The Judah-ites and—"

"You've already told me they are unlikely to show their faces. They take their potshots from behind the trees of the Internet. From whom shall I expect flesh-and-blood opposition within, say, Jerusalem itself? You know my plans."

"Not totally, sir."

"You know enough to know who will be outraged."

"The Orthodox, sir. The devout, religious Jews."

David heard chairs squeak, and it was

obvious Carpathia had stood and Moon followed suit. "Now, Walter. I ask you. How dangerous to me will be the funny-looking men with their beards and their braids and their skullcaps once they have seen one hundred thousand heavily armed troops, there to protect me and those who worship me?"

"Not very, Excellency."

"Not very indeed, Walter. Good day to you."

David guessed Walter still had time to make their appointment. His goal was to schmooze Walter, flatter Mr. Wong, and somehow get rid of them so he could plot with Chang how to get out of there with the other four believers. He sat, earphones in place, ready to shut down his computer. But then he heard Carpathia humming, then singing, as if he were writing a song, trying a line, improving it, starting over. David listened, transfixed.

Finally perfecting it, to a military-sounding tune Carpathia softly sang:

Hail Carpathia, our lord and risen king;
Hail Carpathia, rules over everything.
We'll worship him until we die;

He's our beloved Nicolae.
Hail Carpathia, our lord and risen king.

Just before midnight in Chicago only Rayford and Tsion were awake. All were excited about the expected return of Buck and Albie and their next new member, Ming Toy. Chloe and Leah asked to be awakened as soon as the chopper arrived.

Tsion had been working all day on a new, though brief, message. "I'm about to transmit it," he told Rayford. "But I'd appreciate your looking at it. It's an interesting study, but it's not for the beginners. We have hundreds of thousands of new believers joining our ranks every day, but I have to think also about moving the more mature ones from milk to meat. Perhaps the day will come when someone like Chaim can take over the teaching of the newest."

Rayford eagerly accepted Tsion's hard copy, always feeling privileged when he was among the first to get a glance at something a billion people would benefit from.

Dear ones in Christ:

From your letters to the message board, I sense some questions about certain passages and doctrines, one of which I address today. I am most encouraged that you are reading, studying, curious, and that you so plainly want to learn and grow as believers in Messiah. If you have placed your trust in Christ alone for salvation by grace through faith, you are a true tribulation saint.

While we all rejoice in our new positions before God—we went from old to new, from death to life, from darkness to light—no doubt all are sobered by the reality that we are living on borrowed time, now more than ever.

I have gathered from many that one of your loftiest goals is to survive until the Glorious Appearing. I share that longing but wish to gently remind you that that is not our all in all. The apostle Paul said that to live is Christ but that to die is gain. While it would be thrilling beyond words to see the triumphant Lord Christ return to the earth and set up his thousand-year reign, I believe I could learn to deal with it if I were called to heaven in advance and saw it from that perspective instead.

Beloved, our top priority now is not even thwarting the evils of Antichrist, though I engage in that effort every day. I want to confound him, revile him, enrage him, frustrate him, and get in the way of his plans every way I know how. His primary goal is ascendancy for himself, worship of himself, and the death and destruction of any who might otherwise become tribulation saints.

So, as worthy and noble a goal as it is to go on the offensive against the evil one, I believe we can do that most effectively by focusing on persuading the undecided to come to faith. Knowing that every day could be our last, that we could be found out and dragged to a mark application center, there to make our decision to die for the sake of Christ, we must be more urgent about our task than ever.

Many have written in fear, confessing that they do not believe they have the courage or the character to choose death over life when threatened with the guillotine. As a fellow pilgrim in this journey of faith, let me admit that I do not understand this either. In my flesh I am weak. I want to live. I am afraid of death but even more of dying. The very thought of having my head severed from my body repulses me as much as it does anyone. In my worst nightmare I see myself standing before the GC operatives a weakling, a quivering mass who can do nothing but plead for his life. I envision myself breaking God's heart by denying my Lord. Oh, what an awful picture!

In my most hated imagination I fail at the hour of testing and accept the mark of loyalty that we all know is the cursed mark of the beast, all because I so cherish my own life.

Is that your fear today, friend? Are you all right as long as you are in hiding and somehow able to survive? But have you a foreboding about that day when you will be forced to publicly declare your faith or deny your Savior?

I have good news for you that I have already admitted is difficult to understand, even for me, who has been called to shepherd you and exposit the Word of God for you. The Bible tells us that once one is either sealed by God as a believer or accepts the mark of loyalty to Antichrist, this is a once-and-for-all choice. In other words, if you have decided for Christ and the seal of God is evident on your forehead, you cannot change your mind!

That tells me that somehow, when we face the ultimate test, God miraculously overcomes our evil, selfish flesh and gives us the grace and courage to make the right decision in spite of ourselves. My interpretation of this is that we will be *unable* to deny Jesus, *unable* to even choose the mark that would temporarily save our lives.

Isn't that a blessed thought? I could no more do this in my flesh than I could swim the Pacific. I have heard stories of believers from the past who were asked at gunpoint to denounce their faith, and yet they stood firm, dying for it. I never envisioned myself with that kind of fortitude.

Even since writing to you last, I have heard the story of one who was among the first to face this test. We have no eyewitness account, no one to tell us how the scene unfolded. Yet we know that of all the people herded through the mark application process at this specific venue (which I naturally have to keep confidential), only one man rejected the mark. Knowing the consequences, he chose to die rather than to deny Jesus Christ.

My heart is broken for his loved ones. What an awful mental image to season one's bereavement! And yet how thrilling to know that God was faithful! He was there at the darkest hour. And this beloved saint is one of the martyrs under the altar of God, his robe snow white.

As Antichrist and the false prophet spread their message of lies and hatred and false doctrine around the world, forcing millions to worship Satan himself by threatening to behead those who refuse, it would bode well for us if we would memorize a verse from John's Revelation. In chapter 20 and verse 4, he writes as part of his God-given vision:

"Then I saw the souls of those who had been beheaded for their witness to Jesus and for the word of God, who had not worshiped the beast or his image, and had not received his mark on their foreheads or on their hands. And they lived and reigned with Christ for a thousand years."

Your loved ones who have been called to what the world would call an ignoble and gory end shall return with Christ at his

Glorious Appearing! They shall live and reign with him for a thousand years! Glory be to God the Father and his Son, Jesus the Christ!

And as for you and me, my friend: might we be among those? Oh, the privilege!

Revelation 14:12-13: "Here is the patience of the saints; here are those who keep the commandments of God and the faith of Jesus. Then I heard a voice from heaven saying to me, 'Write: "Blessed are the dead who die in the Lord from now on."' 'Yes,' says the Spirit, 'that they may rest from their labors, and their works follow them.' "

And what of those who enjoy for a season the favor of the ruler of this world? What of those who avoid the guillotine and seem to prosper? As rousing as the Scriptures can be for those who are washed in the blood of the Lamb, look how fearful it can be for those who choose their own way. In Revelation 14:9-11, John quotes an angel, "saying with a loud voice, 'If anyone worships the beast and his image, and receives his mark on his forehead or on his hand, he himself shall also drink of the wine of the wrath of God, which is poured out full strength into the cup of His indignation. He shall be tormented with fire and brimstone in the presence of the holy angels and in the presence of the Lamb. And the smoke of their torment ascends forever and ever; and they have no rest day or night, who worship the beast and his image, and whoever receives the mark of his name.' "

You don't have to be a Bible scholar to understand that.

Now, precious brothers and sisters, let me try to make plain some passages that have resulted in questions from many of you. In Psalm 69:28, the psalmist pleads with the Lord concerning his enemies: "Let them be blotted out of the book of the living, and not be written with the righteous."

Exodus 32:33 says, "And the Lord said to Moses, 'Whoever has sinned against Me, I will blot him out of My book.' "

These references naturally have caused some to fear that they can lose their salvation. But my contention is that the book referred to in those is the book of God the Father, into which are written the names of every person he created.

The New Testament refers to the Book

of Life of the Lamb, and we know that the Lamb is Jesus, for he is the one John the Baptist was referring to (John 1:29) when he said, "Behold! The Lamb of God who takes away the sin of the world!"

Jesus the Christ came into the world to save sinners, and thus the Book of Life of the Lamb is the one in which are entered the names of those who have received his gift of eternal life.

The most important difference between these two books is that it is clear a person can have his name blotted out of the Book of the Living. But in Revelation 3:5, Jesus himself promises, "He who overcomes shall be clothed in white garments, and I will not blot out his name from the Book of Life; but I will confess his name before My Father and before His angels."

The overcomers he is referring to are those clothed in the white garments of Christ himself, guaranteeing that their names cannot be blotted out of the Book of Life of the Lamb.

To me the Book of the Living is a picture of the mercy of God. It is as if in loving anticipation of our salvation, he writes every person's name in that book. If one dies

> without trusting Christ for salvation, his name is blotted out, because he is no longer among the living. But those who have trusted Christ have been written in the Lamb's Book of Life, so that when they die physically, they remain alive spiritually and are never blotted out.

Rayford had to admit to himself that he had also worried about his own response if he were to face the guillotine. He wanted to be true and faithful to the one who died for him, and he wanted to see his family again. But if he failed and proved a coward, he had wondered whether he would lose his standing before God.

"Tsion," he said, "I wouldn't change a word. This will uplift and comfort millions. It sure helped me."

TWENTY

David couldn't sit still. How was he going to pull this off? Maybe he should act uninterested in Chang as an employee. Would anybody fall for that? He stood and paced, straightening his tie and buttoning his uniform jacket.

When Moon, Mr. Wong, and Chang finally arrived, David was disconcerted at Chang's appearance. A slight, fair-skinned seventeen-year-old, he wore khakis, a plain shirt, a light jacket zipped to the neck, and a red baseball cap pulled low over his eyes. He was clearly angry, his eyes darting everywhere but at David.

Moon and Mr. Wong were giddy, laughing, talking loudly. “Ever see a boy so afraid?” Mr. Wong said.

“Can’t say I have!”

Tiffany ushered them in, and David shook hands, first with Walter, then Mr. Wong, who said, “Hat off for meeting, Chang.”

For the first time since he had seen them interact at the Carpathia funeral, David saw Chang ignore his father. The elder reddened and lost his smile, then faked one, pumping David’s hand. “Made hat come off for picture!”

Moon laughed at the memory of it, whatever it was.

David thrust his hand toward Chang, who ignored it. He stood looking down. His father nearly exploded. “Shake hands with boss, Chang!”

The boy lazily reached out, but he did not grip when David did, and it was like shaking a fish. David thought he saw a tear slide next to the boy’s mouth. Maybe this was for the best. If David were to try to bust him out of the place in a few days, it would be better if they didn’t act civil to each other.

Walter Moon said, “He is risen.”

Mr. Wong and David responded, “He is

risen indeed." David was startled to hear Chang mutter, "Christ is risen indeed."

Chang may have considered that godly courage, but David saw it as teenage recklessness. No one else seemed to have heard it.

"Sit, please, gentlemen," David said. "I'd like to spend time alone with the candidate, but it's probably just as well you're both here, Chief Moon and Mr. Wong. I've been studying the personnel manual, and frankly, I don't see any way around the age issue."

"Age issue?" Mr. Wong said, looking stricken. "What's that?"

"Good," Chang said and rose to leave.

"Sit! Mind manners! You guest here and interview for position!"

Chang slowly plopped back, slouching and crossing his feet.

Moon dismissed David's concern with a gesture. "His Excellency has already waived that, and—"

"The policy allows no exceptions," David pressed.

"David," Walter said slowly, reminding him of the way he had just heard Carpathia speak to Moon, "the potentate *is* policy. If he determines that this young man and his off-the-charts intellect and computer savvy will be valuable to the Global Community, then it's a done deal."

David took a breath, deciding to go on the offensive.

But Moon wasn't finished. "You're aware that Potentate Carpathia has already cleared Chang to finish his last year of high school here, and of course we then offer college classes as well."

"I was under the impression the school here was for the benefit of the *children* of employees," David tried.

"I don't think the teachers care who the students' parents are. Tell Mr. Wong what you are envisioning for Chang, David."

Mr. Wong, grinning, leaned forward to drink it in.

Here goes nothing, David thought. "I envision him finishing high school in China and at least beginning his career anywhere but here."

Mr. Wong's smile disappeared. "What?" he said, turning to Moon.

"David!" Walter said. "What the—"

"Look at him," David said, and both men turned to see Chang staring at the floor, hands in his pockets.

"Sit up, boy. You know better. You shame me."

Chang made a halfhearted effort to shift and raised his chin an inch, but he remained a picture of insolence. His father reached to tug at the shoulder of his jacket, and Chang wrenched away. Mr. Wong glowered at him.

"He doesn't want to work here," David said. "He's young, immature, simply not ready. I don't doubt his credentials or his potential, but let him work out the kinks on someone else's money."

"Now, let's not be hasty, David," Moon said. "The boy's just been through a bit of a trauma. He was scared, but he went through with it, and he's clearly still a little shaken."

David cocked his head as if willing to consider the excuse. "Oh?"

"Yes," Mr. Wong said. "He upset. He frightened of needle. Didn't want injection. Scream. Cry. Try to get away, but we hold him down. He thank me someday. Maybe tomorrow."

"And he needed an injection for what?"

"Biochip!" Mr. Wong announced proudly. "One of first to get it! See?"

He reached for the boy's cap, but Chang

stood again and turned his back on his father. David fought to maintain composure. Now what? How had he let this happen?

"When?" he blurted. "How?"

"This morning," Walter said. "I was hoping they'd be ready for him. Took a photog along and everything. But they weren't, not really. We were going to just wait till later, but they could see I had gone to a lot of trouble, so when the first unit was plugged in and ready to go, they tested it and then made him the first recipient here. Not sure the picture's much good though. The boy wasn't any happier there than here."

David said, "Well, that's . . . ah . . . that's—"

"Something, huh?" Walter said. "I think the boy is glad to have it over with, and if he's honest he'll admit it didn't hurt a bit."

"I proud! Son will be soon, you'll see. But he ready for work now. No age problem. No school problem. This is place for him."

"Global Community maybe," David said, his voice hollow. How was he going to explain this to Ming? "But not my department."

"Don't be ridiculous, David. We just explained his attitude. You and I both know there's no better place for him."

"Then you take him. I don't want him. I don't have the energy to try to win him over while training him."

"I'm of a *mind* to take him, David. He's going to make somebody look like a genius. It had might as well be me."

David stood and spread his arms, palms up. "Good to see you all again."

Chang started to rise, but his father stopped him with a hand. The man looked to Walter. "David, sit down," Moon said. "Let us give you a few minutes with Chang, let him win you over."

"There aren't enough flowers or boxes of candy in the United Asian States."

"Find out what's troubling him. If it's just the trauma of the procedure, he deserves another look. What do you say?"

"I suppose you'll go running to the potentate if I don't agree."

Moon stood and motioned David to do the same. He reached for him across the desk and pulled David's ear to his mouth. "This is no way for us to conduct ourselves in front of outsiders, particularly a patriotic GC supporter like Mr. Wong. You're blamed right I'll take this straight back to the top. Now you know Carp—His Excellency wants this boy on staff, so get with the program." He let go of David and turned to Mr. Wong. "Let's give them a few minutes to get acquainted."

Mr. Wong bent to his son as he left. "You make proud, and I mean it." But Chang looked away.

As soon as the door was shut, Chang stood and moved to the center chair facing David. He resumed his defiant posture. David sat and rested an elbow on the desk, chin in hand, staring at Chang, who did not meet his gaze. "Are the blinds open behind me?" the kid muttered, still looking away.

"Yes."

"Close them."

"That would send a wrong signal, Chang. If they're watching, I want them to see me not liking you too much, which is exactly what I feel right now."

"Are they still out there?"

"Yes."

"Then either shut the blinds or tell me when they're gone."

"They're leaving."

"OK, then wait till they're out of sight so you can close the blinds without sending them the wrong signal but I still don't have to worry about anyone else coming by and looking in. Or your secretary."

"Assistant."

"Whatever. Tiffany, right?"

"Observant."

"I don't miss anything, like the fact that she's not a believer."

"I'm trying to figure out a way to work on that."

It was maddening that Chang still sat slumped, looking down. "You can't let her in on where you stand for fear she'll turn you in."

"Of course."

"Could you shut the blinds, please?"

"Not till you tell me what in the world you think you're up to."

"I'll wait," Chang said.

David rose and closed the blinds. "What was I supposed to do, son? I didn't know—"

As David returned to his side of the desk, Chang straightened up. "Don't call me son. I hate that." He whipped off his hat. "Look at me! Look what they did to me!"

David leaned over the desk to study Chang's mark of loyalty. It was the first he had seen other than in a drawing. "That is strange," he said.

"That's news to me?"

"No, I mean, obviously it looks different to me and will to any fellow believers. We can see both marks. The seal of God is still there, Chang." David could barely take his eyes off the small, black tattoo that read *30* and was followed by a half-inch pink scar that would fade to a darker line in a few days. "I still haven't figured the significance of the prefixes," David added.

"You serious?"

"Always."

"Don't tell me you don't even know why Carpathia is so obsessed with 216."

"Of course," David said. "That was rather transparent. Easy."

"Same basic logic as these. Ten different regions or sub-potentateships, as Carpathia likes to call them. We know them as kingdoms. Ten different prefixes, all related to Carpathia. I mean, the fact that one of them is 216 should have been your first clue."

"Don't tell me, Chang. I'll get it."

"Should have had it by now."

"You can lighten up on me. I don't know how I could have prevented this. Your little charade didn't help. Your sister is going to kill me. And, assuming you want out of here as badly as Ming wants you out and as badly as the other four believers want out, how did that help?"

"Can you believe my father and Moon thought I pitched a fit because I was afraid of needles?"

"I'm glad you didn't just scream out that you're a believer."

"Well, what am I now, Hassid?"

"You don't like to be called son—don't call me Hassid."

"Sorry. What's your pleasure?"

"Mr. Hassid or Director Hassid while we're in here. Once we're gone, Mr. or Brother will work."

"You sound like an old guy."

"That's because you're a young guy. As for what you are, with both marks you surely have to be in a special category."

"But all that stuff Dr. Ben-Judah writes about, choosing between the seal of God and the mark of the beast. I chose, and I got both. Now what?"

David sat shaking his head. Chang cocked his head and pursed his lips. "It isn't that I really don't know, *Mr.* Hassid. I just keep testing you. Are you not as bright as they think you are, or are you just short on sleep? Can't figure the prefixes, can't figure—"

"First, I'm *not* as bright as they think I am, but I might surprise *you.*"

"I'm not trying to be disrespectful, sir. I'm really not. But you have already surprised me by how long it takes you to make things make sense."

"I've also been under unusual pressure for months, and worse the last couple of weeks."

"Yeah. I'm sorry about your, ah, were you engaged? Was she your fiancée?"

"Secretly, yes. Thanks."

"That would put anybody off track for a while. That's understandable."

"So, you're mad you got the mark, but you've already made some sense of it?"

Chang sat back and crossed his legs. "You know Ben-Judah personally, huh?"

"Haven't met him, but we work together."

"You have his phone number?"

"Of course."

"Well, you might want to call him to confirm, or let me borrow the number and I'll talk to him myself. . . ."

"I don't think so."

"Fair enough. You call him then and see

if I'm right. I'm a believer. That hasn't changed. The Bible says nothing can separate us from the love of Christ, and that has to include our own selves. And God says we're hidden in the hollow of his hand and that no one can pluck us out. I didn't choose the mark. It was forced on me. I see nothing but benefits."

"Then why the big scene?"

"I don't figure *everything* out immediately. I sure didn't *want* the mark. I was trying to figure a way to get out of it right up to the time they stuck me. I don't have to like it, but what's done is done, and a smart guy like you ought to be able to see the upside of this."

"Tell me, oh great intellect."

"So mock me. Forget it. I shouldn't have to tell you anyway."

David stood and moved to the front of the desk and sat atop it, his knees inches from Chang's. "All right, listen. It's obvious you're a mental prodigy, mind like a steel trap, all that. I'd heard you were a Bible-memory freak, which is saying something when you can't risk being caught with one. All that from reading it on the Net?"

Chang nodded.

David continued. "I'm not hung up on being the smartest guy in the room no matter where I am. That didn't used to be so, especially when I was your age. I enjoyed not only overwhelming older people with my brain but letting them know that we both knew who was the king. You want me on the floor, kissing your feet? Fine. You're the best. You're smarter than I am. I'm a journeyman, a plugger compared to you. That what you want to hear? It doesn't bother me that you're a few steps ahead of me—it really doesn't. What bothers me is your assuming it bothers me, because it would bother you if the shoe were on the other foot. Then I get defensive, trying to prove it doesn't bother me, which only makes it appear that it does. You following this?"

Chang smiled. "Yeah, I got it."

"So enlighten me and quit trying to rub it in. What are you going to do with this 'advantage,' as you call it, being bi-loyal for lack of a better term? And how does acting angry with me help that cause, whatever it is?"

"Glad you asked. May I take it from the top?"

David nodded.

"First, I like the term. Bi-loyal. That's the

way it appears. This forehead is going to really bother fellow believers. They can only assume the seal mark is fake, because no one would fake the mark of the beast. They're going to take some persuading, and if I were them, I might never trust me.

"But the Carpathia loyalists . . . they can't see the mark of God, and they have no reason to believe the loyalty mark is anything but what it appears. Therefore, I am free to live among them—buy and sell, come and go, even work here—without suspicion and—if I'm careful—without risk."

"You're good, Chang. But that last was very teenage thinking."

Chang appeared to think about that, then nodded his concession. "Maybe so. Too bad I won't have an old guy like you around to keep me from being too tempestuous and impulsive."

"I'm starting to feel ancient."

"You are, Director. Think about how few years you have left on this earth as we know it."

"Funny."

"Question is, how do you and your three friends get out of here, and how do I get your job?"

"You're not going to get my job."

"I could do it."

"Maybe you could, but not even Carpathia is foolhardy enough to risk that. You have to work your way up, and I have an idea who might take my spot anyway. You'd wind up working for him."

"That's too bad; if you're right."

"I'm right. You're so smart, have some common sense. They're not going to put a teenager in a director's chair. They're just not. Think about it. I'm the youngest director now by eight years."

"Congratulations."

"That's not the point. If you're going to stay here and be a better mole than I was—because the mark gives you unquestioned credibility—you have to be strategic. Pick your spots. Do what you can."

"Which is what, in your opinion?"

"I can teach you everything I know before I leave."

A smile played at Chang's lips.

"What?" David said. "I know you're dying to say something."

"Just that you teaching me everything you know shouldn't take long. It's a joke. C'mon."

"A real comedian. Well, for as limited as I

am, I'd like to think you'll be amazed by what I've done here and what I have in place. My biggest worry is that my remote access is only good for as long as they stay with the current system."

"You don't have to worry about that anymore," Chang said.

"Because?"

"I'll be here."

"But you're not going to be a director. It won't be your call what system they stay with or change to."

"But I can adapt what you've put in place to work with it, either way."

"You probably could."

"I know I could."

David covered his mouth with a hand, thinking. Why *hadn't* he recognized the possibilities right away? "Some of your confidence is attractive. Part of it is off-putting."

"Most of it is an act, sir."

"Really?"

"Sure. The whole thing in here was an act. Pushing your buttons was just for fun. I'm just showing you how I'd fit in here. Be a little sarcastic, a little condescending. Tweak people. You think they're going to suspect I'm a Judah-ite?"

"I'm just wondering what's really inside you, Chang."

"What do you mean?"

"Spiritually. Your sister is a tough prison guard."

"She could whip my tail."

"But she glows with a spirituality, a humility. She has a real Christlike quality."

"Not around inmates she doesn't."

"I suppose not. But what about you, Chang? Do you know who you are and who you're not? Do you understand the depth of your own depravity and realize that God saved you while you were dead in your sins?"

Chang nodded, maintaining eye contact. "I know I could use a lot more introspection, but yes, I do know. And I appreciate your reminding me."

"All right, I have a plan, Chang."

"That's encouraging. So do I. But I had a little more time to think about mine, so you start."

"I'll start because I'm older, I outrank you, and I am interviewing you. You're not even an employee yet."

"I defer. Mine's going to be better anyway, so go ahead. . . . Kidding!"

"I say you maintain the attitude in front of the people here and your father, but give him a little slack before he leaves. He needs to believe you're at least OK with being here. Don't act impressed with me."

"That won't be hard."

"All right!"

"I'm listening."

"I'll bet. Come reluctantly to the conclusion that you want to work here and that you figure this is the most logical department to work in, though you're not impressed with it. You don't want to appear too eager. They're all excited about you, so let them stay that way. Play a little hard to get. As for me, I won't act much more thrilled than I did in front of Moon, and I'll just assign you to the guy I assume will replace me. After hours, you and I cram—mostly by phone and E-mail—and I'll show you what I've set up. During the day you work with him. Don't alienate him, because you'll quickly be his number-two guy. You might even want to govern yourself so you don't become too much of a star. Let him forget about you while trusting you. That way you'll be most valuable to our cause. Make sense?"

"You thought of that just now?"

"Don't start."

"I'm serious. Those were my thoughts exactly. And there's nothing I want more than to use every gift God gave me to be, like you said, valuable to the cause. Do I get to be a member of the Tribulation Force? Or would I have to live in the safe house for that?"

"They consider me a member. Of course, this is like the nerve center and they depend on what we do here to pave the way for them to come and go and infiltrate."

"So they ought to adopt me soon enough."

"I would imagine."

"May I shake your hand, as long as no one is looking?" David reached for him, and Chang gripped hard. "Don't take me too seriously. I just like to mess with people's minds."

"And I suppose few can compete," David said.

"Well, you sure can."

"I'm going to let you go and not do or say anything. Let them ask what I've decided.

Then I'll reluctantly say I can use you if they insist. That way we keep maintaining distance."

"So when you escape, they won't think I had anything to do with it."

"Sort of. But actually—"

"Excuse me, Mr. Hassid, but have you thought of making your disappearances look like something other than running from taking the mark?"

David shook his head. "You got another few minutes, Chang?"

TWENTY-ONE

One week before the resurrected Nicolae Carpathia's widely advertised triumphal return to Jerusalem, Rayford Steele called an 8 P.M. meeting of the stateside Tribulation Force at the commons near the elevators in the Strong Building.

Grieving for the Greek pastor he had met only briefly and for Laslos's dear wife, he was nervous and fought to keep it from showing. God had restored him to leadership, and he was determined to fulfill his duty. As the others took their places, Rayford reviewed the dog-eared sheets of his legal pad and cleared his throat. He had not expected to become emotional and worried that it would detract from confidence in his command. But he couldn't control his shaky voice from the first word.

Eleven were there, including Rayford, Buck, Chloe—the surviving three original Trib Force members—and Kenny Bruce. In the order that they joined were also Tsion, Leah, Albie, Chaim, Zeke, Hattie, and Ming.

"It's important," Rayford said, "that we always remember our extended family. In Greece, only Laslos remains. In New Babylon we have David, Mac, Abdullah, Hannah Palemoon, and Chang Wong. Maybe sooner than we think, we will all be together. Meanwhile, I am grateful to God for each one on this team."

Rayford asked Tsion to pray, and everyone in the room spontaneously either stood or knelt when he began. "God, our Father, we come to you weak and frail and wounded. So many here have lost so much, and yet we are grateful to you for your grace and for your mercy. You are a good God, full of loving-kindness. We pray for every member of our family and especially for the plans you have for us in just seven days.

"We are comforted by the realization that

you care even more than we do about our loved ones. We look forward to when we shall see you face-to-face, and we pray you will allow us the joy of bringing many more with us. In the name of Jesus Christ. Amen."

As the rest settled back in their places, Rayford began again. "I have assignments for everyone. The following will remain here during what we're calling Operation Eagle: Chloe and Kenny, Ming, Zeke, and Tsion. I foresee using Ming more, but for now her being AWOL from the GC penal system makes her too vulnerable. Changing her appearance is going to be a true test of Zeke's skills. Meanwhile, he has created new personas, looks, names, and documents for all who need them.

"Albie and I will fly the fighter and the Gulfstream to Mizpe Ramon in the Negev tomorrow to supervise the completion of a remote airstrip and refueling center for the airlift. Buck and Chaim will fly commercially to Jerusalem in disguise and under aliases. Chaim will settle into the rebuilt King David Hotel, waiting to confront Carpathia when he enters Jerusalem. Buck will go on to Tel Aviv and be back in Jerusalem in time for Carpathia's return.

"Hattie and Leah will fly commercially to Tel Aviv, where they will process the volunteer vehicles and drivers who will help evacuate believers from Jerusalem to the planes in the Negev when it becomes necessary. They will also monitor Carpathia's arrival, and, like Buck, Hattie will join the crowd watching the air show our New Babylon brothers and sister plan to perform for the potentate and follow the Carpathia entourage to Jerusalem.

"Leah will use a rented vehicle to rendezvous with the New Babylon four in Jordan at the former Queen Alia International Airport, now known as Resurrection International. She will bring the New Babylon contingent to the airlift site, and they will fly back to the States with Albie and me at the conclusion of the airlift. Questions?"

Chaim raised a hand. "I have only a thousand questions. But is it not time for my teacher, who ought to be respectful of his elder, to reveal the city of refuge?"

Tsion smiled and looked to Rayford. "Soon everyone must know where the fleeing saints are headed after they have reached the airlift location in the Negev. Yes, Chaim, you have devoted yourself to your studies and deserve to know where you will lead the people. It is a city you have known about all your life. You have no doubt heard many stories about it, and it would not surprise me to learn that you have actually visited it as a tourist. It is one of the most famous ancient cities in the Middle East. Some call it the Rose Red City."

Chaim's eyes came alive. "Petra!" he said. "In the ancient land of Edom!"

"One and the same," Tsion said.

"I should have known. It will be difficult for *us* to get into, let alone a pursuing army."

"In fact, Chaim, God will make it impossible for them to get in. He has special obstacles planned, the likes of which have not been seen since the days of the first Exodus. Tell me, have you been to Petra?"

"Twice as a youngster. I can never forget it. Oh, Tsion, this is a stroke of genius."

"It ought to be. I agree with countless scholars who say God has planned it for this very purpose from the beginning."

Toughest for David was planning the escape of the four believers without being able to meet with Hannah. It made sense to meet with Mac and Abdullah, who ultimately reported to him. And while David had to be circumspect and not too obvious, he got some time with Chang without raising eyebrows. What he really wanted was to meet with the four of them to carefully plot the entire scenario. By secure-connection phone calls and E-mails, he accomplished the same thing.

Chang worked out better than David could have hoped. While young and impetuous, he was more than a computer genius. He was also a good actor and simply lent his skills to the department and impressed his immediate superior with his industriousness. When his parents returned to China, he was assigned permanent quarters, and he and David designed and installed a computer with an impregnable fire wall that could do everything David's computer did.

The Tribulation Force around the world would have access to everything David had built into the palace system. But first and foremost, Chang would monitor the escape and stay tied in with the computers at the safe house in Chicago. Everyone would know where everyone else was and how the mission was progressing.

Hannah's practical suggestions proved

valuable. She theorized that none of the four should pack or take anything they wouldn't have taken on a real trip of the same duration. "Resist the temptation," she counseled, "to take everything you need for the rest of your life." There should be no hint of closure or finality in how they left their rooms and offices. Of his many computers, David could justify taking only his laptop.

Each of the four planned to leave change on their dressers, things left undone, pictures on the wall, personal items lying about. They were determined to leave anything they would have left if they believed they would be back in a few days. Maybe even a kitchenette light on, a radio playing, favorite clothes or shoes waiting. To-do lists, half-eaten food in the refrigerator, unopened mail.

Mac made a doctor's appointment for the second morning after he was to return. Abdullah sent two uniforms to the palace dry cleaners that he was to pick up the afternoon he returned. David scheduled staff meetings and briefings with key staff members for his entire first week back. He sent memos to colleagues mentioning issues he would like to discuss, "sometime soon when our crazy schedules settle down a bit."

The announcement of Walter Moon's ascension to Supreme Commander was made without pomp and went barely noticed. David, reporting to him officially the first time, asked casually if his own Israel-related plans should be scrapped in light of the change in personnel at the upper-management level.

"And what were those plans, Director Hassid?"

"Mac and Abdullah were to pilot the Phoenix 216 to Tel Aviv, where Potentate Carpathia and his VIPs would inaugurate the first loyalty mark application site open to the public. We understand he has a couple of days of meetings there first."

"Right. He and Reverend Fortunato have extended sessions with the sub-potentates and their religious representatives."

"Mac and Abdullah would return to New Babylon and return in one of the Quasi Twos, bringing with them the young woman from Medical Services who has experience with the biochip-injection system."

"I can tell you right now, David, that I would not want to see that changed. His Excellency is proud of that aircraft and loves to have it shown off to the citizenry."

"Our thought was that Mac would do a little air show, letting people know what that baby can do."

"The potentate will love that," Walter said.

"I would too, if you thought it wasn't too extravagant to let me go along."

"Not at all. You go right on."

"Mac can really make that thing sing. He and his first officer can put it through its paces with the young woman and me aboard, along with the equipment for the application site. Then upon landing, he can introduce the nurse and the equipment while people line up."

"Perfect. His Excellency will get that site rolling, and we move on to Israel, where he has something else planned."

When the day came, Mac and Abdullah were up before dawn, and David supervised the loading of the Phoenix 216 for the potentate and his entourage's flight to Tel Aviv. The biggest chore for a cargo crew that had recently lost its chief was the loading of a gigantic pig that had been driven in the night before from Baghdad. "Were there no pigs in the Holy Land?"

Supreme Commander Moon wanted to know.

A young Russian who had appointed himself acting loadmaster, with David's blessing, said, "The late Mr. Hickman, rest his soul, insisted on the biggest, fattest one in the database, and you're looking at him. Or her."

David liked the Russian because he was by the book, and that came in handy later in the day when Hannah was sent to the hangar to order the loading of cargo onto the Quasi Two. At last, because she had been assigned to David for the work in Israel, she could meet with him in his office without suspicion.

"Worked like a charm," she said. "Look at this."

She slid across his desk the ordering department's copy of the shipping requisition. Handwritten under Special Note:

> *Following repeated efforts by the acting cargo chief to dissuade Ms. Palemoon and her insistence that approval comes straight from Director Hassid, this plane was, in the opinion of said chief, overloaded by at least 20 percent. If this bill of*

> *lading is not countersigned by said director, cargo crew will not be responsible for the airworthiness of this craft.*

"I like it," David said, scribbling his signature. "When we all go down, the investigation will begin and end with our Russian friend. He'll be the grieving hero who wishes we would have listened, will probably be elevated to the position he wants, and we—along with millions of Nicks' worth of plane and cargo—will be sadly explained away as human error. Mine."

"I'm so proud of you," Hannah said, shaking his hand. "You kill me on my first assignment for you." It appeared she was struck by the lack of humor in that, given David's recent loss.

"It's all right, Hannah," he said. "I catch myself using death references all the time, as if even I can't remember."

She sighed. "This really is quite an ingenious plan. I can say that because I had so little to do with it."

"Me too," David said. "If it works, we owe it to Mac and Abdullah. Mac admits to me, if not to Smitty himself, that the best stuff was Abdullah's."

Two mornings later Mac and Abdullah ran through preflight as David and Hannah boarded the Quasi. The Russian fussed and shook his head, trying to get the pilots on his side. Mac told him, "He's the boss. You can only do what you can do, and then you have to remember you're the subordinate."

"Tell yourself that while your plane is going down," he said.

"If I thought it was life or death, I'd stand up to him," Mac said.

"My hands are clean," the Russian said. "Your funeral."

Actually, Hannah had overstated the weight of every piece of equipment she'd loaded onto the plane. The cargo was big and bulky and strained at the cords, but the total weight was well within acceptable limits to allow Mac to navigate without adversely affecting the attitude of the craft.

The only cargo heavier than it appeared were the pilots and passengers. Hannah had reminded them that should anything float to the surface from the wreckage, it should be their suitcases with clothes, shoes, personal belongings, and toiletries. Everyone carried an extra suitcase so they could leave evidence in the water and still have necessities.

"Watch this," Mac said as he maneuvered the sleek jet out of the hangar and onto the runway. As he made his first turn he increased his speed just enough to make the plane sway off course. "That ought to give cargo boy something to shake his head over."

Sure enough, as Mac waited for clearance to take off, ground control asked him if he was aware the acting cargo chief had lodged an overload notice. "Doesn't surprise me, tower," Mac said. "We'll take the heat."

"You know enough to abort early if she's not tracking."

"Roger."

Mac made the plane fishtail slightly as he picked up speed down the runway and heard one more warning from the tower as he lifted off. "Caution noted," Mac said.

He set a course for Tel Aviv, but when they were equidistant from there and Resurrection International in Jordan, he informed both towers that he was going to land in Jordan as a precautionary measure. "To be safe, we have arranged to have some cargo driven to Tel Aviv."

Leah, with a printed order originating from David, had talked her way onto the tarmac in a nondescript van. She pulled up to the cargo bay where the pilots and passengers helped load two guillotines and a half skid of injectors into the van. Satisfied that any curious eyes had long since lost interest, all four occupants crawled into the van and lay on the floor, and Leah slowly drove it between two hangars where Mac could peek through the window and still see the plane.

He communicated with the tower via portable radio and remote controlled the plane's taxi and takeoff. As the Quasi gradually faded from sight, Mac communicated to the tower through an intentionally distorted connection that he believed he was losing radio power. He asked if they could inform Ben Gurion Tower that he was on schedule, would still perform the air show, and would appreciate it if they could be cleared for landing immediately following. He also hinted that he wished he had unloaded a little more cargo, but he was confident he could handle the rest of the trip.

"Advise abandoning show, considering," Resurrection Tower said.

"Repeat?"

"Consider abandoning air show and proceed to immediate conventional landing."

"No copy, tower."

They repeated their advice, but Mac turned off the radio. Leah pulled out of the airport, and she and the four bogus victims headed for Mizpe Ramon. "We can all keep our fingers crossed," Mac said. "I've seen those Quasis do amazing things based solely on what the flight management system onboard computer tells it to do. But this is a long flight on its own, and I've asked it to do some interesting stuff."

"Cross our fingers?" Hannah said. "Only God can make this work. You're the expert, Captain McCullum, but if this thing goes down anywhere but deep in the Mediterranean, it won't take long for someone to discover no one was aboard."

Buck and Chaim had slipped into Israel without incident the day before and checked into the King David. Chaim still seemed out of sorts, having hid two commentaries in his briefcase. Buck thought he looked like a wise old monk in his costume, but privately he wondered whether the old man could command and hold an audience.

From the first time he met Dr. Rosenzweig to interview him as *Global Weekly*'s Man of the Year, Buck had been impressed with how soft-spoken the man was. He carried a heavy Israeli accent, though he had a strong command of English. But his scientific brilliance, his zest for life, and his passion were borne of an intense, distinct, quiet delivery. Would that convey the authority and command the respect he needed to serve as a latter-day Moses? Could this little man with his quiet demeanor lead the remnant of Israel and additional tribulation saints to the promised land of safety?

He would have to challenge the ruler of the world, defy the armies of Antichrist, stand on the front lines against Satan himself. Yes, Chaim had had the fortitude to carry out a murder plot against Carpathia, but by his own admission, he had not known at that time with whom he was dealing.

Buck kept to himself his misgivings and continued to pray. He had inserted himself in so many precarious spots in this very city that somehow the prospect of having a front-row seat to this bit of prophecy seemed par for the course.

It seemed the entire nation had turned out to welcome the potentate at Ben Gurion Airport, then merely waited as anticipation grew for his speech the next day. The initiation of the first public mark application center was one thing, but to see the risen ruler of the nations return to the very city of his death—well, that was what the country was gearing for.

Rumors abounded that His Excellency would flash the ultimate and final nose thumbing at the stubborn Judah-ites by using for himself one of their most sacred traditional sites, the very Via Dolorosa itself. No one could imagine the scene. Would there be opposition? Protesting? The majority of the populace would welcome its idol and admire his pluck. Could Carpathia take the place of the object of worship for many devout believers, humbly and with class paying homage to Jesus, one whom many now considered his predecessor?

And then his plan to address the world from within the rebuilt temple in Jerusalem . . . could he risk offending two major people groups on the same day? It was no secret that Christians, Messianic Jews, and Orthodox Jews were the last holdouts against Carpathianism. But hadn't Carpathia himself and Reverend Fortunato proved his ascendancy through his resurrection and the deadly miracles? It was one thing to read the myths and legends and perhaps eyewitness accounts of a resurrection centuries ago. But to have seen with one's own eyes a man come back from obvious death and to see his right-hand man imbued with supernatural powers—well, there was a religion for today.

Buck, whose *The Truth* coverage of some of the most dramatic incidents of the day had found an enormous audience of Judahites and Carpathianists alike, had engendered worldwide response by his account of some of the first uses of the loyalty enforcement facilitators. He attributed his account to eyewitnesses without identifying himself as one, so no one had a clue where the leak might have come from. He could hope only that even Carpathia sympathizers would be shocked at the inhumanity.

It seemed the entire world was on its way to the Holy Land. Tsion had urged believers to come. Chloe, through the International

Commodity Co-op, had recruited pilots, planes, drivers, and vehicles. Meanwhile, Fortunato had rallied Carpathianists from all over the globe to celebrate the brave return of their idol to the location of his murder.

Somehow Jerusalem civic leaders had found the cash and the personnel to put at least a cosmetic sheen on the city. Banners, signs, and landscaping had sprung up seemingly overnight. While the 10 percent of the city that had been ravaged by the recent earthquake still lay in twisted ruins, the eyes of visitors were redirected to the new. If one didn't look too closely, it resembled again the festive place that had welcomed the Global Gala.

Street vendors and kiosks offered palm branches, perfect for waving or laying in the path of the potentate, for just Nicks apiece. Hats, sandals, sunglasses, buttons bearing Nicolae's picture—you name it—you could buy it.

Tel Aviv was choked with foot and vehicular traffic that led to the seashore and the great makeshift amphitheater that would house the mark application equipment. Everything was in place, including covered areas to blunt the brunt of the sun. All that was left to be installed were the injectors, the enforcement facilitators, and the personnel to man the site. People were already in line, eager to be among the first to pledge their loyalty to Nicolae. Part of Buck wanted to be Moishe or Eli or even Chaim, if he could pull it off. As he parked his rental several blocks from the site, Buck dreamed of abandoning reason and shouting to the uninformed, "Don't do it! You're selling your soul to the devil!"

He looked at his watch and quickened his pace. He wanted the best view of the air show, because he knew how much of a show it would be. As he headed for the shore, he called Rayford. "Four minutes to visual contact," he said. "I allowed just enough time and should be in perfect position."

"Remember every detail."

"Don't insult me, Dad. How will I ever be able to forget this? Are they on schedule?"

"On their way. The airport maneuver was successful. They're worried about the flight management system, since there's no chance to personally monitor it. A malfunction could kill innocents."

"I would be one."

"My point. Mac has communicated with Moon's people by phone, telling them when to expect him and letting him know they have a malfunctioning radio."

"How are things at Eagle central?"

"Amazing. These virtual strangers show up with their parts of the construction plan and no supervision until now, and they simply cooperate, get along, and get the work going. They were further along than Albie and I could believe, and we're ahead of schedule. Dozens of choppers are already here. That'll take care of getting the infirm into Petra without walking the gorge. So far we believe we're still undetected, but that won't last long."

Zeke had done such a thorough job on Buck that he started every time he caught a glimpse of himself. As he camped out near a concession stand, he felt as invisible as he had in the underbrush near where Moishe and Eli had been resurrected. Crowds seemed to materialize from everywhere in anticipation of an actual live appearance by Nicolae himself. And he did not disappoint.

A half dozen SUVs rumbled to the site, and the power elite of the world stepped out and strode quickly to the platform to wild applause. Carpathia was at the top of his game, humbly thanking everyone for coming and for making him and the Reverend Fortunato, the ten sub-potentates, and their respective Carpathianism representatives feel so welcome. He produced his usual blather about the improving state of the world, his renewed energy "after three days of the best sleep I've ever had," and how he looked forward to the rest of his time in Tel Aviv and Jerusalem.

"And now," he said with relish, "before a wonderful surprise for you, I give you the new head of our perfected religion, the Most High Reverend Leon Fortunato."

Leon immediately dropped to one knee and took Nicolae's right hand in both of his and kissed it. When he reached the lectern he said, "Allow me to teach you a new anthem that focuses on the one who died for us and now lives for us." In a surprisingly facile baritone and decent pitch, Leon sang a heartfelt and energetic version of "Hail Carpathia, Our Lord and Risen King."

Buck shuddered. He felt the familiar tingle of expectancy when he caught site of the Quasi in the distance and heard its high drone. The crowd had quickly picked up the lyrics and simple, stirring melody, and as their second attempt at it ended, Carpathia returned to praise the technology evident in the new Quasi Two that was bringing "not only the equipment needed for this site, but also a brief display of its capabilities, ably demonstrated by the pilot of my own Phoenix 216, Captain Mac McCullum. Enjoy."

The crowd exulted as the impressive jet came screaming over the city toward the shore. Buck was surprised how low it was, but the people *oohed* and *aahed,* clearly persuaded that this was part of the show. Buck worried that the computer program had somehow jumped off track and might result in disaster.

The plane surged out along the shoreline, the Mediterranean gleaming in the sun. The craft suddenly picked up speed and rolled up onto one side, then flattened, then onto the other before swooping low again. To Buck it seemed to clear the water by no more than ten feet, and he couldn't imagine Mac's having programmed that thin a margin for error.

A long, low turn brought the frisky craft directly over the dignitaries, who tried to maintain their dignity while squinting into the sky, willing themselves not to give in to the urge to duck, ties flapping in the breeze. The Quasi made another turn toward the Mediterranean, running parallel to the water for a blistering quarter mile, then pointing straight up.

The crowd murmured as the thing ascended like a missile, and they had to wonder as even Buck did, though he knew the craft was empty, what it would feel like to be on board. Any astute spectator knew the plane was in trouble before it became obvious. As it slowed to its apex, it drifted backward, nose over tail for a straight plunge toward the water with its underbelly toward the shore.

People talked excitedly and laughed in anticipation of the pullout that would level the plane at the last possible instant. Just when it appeared there was no more room or time, they knew she would rocket parallel, run out to sea, and then turn back toward Ben Gurion to more applause.

Except that the Quasi never pulled out. This plane was not free-falling toward the Mediterranean. No, this multi-million-Nick marvel of modern technology was accelerating, her afterburner hot, the vapor shimmering in a long trail. The strange attitude and angle sent the craft careening toward the shore approximately three-quarters of a mile south of the crowd.

The Quasi and ostensibly her two-man crew and two passengers slammed the beach perfectly perpendicular at hundreds of miles an hour. The first impression of the shocked-to-silence crowd had to be the same as Buck's. The screaming jet engines still resonated even after the plane disintegrated, hidden in a billowing globe of angry black-and-orange flames. An eerie silence swept in, followed less than half a second later by the nauseating sound of the impact, a thundering explosion accompanied by the roar and hiss of the raging fire.

First one spectator cried out, then another. No one moved. There was no need to run, not away from the crash or toward it. The plane had been there in all its glory, teasing their expectations before fulfilling their worst fears, and now nothing but glowing pieces, the thing all but vaporized in a sand crater.

Another tragedy in a world of pain.

Numbly, people turned toward the sound of the PA system. Carpathia had returned and was speaking so compassionately and softly that they had to strain to catch every word. "Peace be unto you. My peace I give you. Not as the world gives. Would you please quietly make your way from this place, honoring it as the sacred place of the end for four brave employees. I will ask that the loyalty mark application site be appropriately relocated, and thank you for your reverence during this tragedy."

He turned and whispered briefly to Leon, who then stepped to the mike and spread his hands wide, the folds of his robed arms creating great wings. "Beloved, while this sadly preempts and concludes today's activities in Tel Aviv, tomorrow's agenda shall remain in place. We look forward to your presence in Jerusalem."

Buck hurried to his car and phoned Rayford. "The ship is down on the shore. No one could have survived it. On my way back to the voice that will cry in the wilderness."

Buck was struck by an unusual emotion as he merged into traffic that crawled toward the ancient city. It was as if he had seen his comrades go down in that plane.

He knew it was empty, yet there had been such a dramatic finality to the ruse. He wished he knew whether it was the end of something or the beginning of something. Could he hope the GC was too busy to thoroughly investigate the site? Fat chance.

All Buck knew was that what he had endured in three and a half years was a walk in the park compared to what was coming. The entire drive back he spent in silent prayer for every loved one and Trib Force member. Buck had little doubt that the indwelt Antichrist would not hesitate to use his every resource to quash the rebellion scheduled to rise against him the next day.

Buck had never been fearful, never one to back down in the face of mortal danger. But Nicolae Carpathia was evil personified, and the next day Buck would be in the line of fire when the battle of the ages between good and evil for the very souls of men and women would burst from the heavens, and all hell would break loose on earth.

EPILOGUE

Then I heard a loud voice from the temple saying to the seven angels, "Go and pour out the bowls of the wrath of God on the earth."

So the first went and poured out his bowl upon the earth, and a foul and loathsome sore came upon the men who had the mark of the beast and those who worshiped his image.

Revelation 16:1-2

ABOUT THE AUTHORS

Jerry B. Jenkins (www.jerryjenkins.com) is the writer of the Left Behind series. He is author of more than one hundred books, of which ten have reached the *New York Times* best-seller list. Former vice president for publishing for the Moody Bible Institute of Chicago, he also served many years as editor of *Moody* magazine and is now Moody's writer-at-large.

His writing has appeared in publications as varied as *Reader's Digest, Parade,* in-flight magazines, and many Christian periodicals. He has written books in four genres: biography, marriage and family, fiction for children, and fiction for adults.

Jenkins's biographies include books with Hank Aaron, Bill Gaither, Luis Palau, Walter Payton, Orel Hershiser, Nolan Ryan, Brett Butler, and Billy Graham, among many others.

Seven of his apocalyptic novels—*Left Behind, Tribulation Force, Nicolae, Soul Harvest, Apollyon, Assassins,* and *The Indwelling*—have appeared on the Christian Booksellers Association's best-selling fiction list and the *Publishers Weekly* religion best-seller list. *Left Behind* was nominated for Book of the Year by the Evangelical Christian Publishers Association in 1997, 1998, 1999, and 2000. *The Indwelling* was number one on the *New York Times* best-seller list for four consecutive weeks.

As a marriage and family author and speaker, Jenkins has been a frequent guest on Dr. James Dobson's *Focus on the Family* radio program.

Jerry is also the writer of the nationally syndicated sports story comic strip *Gil Thorp,* distributed to newspapers across the United States by Tribune Media Services.

Jerry and his wife, Dianna, live in Colorado.

Dr. Tim LaHaye (www.timlahaye.com), who conceived the idea of fictionalizing an account of the Rapture and the Tribulation, is a noted author, minister, and nationally recognized speaker on Bible prophecy. He is the founder of both Tim LaHaye Ministries and The Pre-Trib Research Center. Presently Dr. LaHaye speaks at many of the major Bible prophecy conferences in the U.S. and Canada, where his nine current prophecy books are very popular.

Dr. LaHaye holds a doctor of ministry degree from Western Theological Seminary and a doctor of literature degree from Liberty University. For twenty-five years he pastored one of the nation's outstanding churches in San Diego, which grew to three locations. It was during that time that he founded two accredited Christian high schools, a Christian school system of ten schools, and Christian Heritage College.

Dr. LaHaye has written over forty books, with over 22 million copies in print in thirty-three languages. He has written books on a wide variety of subjects, such as family life, temperaments, and Bible prophecy. His current fiction works, written with Jerry B. Jenkins—*Left Behind, Tribulation Force, Nicolae, Soul Harvest, Apollyon, Assassins*, and *The Indwelling*—have all reached number one on the Christian best-seller charts. Other works by Dr. LaHaye are *Spirit-Controlled Temperament; How to Be Happy Though Married; Revelation Unveiled; Understanding the Last Days; Rapture under Attack; Are We Living in the End Times?;* and the youth fiction series Left Behind: The Kids.

He is the father of four grown children and grandfather of nine. Snow skiing, waterskiing, motorcycling, golfing, vacationing with family, and jogging are among his leisure activities.